THE VESTIBULE OF HEAVEN

a novel

KATHERINE BOLGER HYDE

ANCIENT FAITH PUBLISHING
CHESTERTON, INDIANA

The Vestibule of Heaven
Copyright © 2024 Katherine Bolger Hyde

Published by:
Ancient Faith Publishing
A Division of Ancient Faith Ministries
1050 Broadway, Suite 6
Chesterton, IN 46304

ISBN: 978-1-955890-60-1

Library of Congress Control Number: 2023952515

Printed in the United States of America

Cover design by Samuel Heble
Image via photoff on Shutterstock
Interior design by Katherine Hyde

To Gloria,
who believed in this book from the beginning

AUTHOR'S NOTE

This is a work of fiction, and as such, it does not purport to teach Orthodox theology. The view of the afterlife and of the interaction between the living and the dead that is presented here is fanciful, having some basis in Orthodox belief but not intended to mirror it exactly.

IN THE VESTIBULE

I KNEW HER, OF COURSE, the first time she came to the house. One of the advantages of being dead is the ability to see beneath the surface.

When I willed the house to Kelly, I hadn't ever seen her, not in all the thirty years since she first slipped into the world. All I had was her first name and one faded little Polaroid picture of her at about a year old. I knew she had June Rose's red hair and Victor's green eyes; beyond that she just looked like a baby.

I gave the lawyers a copy of that picture, though I didn't have much hope they'd be able to find her. But I wasn't counting on the angels. I think they helped. At any rate, eventually—I don't keep track of time anymore; could have been a week, could have been years—the lawyers found her, and she came. My granddaughter came to me at last.

When I made that will, I only thought of her—that I could maybe give her something to make up for everything she'd lost, a piece of the family she'd never had. I never expected to know how it would all work out. But things are different on the other side from what I'd thought, and it looks like leaving her the house was a pretty important thing for me as well.

It turns out there is no purgatory. I always knew the Catholics were wrong about that, though Victor was convinced it was real. He was sure he'd be stuck there for eons for marrying outside the church. When they let me go to be with him, I'll rib him about that. "Now Esther," he'll say, and I'll smile.

But it's not like what we Lutherans thought, either. We don't sleep until Judgment Day, and we don't sit around on clouds in white robes, strumming harps. And it surely to goodness isn't that kind of do-it-yourself heaven so many people seem to be expecting. It is what it is, and you get there or you don't. I made it by the skin of my teeth, in spite of what I'd done, because I'd suffered and shed so many tears, and because Victor and June were praying for me—so the angels said. But I only got as far as what you might call the vestibule of heaven.

Even the vestibule is so much better than anything on Earth, there just aren't any words for it. The light here is only the reflection, the leftovers of the light of Paradise, but even so, you can drink it and bathe in it and wrap it around you like a cloak, and know you'll never need any other sustenance for all eternity. Just being free of the body is like being let out of prison: no more midnight cravings, no more achy joints, no more wondering whether you'll make it to the bathroom this time. No more reading glasses—you see so much better without your eyes. I can see everything at once now, like I'm looking from all angles, up down and sideways, at the same time. And no more brain playing tricks on me. I think that's the best part. I can remember all the good and forget all the bad. I can understand the reasons, too, for everything, and what we understand, we can always forgive.

I might have been content to stay in the vestibule indefinitely, but for one thing: it's lonely here. I miss Victor and June, and I know there are so many others—parents and grandparents, cousins and friends—waiting to greet me as well. Even the saints I came to love through Victor's influence, though I was a good Protestant to the end.

But they're all inside, and so, of course, is the Presence. He's way inside, up in the highest heaven of all. I imagine I'll have to be inside for quite a while before I can bear that much light. But something in me won't be satisfied until I see His face.

Archangel Raphael told me, when he brought me here and promised to help me, there's only one way for me to get past the Vestibule: Kelly has to pray for me. But for that to happen, she has to know who I am and what I've done, she has to forgive me for it, and she has to come to a place where she even knows what it is to pray. It's only God, of course, who can really bring that about; but the task He has set me is to help in whatever way I can.

So without exactly leaving heaven, I have permission for this while to hang around this house that once was mine, to watch Kelly and try to influence her in some way for good. But I'm not allowed to reveal myself to her, not yet, because it would frighten her too much. She's got one of those rational minds, I can tell, wants everything cut-and-dried and explainable. I'll have to soften her up to the other side of things, let the house introduce me to her, let her come to understand the whole story. Then, when she knows me a little and she's ready to forgive, maybe I'll be allowed to show myself and ask for her prayers. Or maybe I won't need to ask.

In the meantime, I can watch her, and that in itself is blessedness.

CHAPTER 1

TWENTY FEET ABOVE the hotel's marble floor, Kelly swayed slightly on the ladder and pulled with all her weight on the chain that held the six-foot brass chandelier. "Is it straight?" she called to her assistant below.

"Looks good from here," Jim yelled back.

"All right, lock 'er down," she said to the workman above her.

She heard a knock, footsteps going to the door, Jim's voice unintelligible below. Then he called up to her, "Kelly! Registered letter for you!"

"I'm a little busy right now."

Jim's voice was low, then rose again. "He needs your signature—says he can't wait."

"Oh, for crying out loud. You done up there, Carlos?"

"I got 'er, you can let go."

She released the chain gradually, waiting to see that the chandelier held firm, then descended the shaky ladder. These high-altitude chores were her least favorite, which was why she always did them herself. A good boss would never shove off on a subordinate what she herself was unwilling to take on.

She wiped her hands on her jeans. "All right, where do I sign?"

The postal worker handed her a clipboard, then frowned at her indecipherable scrawl. "Kelly Mason?"

"Yes, yes. I know you can't read it, but that's me."

With a shrug of the eyebrows, he handed her a thick white envelope with the return address of a legal firm in Santa Cruz.

"What the . . ." Letters from lawyers were a natural component of Kelly's work, but she had no projects in the Santa Cruz area, past, present, or planned. The Isleton Grand Hotel was just about finished, and once she left this sleepy Sacramento River Delta town, she had her eye on a Julia Morgan community center in Marin. The competition would be stiff for that one, but the fact that she was willing to restore it on her own dollar would put her at the head of the pack.

She pulled a screwdriver from her back pocket and slit the envelope open. The stiff white paper crackled as she unfolded it. Under the letterhead of Grayson, Grayson, and Penn, Attorneys at Law, she read:

August 25, 20—

Dear Ms. Mason:

We are pleased to inform you that you have been named as a beneficiary in the last will and testament of our client, Esther Lundquist Hansen, deceased May 12 of this year. Under the will, you inherit Mrs. Hansen's house and all its contents. The property is located at 9773 Journey's End Road, Ben Lomond, California. A plot plan and map are enclosed.

Mrs. Hansen specifically instructed us to give no reason for this bequest, which we understand must come as a surprise to you. However, she did request that you personally inhabit the property for a period of at least three months. We must emphasize that this request does not carry the force of law. The will has been proved, and the property is your own to do with as you like.

If you will call at our office in Santa Cruz at your earliest convenience, we will convey to you the deed and keys to the property. If we can be of any further assistance, please do not hesitate to contact us.

Sincerely,
Richard Grayson, Attorney at Law

Baffled, Kelly turned the letter over, then examined the plot plan and map as if they might conceal some explanation for this windfall. Why on earth would some woman she'd never heard of leave her a house? Houses had been handed over to her before— there was that old guy in San Francisco who wanted his Painted Lady restored for its historical significance but couldn't afford to do it himself. He deeded the house to her and went off to a retirement home, and she fixed it up and donated it as a shelter for runaways.

Maybe this was the same kind of thing, only the owner waited until she was dead to let go of her house. But why not come out and say so? Oh, well. Kelly would go and look at the place, anyway, and if it held no interest, she could always sell it and use the money toward the Morgan. Howard Mason's posthumous pockets were deep, but not inexhaustible, after all.

She looked up from the letter to survey the resplendent lobby of the Gold Rush-era hotel, reveling in the old-mixed-with-new smell that was the restorer's trademark. The little town of Isleton was starting to pull itself back into life after decades of slumber, and this restoration would be a focal point of its renewal: a combination museum, town hall, and bed-and-breakfast. Her mouth tightened in a grim smile as she thought of what Howard, her so-called father, would have made of a town like that—he would have bought out the residents for a pittance, bulldozed the town, and built luxury condos and a shopping mall. He'd writhe in his grave if he could see the use his offspring was making of his ill-gotten hoard.

Jim hovered into view. "So what's up?"

"New house to work on. Over near Santa Cruz, apparently. Some old lady left it to me, no explanation. I'll go take a look, anyway—it'll be a week or two before the Morgan bid is due."

"Want me to come along?"

She glanced at his expression, boyishly eager, and suppressed a sigh. Jim was a good worker, but he'd been too much in her face lately. Always wanting her to have dinner with him, always trying to start a conversation about something other than the work at hand. He was starting to get on her nerves.

"Not this time, Jim, thanks. I need a break. I'll go down myself and check it out, maybe hang out at the beach for a while, get some R&R. I'll call you when I've scoped it out." She read disbelief in his eyes and realized she'd made a faux pas.

"You? Hang out? You don't know the meaning of the word. Look, if you don't want me around, just say so."

Anger lent distinction to his boy-next-door features; no doubt many women would find him attractive. But neither he nor anyone had yet stirred those feelings in Kelly.

Still, she hadn't meant to hurt him. "Jim, I . . ." She put out a helpless hand.

"Forget it. Call me when you're ready to talk about the Morgan." He turned and left the building.

Kelly sighed. Why did he have to take everything personally? Jim was the best contractor she'd ever worked with—competent, reliable, and until now, easy to get along with—not one to question her authority at every turn. But if this sort of thing kept up, they wouldn't be able to work together at all.

She took out her cell phone and called the lawyers' office to make an appointment for the following week.

KELLY CRUISED HER BATTERED TOYOTA pickup down Journey's End Road, looking for number 9773. What a mish-mosh of a neighborhood—here a modest ranch in a kid-friendly yard, there a wet-paint-new remodeling job that had swelled the original house almost to the boundaries of its lot. After that, a log cabin set well back from the street, with a historical marker in the yard—the home, perhaps, of the woman who had named this road. Kelly imagined her being dragged by her fortune-seeking husband across mountain, prairie, and desert to this place, ten miles from the Pacific Ocean, where she said, "Thus far and no farther: I will not budge from this spot."

Across from the cabin sat a smug Cape Cod, freshly painted a fluorescent white with impeccable dark green shutters, presiding over a severely disciplined lawn with rows of red hollyhocks standing at attention along its edges. Kelly shivered, then brightened at the sight of the house two doors down: a smallish Queen Anne restored to all its multicolored glory, in eye-resting tones of sage and peach and cream. She'd done a similar house herself, two or three projects back, and had been rather sorry to move on.

She squinted at the house numbers—a large black 9-7-6-9 marched across the lintel of the Cape Cod; a small sign in front of the Queen Anne read 9777 in sage numerals on cream. The house she was looking for must be between the two, behind that overgrown hedge. She backed up a few feet. Ah yes, there on the mailbox, in faded white painted with a shaky hand, were the numbers 9773. Prepared for anything, Kelly pulled the pickup into the gravel drive and got out.

Not bad. A neat bungalow, set well back in a pleasant garden—neglected all summer, of course, but nicely laid out in the profuse English style. But gardens weren't her thing; she could hire someone to take care of that. It was the house that would have to prove itself worth her time.

She had to admit the town had its charm, despite the architectural hodgepodge—one could always lift one's gaze from an ugly building to the glory of the redwoods that fringed the sky all around. There were two of them here, in this yard—one in the corner near the street and another towering behind the house. She let her eyes travel up the length of the farther tree and wondered if, living here day after day, she would ever cease to feel that little catch of awe in the throat at something so old, so intricate, so impervious to mankind and its hasty ways.

A movement at ground level drew Kelly's eyes downward. Something quick and fluffy disappeared around the corner of the porch. Probably a squirrel. She turned her gaze to the house.

A medium-sized house, two stories, with a low-pitched gable roof. A deep porch ran two-thirds the width of the front, supported by square posts too narrow for a true bungalow. This house might predate the full development of the bungalow style.

Kelly's seventh sense prickled—the one that told her when she was in the presence of a notable building. She stepped around to the gable end, looking closely at the windows and trim. Cream-painted timbers formed a distinctive pattern across the silver-gray shingles. This was a Stickley house. She could picture the illustration from The Craftsman—1905 or '06.

14

Her pulse quickened. She'd been waiting for a Stickley since she began this odd career six years ago. Her fingers itched to turn the key in the lock and see what had been made of the interior, but she restrained herself. Everything decently and in order.

She circled the house, checking for serious structural damage, and found nothing worse than a roof that looked ripe for replacement and some water damage to the eaves where a gutter had broken loose. On the right side of the house, a large branch of a blighted oak hung low over the roof; that should be trimmed at some point. Around back, where the chimney should have been, she saw only a patch of slightly newer-looking asphalt shingles.

As she climbed the steps to the front porch, an orange tabby cat leapt down from the rail and rubbed against her leg, meowing. "Where did you come from?" Kelly said, bending to scratch his head. The meow changed to a purr. Her fingers bumped against a collar. "I bet somebody's missing you."

She knelt down to look at the collar. Dangling from it was a gold-tone tag engraved with "Ginger" on one side and "9773 Journey's End Road" on the other. She stared at the cat in wonder. "This is your house? The will didn't say anything about a cat. Well, I'm glad you seem to like me, because the law thinks this house belongs to me." The cat purred louder and butted his head against her hand.

Kelly straightened and turned toward the front door. Next to it was a double plastic dish, half-filled with dry cat food and water. "Curiouser and curiouser," she murmured, then shrugged and got out the key.

She turned the key in the door—a good, solid door with a nice bit of Craftsman stained glass set into the upper panel—then pushed it open to see another door a few feet ahead. She was standing in a vestibule. The house plan would have called for it, of course, but still she was a little surprised to find it here. Few people building in Santa Cruz County would bother with a vestibule—an airlock designed to keep out the weather—for here the weather was usually welcome.

This tiny room had been put to use, however—coat hooks lined the two short walls. The hooks did not surprise her, but the coats and hats hanging on them did. The will had mentioned "contents," but she'd expected furniture, not personal belongings. Cats and coats: could she have the wrong house? No, the key had fit the lock.

She eased the outer door shut behind her, almost catching the cat's tail as he slipped in. Responding to some unaccountable impulse, she turned the knob of the inner door with exquisite slowness, like a thief, or one about to trespass on a wonder.

The spacious entry hall had the cool, stale feeling of a building long unoccupied, with a slight musty odor that made Kelly's nose twitch. The hall was floored and paneled in dark wood, with wide archways on either side and a U-shaped staircase rising at the back. Over the landing, high leaded windows, in a larger version of the tulip pattern on the front door, cast a stream of warm yellow light across the hall.

Once there was a little red-haired girl who lived in a house made of wood. The floors were wood, the walls were wood, the stairs were wood. And above the stairs was a window made of cream and yellow glass, with golden tulips blooming in the midst of it. And the little girl loved that window, and she played every day on the landing, bathed in its yellow light.

Where had she heard that story? And how did it come to so perfectly describe this house and this window before her? She could hear the story in her mind, told in a sweet and musical

16

woman's voice, a voice that seemed very dear to her . . . Whose voice was it? Certainly not Miriam Mason's.

She shook her head to clear it of that haunting sound, but she could not slow the rapid beating of her heart nor stem the sweat that dewed her frigid palms. Never had a house affected her this way.

The yellow light drew her eyes across the hall to where it glinted off a mirror. A narrow console table stood beneath the mirror; on it were a vase of dried flowers, fuzzy with dust, and a plate stand that held a salad plate of brown Spode.

She moved in slow motion toward the table, then put out a cautious finger and touched the scalloped edge of the plate. It was the twin of one that lay wrapped in layers of tissue in a box in her truck—the most treasured possession of her childhood. She'd spent hours sitting on her bed, tracing the lines of the flowers and leaves in the border, the Tudor manor house and spreading trees in the center. If she'd been allowed, she would have taken the plate to bed with her.

A buzzing filled Kelly's ears. Her seventh sense was shouting now, but it was more than that—a still, small voice that inhabited a region of her heart unexplored until this moment. She blinked, forced herself to breathe deeply, turned, and walked through the archway on her left.

The room might have been inhabited only yesterday. A chintz-covered couch and two cushy chairs surrounded a glass-topped trunk strewn with magazines. In a corner, a round table held a half-finished jigsaw puzzle. Sheet music was spread out on the piano—a true Craftsman upright, Kelly noted with a thrill. And all through the room were photographs—on the tables, on the mantel, on the piano, on the walls—photos of a family, from daguerreotypes to Kodachromes.

The cat at her heels, Kelly made her way around the room, examining the photographs. A large hand-tinted wedding picture in an ornate silver frame held pride of place on the mantel. These must be the previous owners—married just after World War II, by the look of them. The groom was a tall, gangly, pleasant-looking fellow in Army Air Corps dress uniform, with a sprinkling of freckles and a jubilant grin. Kelly warmed to him immediately as a fellow member of the elite society of redheads. The bride wore a high-shouldered, narrow-skirted satin gown, with her blonde hair swept back in rolls off her forehead. She was lovely, in a statuesque Scandinavian style, but there was something a little too decided about the set of her jaw, a hint almost of smugness in her smile.

Kelly followed the photos around the room, watching the couple mature, seeing the setting of what appeared to be a happy marriage shift from someplace with lots of snow to the very house she stood in now. But still the couple were alone, and as the years passed their smiles grew more fixed; the lines around their eyes spoke tension rather than laughter. Then at last, when they looked to be nearing forty, came a large color photo hung next to the archway: man and wife, all lines smoothed from their faces now, beamed down on a little pink-wrapped bundle cradled in the woman's arms. A tiny face topped with a tuft of golden-red hair peeked up at them from the blankets. The three of them looked so intimate, so complete in themselves, that Kelly swallowed and turned away.

The parents faded out of the pictures now, appearing only sporadically in the snapshots that punctuated a series of studio portraits. The portraits showed the little red-haired girl growing from laughing, roly-poly toddler, to schoolgirl with pigtails sticking out like Pippi Longstocking's, to awkward pubescent with swollen lips closed over her teeth—hiding braces, no doubt. The portraits followed her into her high school years, when she began to favor granny dresses and wore her hair long and loose—and then they stopped short. Kelly blinked, shook her head, circled the room again, a desperate premonition tugging at her heart. There were no more pictures. No graduation, no wedding, no grandchildren. Could the daughter have died?

She came back to the last portrait, over the piano. The cat jumped onto the keyboard cover and rubbed against her arm. She picked him up. "I should have guessed she'd disappeared somehow, shouldn't I, Cat?—if she'd been around, the house would have gone to her. But so young?"

She took a closer look at the photograph. The girl's hair had deepened from strawberry blonde to a coppery auburn that fell in undulating waves over her shoulders. Her translucent ivory skin was lightly freckled like her dad's, and her smile echoed his—warm, but a little tentative, as if unsure of a response. She had her mother's high forehead and cheekbones, but her nose was more delicate, her jaw slender, tapering to a narrow chin. Her large, deep brown eyes set her apart from both her parents. Kelly's chest constricted—a girl so young should not know that much sorrow. She looked as if a feather would break her.

Kelly stood mesmerized, feeling a deep kinship with this unknown girl. Not that they looked alike, apart from the coloring; Kelly was tall, strong-boned and strong-featured, with nothing fragile about her. But she had known heartache to equal this girl's.

Surely, though, a different kind of heartache. With Ginger content in her arms, she looked back at the snapshots that showed the family together, mostly on summer camping trips or winter visits to the snowy place they'd come from. That intimacy and completeness she'd seen in the first picture of the three of them never seemed to fade. But there was one later photo, on the piano, of mother and daughter alone. They were trying to smile, but the pinched lines of their faces betrayed them, and the same grief haunted both their eyes.

"Did the father leave them, Cat?" No, impossible—not that grinning redhead in uniform. His smile had deepened over the years but never turned cold or forced. He loved his two girls, she was sure of it. "No, he must have died too."

Kelly felt suddenly cold. She stood in front of the final wall of pictures, hugging the cat and shivering, and didn't know she was crying until she felt a tear drop onto her hand.

OH, HOW I WANTED TO reach out and put my arms around my granddaughter as she stood there crying in front of our pictures. How I wanted to tell her, there and then, "Yes, it was a sad time for all of us, but you're here now, and it's going to be all right." But I'm not allowed to speak or show myself to her—not yet.

All I could do was be there with her, but I think somehow she felt it, because after a while she sort of shook herself and dried her tears and moved on to see the rest of the house. She loved the library, I could tell. I love it too—I'd sit there every evening after Victor passed, at the hour when he and I always used to share a glass of sherry when he came home from work, talking quietly about our day. I can still smell a whiff of his pipe tobacco, though it must be my imagination, after thirty years. But I saw Kelly draw in her nostrils and squint a little, as if she were smelling it too.

She passed through the dining room, looking pleased at the built-in sideboard with the stained glass above it, the Stickley table and chairs, the plate rail all around the top of the walls where

I set out my brown Spode china. It was when she got into the kitchen that I first saw her face fall. And I can't blame her. We redid it in the early seventies, when nobody thought about making a kitchen fit the original style of the house. Who knew those dark wood-veneer cabinets and avocado green appliances would date so quickly? But by the time I got sick of them, Victor was gone, and I didn't have the money to redo it. Well, it will give Kelly something to do, and it appears she likes that kind of thing.

She stayed long enough to turn on the faucet and seemed surprised to see a strong, clean stream of water. Then she headed upstairs.

She looked in Victor's and my room first, to the right of the stairs. I had it done up nice, all in blue, which was always my favorite color but never seemed to belong downstairs with all that woodwork. Up here, there's just a bit of wood trim, and I painted it white. I could see Kelly didn't like that. She clucked her tongue with a little frown, then went into June's room.

I guess it's a weakness in me, but I never touched June's room after she was gone. I couldn't bear it. I straightened it up at first and dusted now and then, but I never got rid of a thing that belonged to her. Kelly started when she opened the door on this teenaged girl's room right out of the seventies, with black-light posters all over the walls and a lava lamp on the dresser, and that awful neon orange bedspread I know June would have outgrown in another year or two. But along with all that, she still kept her dolls and her teddy bears, not stuffed in the closet but sitting up prim on the shelves above her bed and on her pillow.

Kelly stood in the doorway and took it all in, looking a little dazed. I wondered if maybe she was trying to reconcile this room with the picture of the delicate young girl with the soulful eyes she'd seen downstairs. I never could tell, myself, what June saw

21

in all that hippie-type stuff—she wasn't a hippie at all, but a nice normal wholesome girl who wanted to get married and have children and maybe illustrate picture books someday. But I guess we all go through that phase where we have to do a few things just to shock our parents. I was grateful this room was as far as she ever wanted to go in that direction. At least, until . . . Well. I won't talk about that now.

After a minute, Kelly backed out and shut the door, then went into the guest room. I did this room all in butter yellow and cream, with a little apple green and red for accent, because it reminded me of the room in my grandmother's house where I used to stay when I was little. It's a cheerful, peaceful kind of room, a little old-fashioned, with my Wedding Ring quilt on the four-poster and a braided rag rug on the floor. Kelly's face kind of brightened up when she saw it. She sat on the bed and bounced a little, then lay back and gazed at the lace canopy, her hands behind her head. Ginger hopped up next to her as if he owned the place, the little stinker—I never used to allow him on the beds. But I shouldn't fuss at him; I think he contributed to the homey atmosphere. She seemed to like having him there.

After that she took a quick look around the bathroom, tested the toilet (which worked) and the light switches (which didn't), then went downstairs and rummaged around until she found some candles. I always kept some in the sideboard for emergencies. Then she pulled out her cell phone. "I want to cancel my reservation for tonight," she said. "Yes, I'll pay the deposit."

She went out to her truck and came back in with a suitcase and a big heavy instrument case—a cello maybe—which she stuck in the guest room closet. Thank you, Archangel Raphael—at least for tonight, it looks like she's decided to stay.

22

CHAPTER 2

NOT TILL MORNING did Kelly remember the Julia Morgan building. A Stickley was a find, but it couldn't compare to a Morgan. But as she showered (in cold water) and dressed, the very air of the house seemed to embrace her, to call her to stay. Well, the least she could do was to find out more about it.

After calling to get the gas and electricity turned on, she went next door to the lovely Queen Anne to do some research. The next-door neighbors were as likely as anyone to know the history of the house, and should she decide to restore it, she'd trust whoever handled their renovation to contract the heavy work on this one.

She rang the bell, noting with approval the turned posts supporting the porch roof, the fanlight above the door. After a minute the door was opened by a tall, fit man of about sixty with salt-and-pepper hair and a handsome, weathered face. He wore jeans, a chambray work shirt, and a pleasant if questioning expression.

Kelly drew herself straight. "I'm Kelly Mason. I've inherited the house next door, and I'd like to talk to you about it if I may."

The man gazed at her for a moment, then blinked and put

out his hand. "Aidan McCarthy. Pleased to meet you—I've been wondering who you'd turn out to be. Come in, come in, by all means, I'll tell you whatever I can."

Kelly accepted the handshake—his hand was warm and firm—and followed him through a two-story entrance hall with a curving staircase and into a bright, spacious parlor. She was relieved to see that McCarthy (or his wife) had not chosen to decorate the house in period; although she loved Victorian exteriors, she felt suffocated by the lush undergrowth of tables, chairs, and knickknacks that authentically inhabited them. This room had just enough furniture to be comfortable, just enough stuff to be lived in, and all in light warm colors that complemented the sage-and-cream exterior.

She was so taken up with the decor that she didn't notice the old woman sitting by the fireplace until McCarthy introduced her. Bending over the frail form slumped in a wheelchair, he boomed, "Mother, we have a guest. This is Kelly Mason. She's the one Esther left her house to." He straightened and said to Kelly, "This is my mother, Eunice McCarthy. She had a stroke some years ago and doesn't talk much. But I'm convinced she understands every word we say." He gave the old woman's shoulder an affectionate squeeze.

Kelly approached only as near as she felt politeness required. "Pleased to meet you, Mrs. McCarthy." It didn't seem appropriate to try to shake the withered hand curled on the arm of the wheelchair, but she forced herself to look into the watery eyes and found herself agreeing with McCarthy—there was a gleam of intelligence there, although the muscles of the left side of her face drooped uselessly and a line of drool dripped from her toothless mouth. Mrs. McCarthy's short, sparse white hair was clean and neatly combed, and she was dressed in a crisp pink

24

blouse under a white cardigan, with a tartan throw across her lap. With what seemed a great effort, she gave Kelly an infinitesimal nod.

"Have a seat." McCarthy gestured toward an overstuffed chair on the opposite side of the fireplace. "Like some coffee? It's fresh."

"Please." He seemed like a man who would make good coffee. The mud she'd been served with her breakfast at the local greasy spoon was still sour in her mouth.

In her host's brief absence, she looked around the room, noting the mantelpiece, the cornices, the molded ceiling—probably not original plaster, but it certainly fooled the eye. Whoever had charge of this house had done a fine and sensitive job.

In one corner of the room a violin and bow rested on a wooden music stand, reminding her she hadn't practiced her cello for far too long. Now that she had a decent place to live for several months, she'd have to get it out again.

She caught herself and shook her head. She hadn't yet decided to honor Esther Hansen's request that she stay. A great deal more thought—and information—needed to go into that decision.

Kelly's gaze came back to Mrs. McCarthy, who was staring at her intently, her mouth working as if she would speak; but no sound emerged. Kelly managed a smile, hoping conversation with the old woman would not be required of her, and was relieved when McCarthy returned with filled mugs, cream, and sugar on a tray.

She took the mug he offered her but refused the cream and sugar. "Have you lived here long?" she asked while her host was still pouring cream into his cup.

He stirred his coffee and settled on the sofa facing the

fireplace before answering. "I grew up in this house. Moved out as a young man, went to college and—all that. But I came back here—oh, fifteen years ago, when Mother had her second stroke. She's lived here all along."

"So you must have known your neighbors well, then."

"Esther Hansen was my mother's best friend. Victor and my father were close too, but they've both been dead for some time. Esther and Mother were widows together—and Mrs. Perkins, on the other side of you, too, though they weren't as close to her. The locals call this block Widows' Walk."

Kelly set down her mug. "Mr. McCarthy—"

"Aidan, please."

"Aidan, then. What kind of person was Mrs. Hansen? Do you have any idea why she would have left the house to me?"

"I was going to ask you that same question. You're not a relative, I take it?"

"Certainly not. But I am a professional house restorer. I assumed at first she wanted the house restored and donated to the community—that's what I do. But most of the houses I take on are in much worse condition. The neighborhood's wrong too—it doesn't look either disadvantaged or historic. Plus, she left the house completely furnished. It doesn't add up."

Aidan sat forward on the couch and frowned at his hands, pressed fingertip to fingertip between his knees. "No. It doesn't." The tips of his fingers whitened. Then he flexed his hands and sat back. "All I can tell you is this, Miss Mason."

She gave her head a quick shake. "Kelly."

"Kelly. All I can tell you is Esther Hansen was lucid to the end, and she never did anything in her life without a good reason. At least, a reason that seemed good to her. She had no family that I know of. And she did love that house. I know it frustrated her that she couldn't do more with it—she wasn't a wealthy woman after her husband died."

Kelly nodded and sipped her coffee. It was good coffee, now that she took the time to taste it. "The house seems well maintained overall—she must have had at least enough money for that."

"Well, to tell you the truth . . . I did all that for her. She insisted on paying for the materials, but I didn't give her all the receipts. I would've done the major repairs, too, like the chimney and that God-awful kitchen, but she wouldn't hear of it."

Kelly stared at him. "You volunteered your time? All that time? Just for a neighbor?"

He looked steadily back at her. "And what about you? Didn't you just tell me you restore houses and donate them back to the community? That sounds like a full-time volunteer job to me. What's in it for you?"

"That's different." Kelly frowned at her coffee mug, feeling her cheeks go hot. "I inherited a lot of money that was unethically come by. I couldn't live with myself if I didn't give it back."

"Well, I owed Esther a lot. She took care of my mother single-handed for months until I could move back. Besides . . ." He cleared his throat. "Well, anyway, I owed her a lot."

Kelly didn't pursue that; the conversational waters were already getting too deep for her taste. "So I take it you're a carpenter then? Did you do the work on this house?"

"Indeed I did. With help, of course. I'm a general contractor, actually, but I've put my free time over the last ten years into restoring this house. Things are slow in construction right now, and I've just about finished it up."

"You've done an excellent job. I know Queen Anne, and I haven't seen one thing that isn't both authentic and tasteful. Are you as good at Stickley as you are at Queen Anne? I'll be needing a contractor to help me with my house."

She stopped herself, appalled. Again, that automatic response as if she'd be staying, when she'd decided nothing of the kind. And "my house"? None of the houses she'd worked on before had been "my house," though she'd been temporarily legal owner of most of them. And this one she hadn't even chosen—it seemed to have chosen her.

Hastily she added, "That is, if I decide to stay and work on it. I'm still checking things out."

Aidan didn't seem to notice the correction. His mouth turned up at one corner. "I not only know Stickley, I know that house like the back of my hand. If you hired anyone else, I'd be over there every day telling him how to do his job."

Kelly set down her mug and drew herself up. "One thing has to be clear from the start if we're going to work together. I will be calling the shots. I have my own very definite approach to restoration. I'll be happy to listen to your ideas, but the decisions will be mine. Is that understood?"

Aidan raised his palms. "Absolutely. It's your house, and clearly you know what you're doing. What do you have in mind?"

"The kitchen will certainly have to be redone, and the roof, and I want to rebuild the chimney and make the fireplace usable. Beyond that . . ." She clamped her mouth shut on this spate of words. Apparently her professional mind had been working all this out in the absence of her consciousness. "But as I said, I haven't definitely decided to do anything yet. I might just sell it." On the words "sell it," she felt a tug on her solar plexus, as if the words' passing had wrenched something loose.

"Well, in that case, you'd get a much better price if you fixed it up first. You might even want to think about adding on. To get the most out of it you'd need a regular master suite with a bath, plus, oh, a decent laundry room, breakfast nook—with a two-story addition off the back you could add a lot of functionality. And value."

"I don't like additions. Especially on a house like that. I don't want to compromise its integrity."

Aidan shrugged. "It's up to you, but most people think those features are essential these days, and I don't see any way to fit them into the existing footprint. If you don't build them in, a buyer probably will, and most likely make a hash of it. If you and I do it, we can make it look like it's been there from day one."

"That's a good point." She chewed her lip, mentally super-imposing magazine photographs of luxurious master baths, room-sized closets, and gleaming state-of-the-art kitchens on the image of the house as it stood, with its typical Craftsman aesthetic of fine workmanship, honest materials, and decorative restraint. Her gut twisted at the thought of some stranger with more money than taste violating her house.

Not my house, she reminded herself yet again. But it was a house she was responsible for. She'd always adopted needy houses the way some people adopted stray animals. This house needed her, not to rescue it from ruin, but to help its true self shine through.

Kelly frowned, impatient with herself. She'd never been torn like this over a house before. She was known throughout the industry for making quick decisions and sticking to them—and for nearly always being right.

She stood. "I'm going to have to give this some thought. This project came out of the blue, and I'm not sure I can fit it into my schedule."

"Of course. Let me know if I can be of any help." Aidan stood and extended his hand. "Welcome to the neighborhood."

She hesitated, as if accepting the handshake would mean accepting the invitation to be a neighbor. She'd always tried to be a good citizen, but what would it mean to be a neighbor? To have a neighbor? A new and rather terrifying world seemed to open before her in those words.

Seeing confusion dawn in Aidan's eyes as she stood motionless, she gave herself an inward shake and took his hand. A handshake was a social convention; it committed her to nothing.

"I'll get back to you. I need to make a decision soon, today if possible."

She left the house with a feeling of having escaped, but from what she didn't know.

WHEN KELLY CAME BACK FROM McCarthys', she'd hardly got a foot in the yard before Imogene Perkins pounced on her. I declare, that woman would plague the life out of me if I weren't already dead. Now she seems set on plaguing Kelly.

She came tripping over the gravel in that mincing way of hers, saying, "Excuse me! Excuse me!" as if she were afraid of being overlooked, though Kelly had stopped the minute she saw her. She came right up to Kelly and peered up into her face through those ridiculous cat's-eye glasses. How she's managed to save those frames since the sixties I really couldn't tell you. She put out her little hand with its sharp-pointed nails—they almost touched Kelly's stomach, she was standing so close—and said, "I'm Imogene Perkins, from the white house next door? I saw you drive up last night. Are you the new owner?"

"Kelly Mason. Pleased to meet you, Mrs. Perkins." She took Imogene's hand and tried to shake it, but of course you can't shake a jellyfish on the end of a.stick. Kelly pulled her hand away and I could see her fingers twitching, as if she were just itching to wipe her hand off on her jeans—I know I would have been.

Imogene simpered. "Well, now, I do like a young person who knows her manners. You wouldn't credit how many people will up and call me Imogene at our first meeting, as if they'd known me for years! But you know, dear, this formality really isn't necessary between neighbors. After all, Esther Hansen was *such* a close friend, and I do hope you and I can be friends for her sake."

I would've snorted if I still had a nose. Imogene Perkins, my close friend? She'd have to be the last woman on earth, and then I'd think twice. I did call her Imogene, though, couldn't avoid it—but June always called her Mrs. Persnickety.

Kelly cleared her throat and I saw the muscles tighten in her neck, just like Victor's used to do when he was trying not to show his annoyance. "I always like to be on good terms with my neighbors, Mrs. Perkins, but you see, I didn't know Mrs. Hansen at all, and I don't expect to be in the neighborhood any longer than it takes to fix up the house. If that long."

Imogene's eyes widened behind her thick cat's-eye lenses. Maybe she thinks those glasses will help her see like a cat, because she always wants to see every little thing, especially at night. "Oh, do you mean you're going to clean the place up? That will be a wonderful thing for the neighborhood. You know, dear Esther was quite a bit older than I am, and I'm afraid these last few years she was a bit past keeping up with all the work around the house. And especially the garden! Why, you can see for yourself how overgrown it is. Quite a disgrace next to my neat little yard, if I do say so myself. I offered to help her with it time and again, but there, poor thing, I guess she had her pride; she wouldn't let me lift a finger in the garden or the house, either one."

31

Imogene gave one of her sniffs. June used to watch her, hoping one day she'd sniff in a bug. *There was an old lady who sniffed in a fly . . .*

"Of course she let that Aidan McCarthy and his children help out with all kinds of things. But then Eunice always was so pushy. I suppose Esther was afraid of offending her, her being in a wheelchair and all." She peered up at Kelly, sharp and intent like a fox. "Did Aidan say anything about me?"

"Only your name, and that you three were widows together. And I think he said people call this block Widows' Walk?"

Imogene sniffed again. "Widows' Walk indeed!" She dabbed at her eyes with the balled-up tissue she always seems to have in her hand. "I always thought that name was so insensitive, but then people are like that, you know. My dear Oswald has been gone for twenty years, but I still keep his corner of the living room exactly the way he liked it. I never allow anyone to sit in his chair." Of course not—she never allows anyone to sit in any of her chairs. They're all covered in plastic. She hardly sits in them herself—just perches on the edge, like the useless aunts in *A Child's Christmas in Wales.*

Kelly opened her mouth, no doubt to make an excuse and get away, but Imogene kept right on talking. "Now I do hope you'll let me help you with the garden, dear. I know just how it ought to be. Of course, all these weeds would have to go." She swept her hand around to include all my cherished flowers—the alyssum, the Queen Anne's Lace, even my sweet little tea roses. "Then we could put in some nice artificial turf, like mine—no maintenance at all, and it always looks neat. And perhaps some chrysanthemums along the edges—so cheerful, I always think, and no trouble at all to grow." She paused and gazed up at Kelly with a bright smile, looking for all the world like a mockingbird with its eye on a shiny new object for its collection.

Kelly backed away. "Thank you, Mrs. Perkins, but I haven't made any decisions yet about the yard. I have to take care of the house first, and the restoration work can be kind of hard on a garden. Once all that work's done, I'll get someone in to do the garden properly, in a style that fits the house."

Imogene drew herself up to her full four-foot-eleven. "You don't mean to say you're going to have—workmen and—and trucks and—bulldozers and things coming in and out of here?"

"I don't suppose it'll run to bulldozers, but trucks and workmen, certainly. There's quite a bit of work to be done."

"Well, all I can say is they'd better not trespass on my yard! I'd hoped you were going to tidy the place up, not make even more of a mess. We all value our peace and quiet on this street, you know."

Kelly's neck muscles tightened again. "I'll do my best to see you're disturbed as little as possible. But you know you always have to make a bigger mess at first when you're cleaning something up. I promise you the property will look better when I've finished. Now if you'll excuse me, Mrs. Perkins, I have a lot to do."

Imogene sniffed, a real champion sniff, then turned on her sturdy pump heel and marched back to her own artificial turf. Kelly let out a long sigh and headed up the driveway. She'll never let Imogene lay a finger on my place, that much I know.

CHAPTER 3

THE CAT MET Kelly on the porch. He rubbed against her legs, mewling, then sat expectantly next to his food bowl.

She bent down to scratch his neck. "Sorry, Ginger, I don't have any cat food. Or people food, for that matter. Maybe the good fairy who feeds you will come by soon." Ginger purred loudly and she picked him up. "I'll get some cat food when I go to the store. Have to get a few things for myself, anyway." Then she laughed. "Listen to me. I'm talking like I'm staying again. And do you know, I have half a mind to stay and make as much noise and mess as possible, just to spite Mrs. Perkins."

Ginger's purr turned momentarily to a growl.

"Oh, you don't like her either? No surprise there—I bet she hates animals."

Kelly put Ginger down and turned her key in the lock. Mrs. Perkins would clearly be a nuisance, but Kelly had dealt with hostile neighbors before and had never allowed them to interfere with her plans.

A reminder of a bigger problem faced her right here in the vestibule: what to do with all of Esther Hansen's things. She could hardly sell the house with all this stuff in it. These coats, boots, and umbrellas could easily be swept into bags and carted off to Goodwill, but this was only the vestibule. The entire house was filled with all the detritus of a lifetime—three lives, in fact. To judge from the center bedroom upstairs, Esther had never cleared away anything that belonged to her daughter, and the same probably applied to her husband.

Of course, Kelly could hire someone to go through the house, get rid of the worthless things and auction off anything of value. The Spode collection, for instance—that would bring a pretty penny.

She moved to the hall table and picked up the plate she'd noticed there the night before. She traced with her finger the lines of the Elizabethan manor house in which she'd imagined herself living as a child. She'd lie on the crisp white spread of her frameless twin bed in the cold, gray International-style house with its flat roof and unadorned windows, and she'd dream of canopy beds, of time-weathered wood paneling and stone-mullioned windows and bricks that held the residual sun-warmth of centuries. She'd fill the front garden of the manor house with running, laughing children and place an indulgent mother at the first-floor window by the door. When she felt especially bold, she'd add a handsome young father coming up the walk and sweeping a little red-ringleted girl into his arms.

How could she surrender her old daydream to the mercy of auctioneers?

She nestled the plate back into its stand and wandered into the living room. The room seemed full of a suspended life, as if the occupant had stepped into the kitchen to make a cup of tea and would return any moment to add a piece to the jigsaw puzzle, or plump the cushions on the window seat, or play the song that lay open on the piano. Kelly felt an urge to do all those

35

things herself, although she didn't play piano and hadn't touched a puzzle in years.

To strip the room of all its inhabitants would be to kill a living thing.

But the only alternative she could think of was to stay and go through everything herself, one puzzle piece at a time. That could take months. The three months Esther Hansen had requested she stay would be just about right.

In three months—in three *days*—she could lose the Morgan forever. But maybe she could get Jim to bid on the job and run it for her. She could divide her time between this place and Marin. They were only a two-hour drive apart.

A small voice at the back of her mind told her she was dreaming, but she ignored it and pulled out her cell phone. She had a message from Jim.

He'd called several times since they parted in Isleton, and she hadn't picked up. She didn't know what to say to him. He hadn't left a message until now.

She hit the button to listen to voice mail. First she heard him clear his throat. Then came his voice, tight and controlled. "Hi, Kelly. I don't know if you have bad service down there or what. I hope you get this message, because I really need to talk to you about the Morgan. Today."

The message had been left the day before.

Muttering a curse, she pressed Jim's speed-dial number, then drummed her fingers through four rings before he picked up.

"Jim? I just got your message. What's up?"

His silence lasted long enough for a prickle of apprehension to run up Kelly's spine. "They moved up the deadline for bids on the Morgan. To yesterday."

"Holy crap. Did you put in our bid like we talked about?"

"Well . . . not exactly. When I couldn't get hold of you, I figured you weren't interested any more. At least not with me. Squires was after me to work with him on it, so I said yes. We put the bid in just under the wire last night."

"*Squires?! That clown? He'll butcher it!*"

"I'll be there for damage control. It'll come out all right."

"*All right?* The Jim Meriwether I know would never think 'all right' good enough for a Morgan."

Again that chilling pause. "Well, Kelly, I guess you don't know me as well as you thought you did." She heard some static, then, "Listen, I've gotta go." The line went dead.

"Jim?" Kelly shook the phone, then pulled it away from her ear and stared at the words "Call ended" on the screen. Her finger went to the speed-dial button and hovered there.

He hadn't been accidentally disconnected. He'd hung up on her. And wasn't that essentially what she'd done to him, by blowing him off about accompanying her here?

She let her hand fall to her side as she slid down the wall to sit on the floor. The Morgan was gone, and it was her own fault.

With catly opportunism, Ginger appeared and leapt onto her lap. Automatically she put her hand up to stroke him, and he raised his face to touch his nose to hers. The gesture moved her, and incipient tears burned at the back of her eyes. "I bet you arranged that, didn't you, Cat? Don't look so innocent, I know cats have magical powers. You made them move that deadline, you kept Jim's call from getting through, just so you could keep me here to pet you. I know your tricks and your manners." She lifted him and buried her face in his fur. "Well, it worked, and you know what? I'm not sorry. I think I'm actually glad to have an excuse to stay."

NEEDLESS TO SAY, IT WASN'T Ginger who nixed Kelly's deal. It was me. Or rather, Raphael, at my instigation. I guess it was cheating, but I so need her to stay. I want her to be here with her whole heart.

And she seems to have learned a smidgen of humility in the process. That can never hurt.

I'm glad Ginger's there to comfort her, though. There is something a bit uncanny about that cat.

GINGER PRICKED UP HIS EARS, twisted out of Kelly's arms, and trotted to the front door, arriving just as the doorbell rang. Kelly pushed herself up, feeling a decade older than her thirty years, and went to answer it.

On the porch, a dark-haired young woman was pouring cat food into Ginger's dish. Ginger attacked it the moment she finished.

"Ah, the cat food fairy!" Kelly said. "I'd been wondering who was feeding him. He is a him, isn't he? In spite of the name?"

The girl straightened and fastened the food bag with a clip. "Yeah, well, there's kind of a funny story about that."

"I'd love to hear it, but first I'd like to know who you are."

"Oh!" The girl's cheeks went pink and she held out her hand. "Sorry. I'm Kiera McCarthy. Aidan's daughter."

Kiera's smile declared her relationship to Aidan as clearly as did her name. Kelly shook her hand. "Pleased to meet you, Kiera. Got a minute? Come in and tell me the story."

"I've got all day. Pops and I are between jobs right now." Kiera followed Kelly into the hall. "See, there used to be two cats. Esther got them as kittens from some kid on a street corner. The other was a tuxedo cat, a real beauty. Esther called them Fred and Ginger—you know, like Fred Astaire and Ginger Rogers? She didn't know about ginger cats being mostly male. So when she took them to get fixed, she found out Fred was a she and Ginger was a he. But she liked the names so much she refused to change them."

Kelly chuckled. "I think I like this Esther. But what happened to Fred?"

"Oh, she died. A week after Esther. She was a very affectionate cat—she just pined away."

"Ginger seems pretty affectionate too. At least with me."

"Yeah, he used to be more standoffish, but with Fred and Esther both gone I think he's lonely. We tried to adopt him, but he wouldn't adopt. He loves this house." As if to prove her words, Ginger came in from his meal and promenaded around the hall, tail high.

"I'm inclined to agree with him," Kelly said. "There's something special about this place."

"I've always loved it. Esther Hansen was so sweet to me, like a grandmother. Like my own grandmother was before she had her stroke. It's going to be weird having this house belong to someone else."

She broke off and looked sideways at Kelly. "That is—I didn't mean—" She blushed, and Kelly was reminded of a puppy caught tearing a slipper. "There I go putting my foot in it again. Of course I'm glad you're here, I'd hate for the house to sit empty and rot away. And Pops says you might decide to restore it, so that's all good." Kiera looked down, her thick dark lashes shadowing her cheeks. "I just wondered—what are you going to do with all her stuff?"

"To tell you the truth, I've been wondering that myself." Kelly surveyed the hall, running a hand through her short, spiky hair. "It's kind of overwhelming. Not only the amount of stuff, but—well, it feels like I'm invading someone's privacy. These people may be dead, but their stuff seems very much alive. For me to come in here, a stranger, and haul everything off to Goodwill—it's like I'd be dumping their lives down the drain. It feels—disrespectful, I guess." She turned to Kiera. "Your family seems to have been so close to her—I wonder she didn't leave it all to you."

Kiera shrugged, her eyes glistening. "Oh, well, I'm sure she had her reasons. I mean it's not like we need it or anything. Only . . ."

"What is it?"

"Well—would you mind if I took some little memento for myself? Nothing valuable, just something to remind me of her."

"Of course. Help yourself—whatever you want."

Kiera smiled and wiped a quick hand under her eye. "Thanks. I don't know yet what I want, but I'll know it when I see it. In fact—here's an idea. Why don't I help you pack things up? Or even—no, that's crazy, you'd never want to do that."

"Do what? Sometimes crazy ideas are the best."

"Well, I thought . . . I don't know how much work there is to do here. If you don't have to gut the place or anything . . . Maybe we could move things from room to room to clear the space as you need it. When you're all done you could decide what you want to keep." She gave a little laugh. "Or after schlepping it around all that time, maybe you won't want to keep anything."

Kelly gazed at Kiera, her mind working. It was a little crazy, but after all, why not? If the main systems of the house were in good shape—and Aidan had probably seen to that—she'd only need to tear apart the kitchen and bathroom. Kiera's plan might work, and it would put off the evil day of decision for months.

Kiera's brow crinkled. "I told you it was crazy."

"No, no, I was just thinking it through. I think it's a great idea. Provided I don't have to do major plumbing or electrical work, and I don't expect that."

"Terrific! It'll be an adventure."

The two women stood smiling at each other for a moment, Kelly wondering what made her feel so at ease with this person she'd only just met. Kiera's petite, slender frame, her glossy dark hair caught hastily into a ponytail, the bright color that came and went along with the dimples in her cheeks—and above all her forthright, enthusiastic manner—added up to the impression of an overgrown child. That was it. You could trust a child—they had no hidden agendas.

"So what do you plan to do first?" Kiera asked.

"Can't say I have a plan. To tell you the truth, I only decided about ten minutes ago to do anything. But the roof and the chimney will be top priority, I guess."

"Great! That'll give us time to do stuff in here while the guys work outside. My pop's got a great crew, you'll love them." Kiera clapped a hand to her mouth. "Oh, wait—if you just decided, that means you haven't actually hired him, have you?"

"Not yet. But I will. Your own house is the best recommendation I could ask for."

"Whew! So that's all right. You won't be sorry, he's the best. Anyway, like I was saying, my brother Kyle's our mason, so I'm sure he'll be doing the chimney. We're twins, but you'd never know it to look at us—he'd make two of me."

Kelly could easily believe it. "So it's a family business then."

"Yup, I work with them too—did Pops tell you? I'm a

kitchen designer. Any chance you'll redo the kitchen?"

"Are you kidding? The thing's a horror. I'd like to lift it out bodily and donate it to the Museum of American Kitsch."

Kiera laughed, a high, bubbly, contagious laugh. "I'd love to help you redesign it—I've been redoing it in my head for years. But you don't have to hire me—I'm not part of a package deal. Maybe you'd rather do all that yourself."

Kelly hesitated. In the past she'd always done her own designing; what was the point of having a degree in architecture and design if she wasn't going to use it? But it might be nice to work with someone else for a change. "Let's talk about it. I'd like to hear your ideas. Maybe two heads will be better than one." Or make that three heads, counting Aidan's. What was she getting herself into?

"Terrific! When do you want to start?"

"How about tomorrow? I need to get the lie of the land first—I only had a quick look last night."

"Perfect. I'll dig out my sketches." Kiera blushed again. "The truth is, I haven't only done it in my head—I used this kitchen for my senior project in college a couple years ago."

Kelly quailed internally. Apparently she'd be dealing with the plans and preconceptions of a whole family. She might be in for quite a time.

OH, THANK THE LORD, SHE'S not going to throw away my things. Not that I care about things anymore, but they're the only way I have to get through to her. If she can feel something toward my belongings, she must be able to feel my presence here in some way. She'll go through the whole house, and in time she'll find everything I need her to find, and then she'll understand.

CHAPTER 4

KELLY WAS ABOUT to show Kiera out when the doorbell rang again. This time it was Aidan.

"Hey, Pops," said Kiera.

Aidan gave her a squeeze and kissed the top of her head. "You got over here pretty quick for a sleepyhead."

Something twisted in Kelly's gut as Kiera leaned into her father's embrace.

"Yeah, well, I couldn't wait to meet Kelly, and guess what? She's going to keep all Esther's stuff for now, and she's going to let me help design the new kitchen." Kiera might have been a four-year-old bragging that Mommy was going to let her help clean house. "Oh, and by the way, she's going to hire you too." She touched her finger to his nose.

Aidan turned a questioning look toward Kelly. She nodded. "I've decided to stay and restore the house. I don't think I'll find a better person to help me than you." She put out her hand, and they shook.

"Well, that's a relief, I must say. I couldn't stomach the house being sold and some other fellow getting his mitts on it. But you're really going to keep all this stuff?"

"I thought I might. Just for now. Do you think it'll get in the way?"

"I guess we can work around it, but where will you put your own stuff?"

"My 'stuff,' as you call it, is all in my truck—except for what I brought upstairs last night. I don't think it'll be a problem."

Aidan and Kiera stared at her with identically gaping mouths until Kelly wanted to laugh. "I don't exactly have a permanent home, and I like to travel light."

Aidan whistled. Kiera said, "So you just sort of camp out from house to house while you're working on them?"

"That, or stay in a motel if the house is too torn up. Sheesh, don't look at me like that. I like living that way. Nothing to tie me down."

Aidan blinked. "Well, to each his own, I guess. But you might find living with actual furniture habit-forming."

Kelly looked around the room. "I might, at that."

Aidan held up a roll of papers. "I found an old set of plans Esther gave me. Want to go over them now?"

"Absolutely." She led the way into the dining room, where they clustered at one end of the big oak table.

"The plumbing and electrical are in good shape," Aidan said. "You might want to add some outlets, though. Structurally the house is sound. The only big change to the original house is that powder room off the back hall. Esther had to have it—she couldn't handle going up and down stairs during the day. I put it in for her and talked her into using period fixtures."

Kelly nodded. "That's a keeper."

"The roof and the chimney we already talked about. Other than that, the exterior's in good shape. The foundation's solid— we patched it up after the eighty-nine quake. The shingles and sills are all redwood—they'll last forever. And the wood inside's in good shape too, unless you want to refinish it just to brighten things up. The floors are way overdue for a refinish."

Kelly looked down at the pitted and discolored boards beneath her chair. "So I see."

"So that covers the essentials. Anything else is up to you."

"Yeah. I haven't had a chance to think about that yet. If you'll leave me the plans, I'll see what I can come up with."

"No problem." Aidan pushed himself up with his palms on the table. "I'll leave you to it, then. Coming, Kierabeera?"

He gave Kiera's ponytail a gentle tug. She got up to follow him out. Ginger appeared as if to say goodbye, and Kiera turned back. "Oh, listen, I meant to ask—are you okay with Ginger here? If he's a problem we can try adopting him again."

"No, it's fine, I like cats. I've always wanted one, actually, but it would never work, the way I move around. I'll take over feeding him from now on."

First a house, then a houseful of stuff, and now a cat. Kelly couldn't remember when she'd had so much to weigh her down.

WHEN AIDAN AND KIERA HAD gone, Kelly sat for a few minutes gathering her wits, which felt scattered by a solid morning of contact with new people. Although her work required her to constantly meet new people, she preferred to encounter them one at a time and was careful to limit the conversation to essential matters concerning their mutual work. This morning had been completely outside her normal pattern of life, and she didn't know quite what to make of it.

But the plans on the table drew her. She pored over them but found no surprises; Aidan seemed to have covered the bases thoroughly. Nothing was left to her now except to face the issue of adding on.

She walked into the kitchen again. It was an adequate size for a simple kitchen—11' x 13', according to the plans—but upscale buyers would no doubt find it cramped. Because of its position— abutting the fireplace wall of the living room and across the entry hall from the dining room—it was impossible to open up the space without completely reconfiguring the house. A remodeler, as opposed to the restorer/renovator she had pledged herself to be, would probably move the kitchen to the other side of the entry hall, converting the adjoining dining room and library into a contemporary kitchen/dining/family room complex and making the existing kitchen into an office or media room.

She circled the dining room once more, trailing her fingers along the darkened redwood wainscoting that filled the wall up to the plate rail, then the built-in sideboard with the stained glass above. She paused to open a drawer; it slid out with a tiny squeak to reveal linen napkins with an elaborate H hand-monogrammed in one corner. She passed into the library, where her hand continued its journey along the shelves, on which venerable leather bindings leaned companionably against brash paperback upstarts.

At the library window seat she stopped and sank onto the velveteen cushion. Within these lovingly crafted walls was embedded an older, more gracious style of living, one that took time for beauty and the life of the mind, one in which two parents would sit down with their child for dinner every night at a polished oak table set with embroidered linen and brown Spode. Not in this house would the maid feed the child in the kitchen while the mother went out to bridge-and-supper parties and the father stayed away for months at a time.

She could not rip out these walls and destroy the ghosts of that gracious life, even if the people who had lived it were gone. The kitchen would stay the kitchen.

Aidan's suggestion of an addition nagged at her. It would, of course, be possible to add a full room onto the existing kitchen. And if she made it a two-story addition, she could solve some problems upstairs as well.

Ginger at her heels, she mounted the stairs but slowed to a stop on the landing. The yellow light from the tulip window flooded her face and brought that voice into her head again: *Once there was a little girl who lived in a house made of wood . . .* Somehow Kelly was convinced that little girl had lived, not just in a house like this one, but in this very house. She knew—not in her head, but in her heart, her bones—that she must not destroy the memories embedded within these walls, these floors, these windows. Whatever she did here must be done with a gentle hand.

She continued up the stairs, caressing the well-worn patina of the handrail, to explore the second floor once more. One bathroom, and an odd one at that, long and narrow with all the fixtures in a row. No linen closet. The bedroom closets were dark tunnels with a narrow door at one end. The largest bedroom, under the central dormer, had the smallest, pokiest closet of all. These days, buyers who could pay the kind of price a renovated Stickley would command expected a sybaritic mini-spa for a master suite. Short of sacrificing one of the smaller bedrooms, which would not be smart, a full-room addition would be the only way to create that here.

But if she did that, the little girl's memories would surely be demolished. Her spirit would never return.

Kelly shook her head, blinking. She wasn't one to think about spirits returning. What was this house doing to her?

She sat on the rocker in the blue bedroom to collect her thoughts, and immediately Ginger leapt into her lap. Absently she petted him. "A pox on these buyers! Who do they think they are, coming in here and wreaking havoc with our beautiful house? Well, we're not having it, are we, Cat? We'll have to find some buyers who have more sense."

But who would they be? Not the growing family Aidan was envisioning. A young couple just starting out? No— they wouldn't be able to afford it. A couple who could afford it wouldn't want to live here in the boonies; they'd want a condo in the city, close to jobs and nightlife. An older couple? Not elderly, because of the stairs, but maybe in their fifties. They've made their pile, gotten the kids out of the house, and now they want a slower, simpler lifestyle. They'll retire, or maybe work from home; the library would be perfect for that. They won't want tons of space because they'd only have to clean it; a couple of extra bedrooms for the kids and grandkids to visit would be just right. One and a half bathrooms are plenty. Of course they'll want a decent laundry room, and they'll need better storage too—a pantry, a linen closet, better access to the closets upstairs.

Kelly warmed to this imaginary couple. They'd been good parents, loving their children, spending time with them, teaching them to appreciate the important things in life. Now they could be rewarded with a beautiful house in which to spend the years of leisure they'd earned.

She brought her drawing board in from the truck and set it up in the library. When the plans were final, she'd transfer them to the CAD program on her laptop and get them printed, but she liked to do the preliminary sketches by hand; it helped her get a tangible sense of what she was creating.

By evening she had a rough set of sketches made. She walked

to the greasy spoon for supper, stopped at the local market for coffee and cat food, then climbed the stairs to her cream-and-yellow bedroom with a sense of work well done. The room seemed to welcome her. She set out her few toiletries on the dressing table, hung her shirts and jeans in the cedar-lined closet, and folded her underwear into the lavender-scented drawers of the mahogany tallboy. She turned down the quilt on the four-poster—like the one she used to imagine herself in as a child—and felt a sense of settling and peace.

She stroked Ginger, enthroned on the spare blanket folded at the foot of the bed, and said to him, "I wonder—is this what it's like to have a home?"

WELL, PRAISE THE LORD AND pass the ammunition, as Victor used to say—they're going to gut the kitchen. I listened to Kelly and that sweet little Kiera plan it all out, sitting right there at my old Formica table and plotting destruction to everything in sight.

I was afraid at first they might have some disagreements—Kelly seems to be a little strong-minded, like people used to say about me. Kiera's a pushover in a lot of things, but not where her work is concerned. But in the end they came up with a pretty good plan to cooperate.

"I have one serious handicap in planning a kitchen," Kelly said. "I can't cook."

Kiera's brown eyes opened wide. "Not at all?"

"Not one little bit. If it can't be made by adding hot water or nuking it in the microwave, I don't make it."

I was as shocked as Kiera. A granddaughter of mine not know how to cook? It looks like I got her here just in time.

Kiera stared a moment longer, then blinked. "So we're doing this just for the look of the thing?"

"Well, no." Kelly doodled on her notepad. "I plan to sell the place when it's all fixed up. A buyer will need a workable kitchen."

Uh-oh. I should have seen that coming, but I did so hope she'd stay. If she's going to sell, I'll have to win her forgiveness in the time it takes her to fix up the house. I can see I have my work cut out for me.

"Sell? I hoped you were going to live here. It'd be so great to have a neighbor near my own age."

Kelly's mouth jerked into what might be taken for a smile. I wanted to get an oilcan and grease her smile muscles up good. "Sorry, but with my career, it wouldn't work for me to settle down. I have to be ready to pick up and go wherever the jobs are."

She said that all brisk and businesslike, but her eyes betrayed her. She wants to stay—she just won't admit it.

"I see. Well." Kiera blinked a few times and cleared her throat. "Right. So, since you don't know much about how kitchens work, I propose a division of labor. I decide what goes where, how to arrange the storage and whatnot, and you concentrate on the finishes. I don't know that much about Craftsman style, so I'll gladly leave all that to you."

Kelly hesitated. I could see she was reluctant to let go of that much control. But in the end she stuck out her hand. "Deal."

Kiera shook hands, then pulled out the sheaf of papers she'd brought with her. "First we need to know what space we're dealing with and what we have to fit into it. Have you decided what you're going to do with the rest of the house?"

"Pretty much. I don't want to do any major reconfiguring, and I don't want to do a big addition. I think we can make it work with a few tweaks here and there." Kelly produced some sketches of her own. "I want to put a laundry room upstairs, here in the attic storage space. Then we'll add a linen closet here, off the hall, and rearrange the bedroom closets like this."

"Good. Then we can use the back porch for something else. It was never a great place for laundry anyway."

Kiera honey, you can say that again—oh, how I hated lugging all those baskets up and down the stairs, especially after my knees went bad.

"I was thinking a combination mudroom and pantry?"

"Perfect." Kiera studied the sketches, tapping a pencil against her lips. "Most people want some kind of casual eating area. Have you thought about that at all?"

"I guess I was hoping we could fit it in here. Esther had this table."

"Yeah, and Esther had a really bare-bones setup here, too—no microwave, pokey little fridge, hardly any counter space. I guess it suited her; she was alone for so long, and she was an old-fashioned kind of cook. But most buyers nowadays wouldn't go for that."

"No, I suppose not." Kelly sat with one foot swinging, fingers of one hand drumming on the tabletop. She shrugged. "I'm clueless. What do you suggest?"

Kiera looked around the room with narrowed eyes. "What if we were to build the tiniest possible addition—just extend the back porch a few feet over this direction—and make that extra space into a breakfast nook? A little booth, you know, like in a restaurant. That's authentic for a bungalow, isn't it? With big windows all around? This room needs more light."

Kelly squinted toward the back wall, screwing up her mouth. "I guess I could see that. It would blend right in on the outside, and we have to redo the roof anyway. And you're right about the light." She gave a brisk nod. "Let's go for it."

That big smile of hers spread across Kiera's face. She really is a doll. I used to imagine she was my granddaughter, and that made the ache a little less. "Great!" she said. "Now here's what I see for the kitchen itself."

From there on it was smooth sailing. They're both clever girls, and their ideas seemed to feed off each other. And I guess Kelly has plenty of money, so anything they can dream up, she can do.

It was quite a revelation to me, all the newfangled gadgets and custom-built units and whatnot they're going to cram in there— and still make it look like it belongs in a Stickley house. There's going to be a great big stainless-steel refrigerator, a dishwasher inside a drawer of all things, and a clever pantry with layers of shallow shelves. They're even talking about an island with a vegetable sink. To think of the steps and the bending and the time it would have saved me to have all those things! I may have been an old-fashioned cook, but it wasn't altogether from choice. I'd have been happy to move with the times, only there wasn't any money after Victor passed.

If only I'd found Kelly while I was still alive, I might have had all this to enjoy in my own time. But if-onlys aren't allowed up here. We only have what is.

CHAPTER 5

KELLY REVISED HER sketches to include a breakfast nook, then showed them to Aidan, who suggested a couple of minor amendments to satisfy the local building code. She set up her laptop in the library and drew the final plans. All they needed now was a building permit.

"This is where we have to watch our step," Aidan warned her. "Getting permits in this county is a fine art. You can build all you want down the road in Scotts Valley, but up here we're unincorporated. And the county is so paranoid about uncontrolled growth, they won't even let you build a carport without a complete environmental impact analysis."

"Are you serious? That would take months!"

"Well, I'm exaggerating a little. Actually, you don't need that unless you're adding five hundred square feet. We come in well under that, thank God. We should be able to get permits in a couple of weeks, with luck. But it's going to cost plenty."

Kelly waved a hand. "I don't care about the cost, as long as we can move ahead."

"Right. A lot depends on the first interview. Ordinarily, it's best for the homeowner to take care of it. They're nicer to people they think don't know anything about building. But since you're also the architect—it's probably best if I put in the application."

So he did, and reported that the process had gone fairly smoothly. Even so, it would be at least a couple of weeks before final approval would come through.

Kelly chafed at the delay, but at least she had plenty to keep her busy. She and Kiera began by cleaning out the back porch. There was little fodder for sentimentality in the litter of mops and brooms, cleaning supplies and old newspapers they found there. Kelly made a place in the house for the few things that would be useful, while Kiera took the rest to the trash.

The kitchen was a much bigger job. The cupboards were stuffed to capacity with dented pots, empty margarine tubs, and small appliances, some of them still in their boxes, while the drawers overflowed with paper and plastic bags, neatly folded pieces of used foil, and sandwich bags washed out for reuse. Alongside full sets of flatware and Fiestaware were odd pieces from at least half a dozen old patterns.

"Esther seems to have been a thrifty soul," Kelly said drily.

Kiera bubbled with laughter. "Oh my word, that woman never threw a toothpick away—it might come in useful some-day. I think she considered it her personal mission to keep the landfills from overflowing. She wouldn't get rid of a gift, either, even if she'd never use it—hence the four blenders."

"Well, I think I'll have to stretch the point about hanging onto her stuff. Three-quarters of this no one could ever possibly use."

Kiera agreed, and they filled a number of bags for trash and recycling as well as several boxes earmarked for the thrift store. Ginger had a heyday rooting through all the castoffs. That left the basic appliances, a good set of pots and pans, the flatware and Fiestaware, an eclectic assortment of serving pieces and canisters, and a collection of cookbooks.

Kelly sat at the Formica table, turning over the cookbooks. Every major European and Asian ethnicity seemed to be represented, along with *Death by Chocolate, Cooking for One or Two, Dinner in Half an Hour,* and *Luscious Leftovers.* "Did she really use all these?"

"I highly doubt it. She loved to bake, but as for all the ethnic stuff, I think she just liked to look and dream. Back when her husband and daughter were alive, she might have done some fancy cooking, but when I knew her, she only ate to live."

"What happened to her husband and daughter? How did they die?"

"I think Victor died of a heart attack or something. It was before I was born. And June . . . There seems to be some kind of mystery about June. Nobody would ever talk about her. Esther would say, 'I lost my baby when she was just seventeen,' but she would never tell me how." Kiera shrugged. "I'm sure Grammy knows, but she couldn't tell if she wanted to."

Kelly's throat constricted to think that lovely young girl should have passed out of all memory, with only photographs to show she had ever existed. Abstractedly she picked up a binder full of handwritten recipes and began to leaf through it.

Kiera finished packing the canisters into a box, then lingered over a cookie jar in the shape of one of the Oliver Hardy-esque bakers from Maurice Sendak's *In the Night Kitchen.*

"Is that what you'd like to have for your memento?" Kelly asked.

"Oh, could I?" She clutched the jar to her chest. "This jar has such memories. Kyle and I used to come over here every afternoon after school, before Pops got off work, and Esther would give us homemade cookies out of this jar. She made the best chocolate-chip-peanut-butter cookies you've ever tasted."

"Didn't your mother mind you being over here so much?"

"Mom died when we were seven—before we moved back here. Pops was happy to have us spend time with Esther. Of course, when we got older, I had to help out with Grammy more."

Kelly felt that same wrenching in her gut she'd felt at watching Aidan hug his daughter. "The jar's yours, Kiera. Just make me some of Esther's cookies sometime—if you have the recipe."

"It's probably in that binder."

She turned a few more pages. Then one title, written in Parker-perfect handwriting in blue ink, leapt off the page and knocked her back in her chair.

"Crustimony Proseedcake," Kelly said. "My mother said she invented that."

"Crustimony Proseedcake? No way. That was Esther's original recipe. She told me all about it. When June was little, they read that story where Owl tells Pooh that something-or-other is 'customary procedure' and Pooh hears it as 'crustimony proseedcake,' and June wanted to know how crustimony proseedcake tasted. So Esther made something up." She paused, but Kelly did not respond. "Maybe your mom made up a different recipe and gave it the same name."

Kelly had been scanning the ingredients as Kiera talked. "No. It's exactly the same. This is the one thing I ever learned to cook, and I remember it perfectly. The ingredients, the process, even the wording. *Exactly* the same." She looked up and saw her own consternation mirrored in Kiera's eyes.

"That's creepy," Kiera said.

"Maybe they both copied it out of the same magazine and

just said they made it up. That's the sort of thing my mother would've done."

"Not Esther. She couldn't stand any kind of sneakiness. Once I told her a tiny little fib—said I hadn't had dessert at home when I had, so she'd give me a piece of cake—and when she found out about it, she wouldn't give me any cookies for a week."

Kelly stared at Kiera another moment, then briskly shook her head. "Well, there's got to be some explanation. Maybe it got passed around. I grew up in San Francisco, not so far from here. They could have had a friend in common." But even as she said the words, she knew they couldn't be true. Miriam Mason had no real friends, and she'd never traded recipes with another woman in her life.

WELL, WHAT DO YOU KNOW about that. Crustimony Proseedcake. My job might be easier than I thought. It looks like there could be all kinds of little connections I don't even know about, to let Kelly know how much she belongs here. Raphael, I bet you had a hand in that—a hand that goes right back through all those years to when it all began. What can I say but thank you?

THE NEXT MORNING, AIDAN APPEARED at the front door with a younger man in tow. "This is Nathaniel Erikson. He's the best cabinetmaker and finisher in the county, with a great eye for period detail. I wanted him to get the lie of the land before we get started."

Nathaniel put out his hand. He was thirtyish, tall and muscular, with long medium-brown hair tied back in a ponytail and strong, high-boned Scandinavian features. But Kelly noticed these things only later, because as their hands touched, his grey-blue eyes fastened on hers and held them. She fell through his eyes and saw a rough grey sea and a rugged pine-forested shore, with dragon-prowed boats drawn up on a narrow strip of beach. Men in iron helmets came and went from the boats, but to her surprise Nathaniel was not among them; his face belonged to the lone figure off to the side, in a hooded robe of brown homespun, his hand raised in the sign of the cross. Nathaniel had the body of a Viking and the eyes of a saint.

Kelly awoke from her dream, pulled her hand back, and said, "Pleased to meet you," in the most neutral tone she could muster. "I always like to work with the best. The best materials and the best craftsmen. This house will be a showplace by the time we're through."

He smiled, and the severe northern landscape of his face was transfigured as if by the rising sun. "It's beautiful as it is," he said, his eyes still fixed on hers.

Kelly felt a hot flush creep up her neck and mentally slapped herself. Ridiculous to be discomposed by a handsome face, like a silly schoolgirl. She cleared her throat, frowning. "The plans are in the dining room. But maybe you'd like to look at the woodwork in the front rooms on the way. I'd like your opinion about refinishing."

Nathaniel nodded, then began a slow circuit of the living room, hall, and library, inspecting the woodwork of the wainscoting, windows, and inglenook, making little noises of recognition and appreciation in his throat. Ginger trotted at his heels as if they were old friends, though they hadn't even been properly introduced. Kelly felt vaguely resentful of this familiarity.

At last she followed Nathaniel into the dining room, where he examined the built-in sideboard with its carved fig motif on the central door, his long slender fingers caressing the wood as if it were a woman's skin.

Kelly shook off that thought. "What do you think?"

He straightened. "We're looking at redwood with a clear shellac finish. It's all beautifully done, well cared for, mostly in pretty good condition. A few nicks and nail holes, not hard to fix. As far as the finish is concerned—there's some darkening, especially in the inglenook, and some crackling here and there.

"Your options are basically, one, you could strip and refinish everything. That would take a lot of work, but it would look like new when we're done. Short of that, we could try a good cleaning and smooth out the crackled spots with alcohol. That would leave the finish a little darker than it was to begin with, but smoother and brighter than it is now. Or, three, if you like the old lived-in look, you could leave it alone."

Kelly pivoted, scanning the room, and pulled at her bottom lip. All those candlelit dinners, all those evenings with the family sitting companionably by the living room fire—some residue of those evenings was impregnated in the finish of the wood. Yet she didn't want it to look rundown.

"I think I'll take the middle road," she said, turning to face Nathaniel again. "Cleaning and smoothing. If I don't like the result, we still have the option of stripping, right?"

"Sure thing." He gave her a smile that said hers was the course he would have chosen. The schoolgirl in her was as gratified as if her favorite teacher had given her an A-plus.

She turned to the table. "Here are the kitchen plans." Nathaniel moved to stand behind her left shoulder; she could feel his warm breath on her neck, and when she spoke again her voice broke. She cleared her throat furiously and took a step to her right.

"We'll be using some standard-size cabinets, here, here, and here," she said, pointing with a pencil and avoiding the direct gaze of his disconcerting fjord-colored eyes. "But the doors, the island, the pantry, and the breakfast nook will need to be custom-built. I want all this to coordinate with the rest of the house."

Nathaniel nodded and bent over the plans, absorbing each detail. "This all looks doable. It's going to take some custom millwork, though, for that trim. Is that in the budget?"

Kelly felt his gaze on her but did not look up. "Not a problem. I'm committed to spending what it takes to do it right."

"You're my kind of boss." He straightened and looked from Kelly to Aidan. "When do we start?"

Aidan grimaced. "Soon as the permits come through. But I figure we can get away with tearing out the old kitchen before that. I'd like to start that tomorrow, if Kelly's game. And you could go ahead with the custom doors off site."

"Right." Nathaniel extended his hand toward Kelly again. "Good to meet you, Kelly. I look forward to working with you."

Kelly told herself it was only because of his craftsmanship that she was able to answer sincerely, "Same here."

CHAPTER 6

WELL, THAT WAS an interesting encounter, I must say! It seems Kelly may not be quite so self-sufficient as she'd like to think. Clearly that Nathaniel made quite an impression on her. More power to him, I say—if she falls in love, she'll be that much more likely to stick around.

The next morning Aidan brought in the rest of his crew. "My son, Kyle," he told Kelly. Now, Kyle is as tall and beefy as Kiera is petite and fine-boned. But they've got that same open, childlike smile. Kiera was always my favorite because she's a girl, and I'd lost a girl; but Kyle's as sweet as they come.

"Want to see some pictures of my little guy?" he said, reaching for his wallet.

Aidan laughed. "Not now, Kyle. His wife Mindy just had a baby boy, and Kyle's about to bust. You can show her the pictures later, son." Kyle put his wallet away, looking crestfallen.

"Kyle's a topnotch mason; he'll be working on the chimney when we get to that point. But for now he'll be tearing up the kitchen with the other guys."

Kyle grinned. "I love to bust things up. Almost as much as I love building them again."

Kelly shook hands with the other two workers, but her eyes kept straying beyond them as if looking for someone else. I wondered if she was disappointed that Nathaniel wasn't with them—but she must have known he'd be working off site.

Aidan said, "Right. We'll get to work then," and in no time the kitchen was bursting with the din of pounding sledgehammers and splintering wood. Good thing I don't have ears anymore—I wouldn't be able to take it Ginger made himself scarce with the first hammer blow.

Kelly covered her ears and mouthed to Kiera, "How about we work upstairs today?"

THE LONG, NARROW BATHROOM WAS on the opposite side of the house, so that was a good place to start. The din of demolition reached them, slightly muted, through the one small window.

"Well, this should go quickly, anyway," Kelly said, looking around the bare little room. A few wicker shelves over the tank, a mirrored metal medicine cabinet, and the vanity were the only storage places in the room, and the surfaces held nothing but a pink seashell-shaped plastic soap dish.

Kiera started on the medicine cabinet. Several amber plastic pill bottles spilled out into the sink when she opened the door. She rummaged about for a minute, then said, "Good grief, here's a bottle with one pill in it from 1978!"

Kelly pulled a towel off one of the wicker shelves and shook it out. "I think this towel's about the same vintage. It doesn't have enough nap to dry a lizard." She tossed it into a garbage bag and followed it up with the other towels on the two bottom shelves.

From the top shelf she reached down a dust-encrusted but

nearly full jar of bath salts. "This might be useful." She strained at the lid till it came unscrewed with a grinding jerk, then put the jar to her nose and inhaled a faint smell of jasmine. Without thinking she said, "My mother used to use this scent."

"Crustimony Proseedcake and jasmine bath salts—Esther and your mother seem to have had a lot in common."

"No, not her," Kelly said absently, as if the jasmine had drugged her. "My other mother."

The sound of her own words penetrated the stupor, and she sat down hard on the closed lid of the toilet. "What did I just say?"

"You said 'my other mother.' Did your father remarry or something?"

Kelly slowly shook her head. "I only have one mother. My parents hated each other, but they stayed married until he died. I can't imagine what made me say that."

Something teased at the edges of her consciousness, an image as ungraspable as a fading dream. Her tiny self in a bath-tub, and a woman bending over her—a woman she adored as she had never loved Miriam Mason—but the image dissolved before she could make out a face.

She screwed the lid back on the bath salts and dropped them into the trash. "Something in this house is getting to me," she said lightly. "Now I'm seeing things."

AT QUITTING TIME, KYLE MET Kelly on her way to the dumpster with the bathroom trash. "Can I show you my baby pictures now?"

"Sure." As a matter of fact, Kelly was a sucker for babies and would have been happy to look at the pictures that morning, when Kyle first offered.

He reached for his wallet, then stopped with it half out of

his pocket. "Or better yet, come and meet the little guy in person. I live right on the other side of Mrs. Perkins. Why don't you come for dinner? You can get to know my wife. You'll love her."

"That's very kind of you, but are you sure your wife would be up to having dinner guests? Didn't she just give birth a few days ago?"

Kyle's brow wrinkled in consternation. "Oh. I guess you're right. Hadn't thought about that." He brightened. "But come meet him anyway. I know Mindy won't mind."

His enthusiasm was irresistible. "All right. Just let me get rid of this." She hefted the trash bag.

"I'll take it."

She surrendered the bag and washed her hands, and they set off. Ginger followed them to the border of Mrs. Perkins' yard, then turned and stalked back. As they walked past Mrs. Perkins' manicured turf, Kelly glanced toward the house and was almost certain she saw the curtains drop into place.

Kyle lived in a small one-story yellow cottage, which he explained was one of many built in the 1920s when the area was a favorite vacation spot for Hollywood royalty. The interior was light and airy, with the original multipaned windows and white beadboard walls. Kelly loved it on sight.

"Mindy!" Kyle called as they entered. "I brought Kelly to see the little guy."

"Shhh!" came the whispered reply from the back bedroom. "I've just gotten him to sleep."

Kyle made a guilty face and tiptoed into the bedroom. Watching that burly frame move in cartoonishly exaggerated silence, Kelly could hardly keep her countenance. He emerged a minute later and whispered loudly, "Come on in. She doesn't want to move him."

Kelly hesitated, then followed him. She peeped cautiously around the door to see a disheveled but pretty young woman in a bathrobe sitting in a rocking chair, with a bundle of blankets cradled in her arms. Mindy smiled the proud, demure smile of new motherhood and beckoned Kelly closer, pulling down a corner of blanket to reveal a small round face and one minuscule red clenched fist.

He was too young yet to show much individuality, but his sheer babyness was enough to win Kelly's heart. A faint flush warmed his waxen cheeks, and the pink underlip pulled in and out with his sleeping breath. She longed to kiss the dark downy head but feared to wake him, so she contented herself with touching a cautious finger to the tiny wrinkled hand.

"He's beautiful," she said, and the new parents beamed. "You're a very lucky woman."

Mindy dimpled and blushed pink. "I know."

Kelly straightened and made way for Kyle to bend over his son. Had anyone ever hovered over her like that? Had anyone ever loved her as this baby was loved, as the little red-haired girl in the pictures had been loved? Not Miriam Mason, certainly. Maybe that "other mother" whose face and voice had tantalized her for a fleeting moment, and for whom she now yearned with an orphan's intensity.

Please, she thought urgently, not knowing to whom she spoke or for what she was asking. *Please.*

WITHIN A FEW DAYS, MY kitchen was an empty shell. They'd stripped the floor down to plywood, and the walls looked like careless patchwork, with the outlines of appliances and cabinets stamped in the old white paint against my autumn gold.

Kiera stood in the midst of the devastation and said to Kelly, "How are you going to eat? Obviously you can't cook in here. You'd better come and eat at our house for the duration."

"I've got a microwave in my truck. I'll rent a portable fridge, set those and the coffeemaker up in the dining room, and be good to go. There's water in the powder room, so I've got all I need."

Kiera sighed theatrically. "You're hopeless. But I like hopeless causes. I'm making it my mission to domesticate you before this project is through."

Kelly laughed, but behind the laugh I sensed a deep uneasiness. I think she's afraid Kiera's mission might succeed.

Meanwhile, Aidan paced around the kitchen like a tiger in a cage. He was antsy for the permits to be approved.

"A week is nothing, really," he said. "Two weeks is minimum, a month—nothing to worry about. But it's the middle of September already. If we don't get going we might not get the roof done before the rain." Around here we often don't see a cloud all summer long. But October gets iffy, and by November you can just about count on some serious storms.

Kelly frowned and chewed her bottom lip. "What can we do? I don't want you to risk getting in trouble, working without permits."

"We could go ahead with the demolition on the back porch. Technically you need a permit for that, but what can they do? They can't red-tag a structure that isn't there."

"Let's do it. The permits are sure to come through eventually, right?"

Aidan tossed an "Oh, sure," over his shoulder as he strode out the back door, not willing to lose a second. But I wouldn't be quite so certain. I've seen Imogene Perkins poking her nose through the hedge, peering over at the house from her upstairs window, watching the workmen come and go. I know how her mind works, and I know she's got a nephew in the county planning office. She feels like she's been snubbed, and I'd bet a batch of my chocolate-chip-peanut-butter cookies she'll be out to get her revenge.

THE NEXT MORNING, I SAW a white pickup with the County Planning logo on the door pull up in the driveway. A short, pudgy bald man opened the driver's door and jumped to the ground—his legs were too short to step out the normal way. Glaring through black horn-rimmed glasses, he stomped up the drive and around to the back, where the noise was coming from. I'd never met the man, but he had Perkins written all over him.

He stopped in front of the half-demolished back porch and bellowed, "Who's in charge here?"

Aidan stepped out from the midst of the rubble. "I am." He put out his hand. "Aidan McCarthy, McCarthy Construction, at your service."

Perkins kept his fists clenched at his sides. His beady eyes narrowed at Aidan. "I've had a report of unauthorized construction going on here."

Aidan lowered his hand and slowly wiped it down the side of his jeans. "And you are—?"

"Perkins. County Planning."

Aidan said coolly, "May I see some identification, please?" although the man's badge was in plain sight, clipped to his pocket.

"Don't change the object." Aidan's mouth twitched at the malapropism. "We're talking about unauthorized construction. Now what about it?"

"Construction? We're not constructing anything. All we're doing is tearing down this old porch."

A dull red flush spread up Perkins' neck. "Oh, sure, today you're tearing down, but tomorrow you'll start building. I've seen those plans you filed. You can't put some over on me."

Aidan drew himself up and his eyes flashed steel. I was so proud of him in that moment. "Unless I am grossly misinformed, in the United States of America a person cannot be accused of a violation he has yet to commit."

Perkins' jowls began to wobble, and the few hairs slicked across his scalp came loose and flapped in the breeze. "I demand to see the owner!" he squeaked. Well, he tried to bellow, but it turned into a squeak halfway through.

Kelly, with Ginger behind her, had appeared in the doorway while Aidan was talking. "What seems to be the problem here?"

"No problem. It seems our friend Mr. Perkins here was slightly misinformed. He thought we were constructing some-thing, when of course all we're actually doing is tearing something down. That little misunderstanding is all cleared up now, and Mr. Perkins was just leaving." He turned to Perkins, steel in his eyes again. "Weren't you?"

What Aidan missed when he was talking to Kelly was the look that came across Perkins' face when she first spoke. I don't know if you've ever seen rage and lust competing in one ugly counte-nance, but I can tell you it's not a pretty sight. Ginger didn't like it either—he crouched before her, tail waving, fire in his eyes.

I may have neglected to mention it before, but Kelly is quite a beautiful girl. Young woman, I should say, but anyone under forty seems like a girl to me. She does her best to hide it, wearing baggy clothes and keeping her hair so spiky-short, but she's got good bones, pure ivory skin, and the clearest grey-green eyes you ever saw. Her figure's nothing to sneeze at either, tall and slender with fine broad shoulders and all the right curves. She looks like a Norse goddess. And that sniveling dwarf Perkins dared to cast his eyes on her!

He spluttered and simpered, torn between his two besetting sins, and his face got redder and redder. Finally he stammered, "I'll be back," whipped a handkerchief out of his back pocket, and stomped off down the driveway, mopping his brow.

Kelly stood in the doorway, arms crossed, drumming her fingers against her arm. "I didn't expect this kind of trouble so soon."

"Neither did I." Aidan stood arms akimbo, frowning after Perkins. "But did you notice the name? I'd bet my license he's related to our dear neighbor." He jerked his head in the direction of Imogene's house. "A hundred to nothing she turned us in."

"Guess I'll have to go talk to her." Kelly dusted off her hands. "See if I can smooth down her feathers."

"Good luck. That woman was born ruffled. But I wouldn't worry too much about Perkins. He's all bark and no bite. Heck, I wouldn't even dignify him with the name of dog—he's just a flea."

"Maybe. But fleas can be awfully hard to get rid of once they've settled in."

KELLY TOOK A DEEP BREATH and stepped onto the pristine cement path that precisely bisected Mrs. Perkins' preternaturally green lawn. She half expected the path to rise up against her and each blade of turf to shriek, "Intruder! Intruder!" Instead, a frosty silence reigned, into which the tinny chimes of the doorbell fell like klaxons.

The door opened exactly two inches and Mrs. Perkins' pink-tipped nose poked into the crack. "Oh, Kelly, dear, it's you." The gap narrowed, a chain rasped, and the door swung open. "Do come in."

"Thank you." Kelly stepped over the threshold onto a plastic runner that led across the white carpet to the tile-floored kitchen beyond.

Mrs. Perkins beckoned her in a few feet farther. "I'll just close this door, dear. The dust does blow in so."

No speck of dust would dare to fall on Mrs. Perkins' property, nor was there any breeze to blow it if it had; but Kelly stepped aside.

"Now, what can I do for you?" Her head on one side, bony hands clasped before her concave chest, Mrs. Perkins' bright birdlike eyes peered up at Kelly.

Years of experience with hostile neighbors had honed Kelly's conciliation skills. "I just wanted to apologize if our noise has been disturbing you at all."

"Oh, no, dear. Not disturbing me. Although I must say my dear little budgies have been sadly upset." She gestured toward the kitchen window, where two covered cages emitted a volley of squawks and twitterings.

With some effort Kelly kept a straight face. "Well, I am sorry about that, Mrs. Perkins. But the demolition is by far the noisiest part of the process. We'll be finished with that in another day or two."

"The noisiest part of the process? Do you mean to say there will be more?"

"Well, yes. We're going to rebuild the back porch a little larger, to make room for a breakfast nook. There'll be some hammering and whatnot, of course, but it won't be as bad as the demolition. And once we have the shell up and move on to the inside finishing, you won't hear much at all."

"You do surprise me, Kelly. It was my understanding your construction permits had yet to come through."

"And where would you have heard that, Mrs. Perkins? It was my understanding that such matters were between the homeowner and the county."

Mrs. Perkins sputtered. "Well, I don't know—I'm sure I heard it somewhere. Perhaps that nice Kyle McCarthy mentioned it when we were chatting over the fence the other day."

Kelly was sure Kyle would avoid any "chatting" with Mrs. Perkins as strenuously as she would herself, were she not forced into it. "We're confident the permits will come through in good time. Meanwhile, we have to go ahead with construction or we won't be able to finish while the weather's good. You must see that, Mrs. Perkins."

Mrs. Perkins sniffed and applied her balled-up tissue to the pink tip of her nose.

Kelly went on. "When everything's finished, the house will go up in value quite a bit. And as I'm sure you know, that will improve the value of all the properties in the neighborhood. Not to mention the view from your upstairs window will be nicer as well." She watched that shaft go home.

Mrs. Perkins' eyes widened and she fluttered her hands before her face. "Yes, yes, I see all that of course. Now if you'll excuse me, I really must get back to my cleaning." She edged past Kelly and opened the door. "Good day, Kelly dear."

Kelly left the battlefield unsure of whether she'd achieved a victory or merely a draw. It was hard to fight an enemy who would do nothing but dodge and call you "dear."

CHAPTER 7

WHILE THE BOYS were having fun tearing down the porch wall, Kelly and Kiera proceeded to clean out what I used to call the attic—the undereave storage that opens off my bedroom. This house doesn't have a lot of storage, what with the lack of a basement, which is a thing I never could understand how people can do without. So I have to admit I'd crammed an awful lot of stuff into that little space. It's the width of the bedroom and about six feet deep, only three of which you can stand upright in.

When I saw Kelly's face, I did feel bad for her, having to deal with all my junk. And a lot of it is just junk. I don't even remember what's in the boxes at the back; I haven't been able to get to them for years. But there are a few things here that I want—need—her to see. Some she may even want to keep, once she knows my history is her history too.

Kelly stood in the doorway with Kiera and ran a hand through her hair, which isn't quite as spiky now as when she first came. She took a deep breath and blew it out through puffed lips.

"Well," Kiera said, "we could just lug it all to the dumpster."

I held my breath, figuratively speaking. Please, Raphael, don't let her dump it all unseen.

"That would be the sensible thing. It'd take forever to go through all this. And the dust!" Kelly sneezed three times in a row. "Listen to me. And we haven't even moved anything yet."

She blew her nose, then nipped down the hall to her bedroom and returned with two clean bandannas. She handed one to Kiera and tied the other over her own nose and mouth.

Kiera giggled as she tied hers on. "We look like bandits."

Kelly sighed. "I feel like a bandit, throwing out all this stuff."

Ginger appeared, darted between their legs, and began to root among the boxes, probably scenting mouse. He pawed at a decaying box in a corner and dislodged its contents with a clatter.

"What have you got there, Ginger?" Kelly went to look. "Kiera, look at this! It looks like one of the original glass doorknobs. And here's a light fixture. That settles it—we're going through all of this. There could be all kinds of treasure buried in here."

I did a little bodiless victory dance at those words. Oh, thank you, Raphael! And you too, Ginger. I'd give you a kitty treat if I could.

So they went through it all, box by box. They pulled out all kinds of old stuff from the house that I never even knew was there. And of course, a lot of trash did end up in the dumpster, or in the back of Kelly's truck awaiting a trip to the thrift store; and good riddance, too. A few things, like the plastic boxes of Christmas decorations, they glanced at, then stacked at the far end of the room. But they lingered over the two big cedar trunks, which is just what I wanted them to do.

I had embroidered linens in there that my grandmother brought over from Sweden. Hand-pieced quilts my mother made—I can remember her stitching on them as she rocked by the fire. Darling little smocked and tucked and flouncy-lacy dresses I made for June when she was small and could never bear to part with. And a

73

couple of old photo albums—I didn't hang all the pictures on the living room walls.

Kelly fingered the linens with a reverence I couldn't have bettered and paged through the albums with the rapt attention of a genealogical sleuth. "Some of these pictures must go back to the invention of the camera. Look at these people—they look so grim." She pointed to a wedding picture of my great-grandparents, him seated, her standing next to his chair. They do look as if they were facing a firing squad, but I know they were kind and jolly people who had a long and happy life together.

Kiera looked over Kelly's shoulder. "That's because they had to hold a pose for a full minute while the exposure took. They couldn't risk a smile."

They looked on through the generations—the farm my grandparents left in Sweden, the new one they carved out of the Minnesota prairie and handed down to my parents; my girlhood, my courtship with Victor, the proverbial boy next door; Victor in uniform; then more photos like the ones she'd seen downstairs, of our wedding and our life together. Kelly lingered over the last few pictures of June, where she'd dressed up like a Renaissance painting for a play she did at school.

"She's so lovely," she said, and I couldn't agree more. She looked up at Kiera. "I feel I know these people. It doesn't make sense, does it—from the little you've told me, and seeing their pictures and their things. But I feel connected to them, as if—" Her voice dropped to an awe-filled whisper. "As if—I belonged here."

Oh, you do belong here, honey, you do! Oh, Raphael, it's working! I *knew* there was some point in hanging onto all these things.

She blinked hard. "My parents never kept any of this kind of stuff. They didn't have one thing in the house that reflected any kind of family history at all. I never even met my grandparents. It's like I'm cut off from all the world, just alone."

She turned her head and looked at Kiera as if she'd forgotten she was there. "I want to be part of this family, the Hansen family. Can people adopt you after they're dead?"

Kiera, that dear sweet child, put her arm around Kelly's shoulders. "I don't think so, honey. But my family would adopt you in a heartbeat. Would you settle for being a McCarthy instead?"

Kelly sat up straight, shrugging off Kiera's arm. She tried for a smile, but it wasn't very convincing. "I'm being silly. I'm a grown woman, I'm fine on my own." She turned to face Kiera, who looked the way a little girl might look if her mother took the bouquet she'd picked for her and tossed it in the trash. "But thanks for the offer. It really was sweet of you." She gave Kiera an awkward little hug.

"Well, the offer stays open in case you ever change your mind." Kiera composed herself, then stood and went over to open the second trunk. Off the top she picked a fat packet wrapped in tissue paper and tied with a red ribbon. "Look at this. I bet these are Victor's love letters." She handed the packet to Kelly.

Kelly gingerly unwrapped the tissue and pulled open the bow. She unfolded the top letter as if it might crumble in her hands and glanced at the date, the greeting, the signature. "Yep. Written from overseas during the war."

She settled herself cross-legged with her back against the trunk and read aloud.

Dearest Esther, star of my heart,

We're in France now. That's all I'm allowed to say. I can't describe the countryside to you, but I can tell you that every night I look at the sunset, and it looks just like the sunsets we used to watch over the prairie back home. I watch the sun as it sinks into the trees, shedding its benign yellow mask and revealing itself as the gigantic red fireball it really is, and I know that in a few hours it will be setting in Minnesota and you'll be watching it, as we agreed. I send it messages to take to you—are you getting them? Does the sun tell you every evening how much I love you, how my life is anchored and centered in you, how the thought of you sings me to sleep through the distant shellfire, graces my dreams with sweet longing, and wakes me gently in the morning with enough strength to face the horrors of the day?

Kelly's voice broke. She put the letter down and wiped the back of her hand across her eyes. I was getting pretty choked up myself. I'd forgotten what a poet Victor could be; but in all our years together, he never let me forget how much he cared. Oh, Kelly, you've got to let me get through to you so I can go to be with him again.

"Wow," Kiera said. "Can you imagine being loved like that?"

Kelly shook her head, and my dead heart broke all over again. "No," she said. "No, I absolutely cannot."

THE NOISIEST PART OF THE demolition was finished in a couple of days, and it was safe to work downstairs again. Nathaniel returned to help Kelly clean up the woodwork.

"Why don't we start with the living room?" Kelly said. "I have a feeling the inglenook will be the dirtiest. I like to get the worst jobs out of the way right at the beginning."

"Right." He nodded. "Eat the liver first, then dessert tastes all the better."

She laughed, then caught him looking at her, his North Sea

eyes calm and contemplative. "You should laugh more often," he said. "It suits you."

She turned away in confusion and lugged her bucket into the living room. The inglenook filled the far end of the room—two built-in benches facing each other and turning the corners to meet the edges of a wide stone hearth.

Nathaniel stood for a moment admiring the workmanship of the fireplace and mantel. "You're going to rebuild the chimney, aren't you? Make this a working fireplace again?"

"Absolutely. A house is not a home without a working fireplace." *Listen to the expert on what makes a home.*

"You'll have some nice cozy winter evenings curled up on these benches."

"Mmm. With a mug of hot chocolate and a nice long book." Kelly could feel herself in that scene right now. In her vision she snuggled into the cushions, warmed her toes at the flames, and glanced up from *Bleak House* to see a man's long legs stretched out on the opposite bench. Her gaze traveled up that tall form to watch the firelight flicker over the sculpted planes of a familiar face, bent over a book of his own. Nathaniel's face.

She shook herself, forcing the rogue thoughts of home comforts and a friend to share them with down to the subterranean reaches of her mind. "Too bad I won't be here for many winter evenings. We should be finished before December, and then I'm selling the place."

His eyebrows lifted. "Oh, I see. I thought you were doing this for yourself. Well, it'll be nice for someone, at any rate."

Nathaniel sought out a spot on the mantel where the shellac had crackled; areas like this would have to be smoothed before they could be cleaned. Kelly watched him moisten a cloth with alcohol, dab it over the jagged edges of crumbling shellac, then

77

as they softened, gingerly rub them down until they melted back into a smooth finish. Again she noted the grace and gentleness of his long, delicate fingers. She would never have pegged those hands for the hands of a workman.

He worked quietly, absorbed in his task, not seeming to mind her presence as she watched over his shoulder. But when he finished the first patch, he cocked an eyebrow at her, and she was suddenly conscious of the way she'd been staring at his hands. "Want to try the next bit?" he asked her.

"Not right now. You're doing great. I'll find a smooth place and start cleaning."

She moved to the far end of a bench, set her bucket on the seat, and dipped her sponge into the solution of water and Murphy's Oil Soap. She rubbed at the wood until the years of accumulated soot began to come off on the sponge.

Both absorbed in their tasks, they spoke little beyond the occasional, "Oy, that was a tough spot," or, "That's done it— look at this grain!" But even in the long silences, she was aware of his presence at every moment, and when he occasionally brushed her sleeve in passing, every hair on her arm stood at attention.

The work was indeed difficult, with many spots needing superfine steel wool to restore the wood to something like its original color. By noon Kelly's arms and shoulders were aching, though she was not unaccustomed to similar kinds of work.

She finished the bench, then dropped onto the damp seat. "I've had it. Let's break for lunch."

"You're the boss." He set his cloth and bottle of alcohol on the mantel and stretched his arms over his head. Kelly averted her eyes from the glimpse of taut, tanned abdomen his shirt afforded as it rose.

He exited the inglenook, then stopped by the piano just outside it.

"This is a real Stickley piano, isn't it?"

"Far as I can tell."

"Don't suppose it's in tune?"

"Wouldn't know. Haven't tried it."

He opened the keyboard cover and his slender fingers caressed the ivory keys. "Mind if I have a go?"

"Help yourself."

He sat on the piano bench and flexed his fingers, then played the opening bars of a Mozart minuet. Several of the keys rang sour, but his touch was masterful.

"Nope," he said. "Definitely not in tune."

"No. But you play beautifully."

"How about you? Do you play?"

"Not piano. I play cello."

He looked at her for a moment, his head on one side. She forced herself to meet his gaze. There was nothing in this conversation to frighten her, but her heart raced nevertheless.

At last he said, "I could tune it for you if you like."

"You're a tuner?" Was there no end to his talents?

He shrugged. "I have perfect pitch, so it seemed like a good skill to pick up. Then maybe we could play something together. Aidan plays violin, did you know? We could do a trio."

He paused, then added, "If you like."

She flexed her arms in front of her, and her fingers tingled with longing to feel the smooth wooden hollow of the bow, the tough give and tensing of the strings. "All right. Yes. I like."

"I'll bring my tools tomorrow and tune it after I finish work."

AIDAN RECEIVED THE IDEA OF playing a trio with enthusiasm. "I haven't played much lately, though. I'll need some time to practice."

"Me too," Kelly said. "I haven't had my cello out in weeks."

They agreed to give themselves a week and get together the following Sunday evening to play through Mozart's second piano trio. Kyle and Kiera insisted on being present, though all three players protested they weren't ready for an audience. "We'll bring Grammy over, too," Kiera said. "She loves music. And Kyle can bring Mindy and the baby."

Kelly put her hands on her hips. "Excuse me, but last time I checked, this was my house. I'm not very up on the etiquette of being a homeowner, but I believe it does give me the right to invite my own guests."

"Oh. Right." Kiera's voice went small and her cheeks red. "Sorry."

Oh, blast, she'd done it again—hurt this innocent, affectionate creature who only wanted to get close to her. Kelly threw up her hands. "But what the heck—invite the whole neighborhood if you want. If I'm going to make a fool of myself, it may as well be in public. Just spare me Mrs. Perkins, please."

Kiera's laugh told her she was forgiven.

ON MONDAY THE PERMITS CAME through, which surprised me a little; I was sure Perkins would manage to hang things up somehow. But I guess he's just an inspector and doesn't have the power to deny a permit.

Aidan got the men right to work pouring the foundation for the new breakfast nook. They poured it over where the old back stairs used to be, then made new concrete steps heading ninety degrees off the back of the "mudroom," as they call it. That'll be a lot more convenient for Kelly, as the garage is on that side. I don't know why the original builders made me take all those extra steps instead of just flipping the back porch around to face the garage. Maybe the garage was added later.

Kelly and that nice young Nathaniel spent most of the week polishing up the paneling and whatnot in the living room. My goodness, if I'd had any idea how much difference a little scrubbing could make, I'd have done it myself years ago. Of course, I dusted all the wood regularly, but that's not the same thing. I guess it darkened so gradually over the years, I didn't notice. But it sure looks pretty now.

I never met Nathaniel in my lifetime, but I surely do like him. I like the way he looks at Kelly, as if he'd be pleased to cherish her forever, and the way he's so respectful toward her. I know as certain as the sun will rise she likes him too, but she's trying hard not to show it. It makes my heart ache—yes, I know my physical heart is moldering in the grave, but I still have a heart nonetheless—and it aches to see how she pushes people away when all they want to do is love her. Those people she grew up with must have been awful to her. Oh, Lord, if only I could have had her here with me! It's all my fault, of course, and I know He had His reasons not to let me find her and bring her back. But I do pray she'll open up and let herself be healed now.

CHAPTER 8

THE MEN TOOK the weekend off, but Kiera came over on Saturday to help Kelly clean out the small corner closet in the back hall, which she planned to replace with a telephone desk and mail-sorting area.

Tying up a yard-sized bag of trash, Kiera said, "Want to come to church with us tomorrow?"

Kelly turned on the step stool with a box of used wrapping paper in her arms. "Church? What church? What for?"

Kiera made a face at her. "What for, she says! If you don't know that, I can't tell you. But to answer your more sensible question, Saint Innocent's. The Orthodox church in Boulder Creek."

"Hm. No thanks. I went to an Orthodox church in San Francisco once, just because the architecture intrigued me and I could only get inside when a service was on. I couldn't understand a word they were saying, and nothing they did made any sense."

"Oh, our church isn't like that. Our service is all in English. Some of it might look a little weird, I grant you, but I could explain all that as we went along." A sly look crept into her eyes. "Nathaniel goes there too, you know."

At that name Kelly felt a small jolt, like a static-electric shock. She flattened her tone as she climbed down and set down her box. "Why would you think that would make a difference?"

"Oh, come on, Kelly. It's plain as grape juice on a white rug you're attracted to each other. And why not? He's a terrific guy."

So it wasn't her imagination, the way Nathaniel looked at her; Kiera had seen it too. And seen something more that Kelly'd hoped she'd kept hidden.

"I can't be held responsible for what my hormones choose to do. A—relationship—" she could hardly bring her lips to form the word— "is not in my plans right now." She climbed back on the step stool. "Or ever."

Kiera was silent a moment. Then her lip trembled as she said, "You won't let us adopt you, you won't come to church, you won't let yourself fall in love. Sometimes I think you'd rather the world had only houses in it and no people to live in them."

Kelly felt as if a very small and private earthquake had agitated her molten core and sent fault lines through her outer crust. She climbed back down and with slow, deliberate movements willed her hands to lift and rest on Kiera's shoulders. Kiera's moist brown eyes fixed on hers with a glimmer of hope.

"I grew up with people I couldn't trust. I've never really learned to trust anyone. I think I may have found some trustworthy people here—you especially. But it's a hard lesson, Kiera. Please—be patient with me." Her voice crumbled to a whisper. "And don't give up."

Kiera's face lit in a teary smile and she wrapped her arms around Kelly, who stiffened at first, then softened into the embrace. "I won't give up. I always wanted a sister like you."

HAVING REFUSED CHURCH, KELLY WAS left to fill her time on Sunday as best she might. She decided to put the living room in order in preparation for the evening and then get in some practice time.

She stood in the archway to the living room, hands on hips, assessing the task before her. The woodwork gleamed with a soft reddish glow, the fruit of the week's labor. But the furnishings were all in disarray, as she and Nathaniel had shoved things about to get to the paneling. The couch and chairs stood at crazy angles, like guests at a party where no one knows anyone else. Books from the shelves that flanked the front window lay in toppling piles on the window-seat cushion, which had been tossed to the floor. Ginger reveled in the chaos, pawing and sniffing at the books and pillows as if he'd never seen them before.

Ignoring his protests, Kelly stacked the books back on the now-dry shelves, noticing a decided trend toward mysteries by dead Englishwomen—Dorothy L. Sayers, Ngaio Marsh, Margery Allingham, Patricia Wentworth, Agatha Christie. Guessing these were Esther's books—Victor had the whole library across the hall—Kelly approved her taste. These would make for many a pleasant fall evening curled up by the fire. Already, at the end of September, the morning air held a bite that made her look forward to having a working fireplace.

Rather than return the couch and chairs to their original positions, she regrouped them to face the piano, leaving space for straight chairs for herself and Aidan near the piano, and for Eunice's wheelchair next to the couch. But the folding table with the jigsaw puzzle was decidedly in the way. Shame—she'd meant to work on the puzzle in her evening spare time, but between drawing plans and practicing the cello, she hadn't had any spare time.

She hated to take it apart, though. It represented one of her favorite paintings—Botticelli's Birth of Venus. That print had hung on the wall of her bedroom in the cold gray house, the only picture in the room. An odd choice for a child's room, perhaps, but she loved it—the soft bright tones of coral and aqua, the boisterous winds on one side, the solicitous handmaiden on the other, and most of all Venus herself in the middle, emerging from the sea on her scallop shell, demurely covering herself with her fantastically long red-gold hair. Her face looked more like the Madonna, the ideal mother, than like the pagan goddess of erotic love. Kelly had gazed at that face hour after hour, wishing she had a mother capable of that much tenderness.

Shooing Ginger, who pounced on the puzzle pieces as if they were live prey, Kelly studied the face on the box; then her head jerked up to scan the wall of pictures across the room. She strode over to the last picture of the daughter—June, had Kiera called her?—and cut her eyes back and forth from that face to the one on the puzzle box. The resemblance was uncanny. The same ivory skin, the same oval shape, the same tender and sad expression.

Why that should so move her, Kelly didn't know. It was natural that Esther should be drawn to a puzzle that reminded her of her lost daughter, and it was no such startling coincidence that the same famous painting should have hung on Kelly's wall. And yet . . . and yet. There was something about that face.

As she looked from one picture to the other, her vision from the bathroom floated before her eyes, and for an instant the woman bending over her infant self in the tub took on the combined faces of June and Venus. "My other mother," she whispered as the blood rushed from her head and she swayed toward the wall. She put out a hand to steady herself, and the vision

85

faded. "No. It couldn't be. It's just the power of suggestion."

But in the end, she picked up the folding table and carried it into the library, puzzle and all.

AN AFTERNOON OF PRACTICING STEADIED Kelly's nerves. She had a quick supper of microwaved macaroni and cheese and got ready to receive her guests.

The occasion seemed to call for something a little more formal than her usual T-shirt and jeans. She pawed through the few garments hanging in the guest room closet—she still thought of it as the guest room although she, the owner, was its only guest—and pulled out the grey fitted suit she wore for business appointments. That would never do; she couldn't move her arms or hold a cello between her knees in that. The only other option was a long, flared black velvet skirt she'd worn for recitals in college. A cream silk blouse and black pumps completed the outfit.

When she was dressed, feeling ridiculously self-conscious, she sat at the dressing table to brush her hair. The proper time for a trim was long past; she'd been too busy to think about it. Her usual spiky look didn't work at this length. She brushed the hair softly back from her face at the sides and pulled bangs down over her forehead. It looked, surprisingly, not bad.

She went downstairs and surveyed the living room, which looked both tidy and welcoming. Most of those who would be here tonight had been in and out of the house constantly for the last few weeks, regarding it as a workplace rather than a home. But tonight she wanted them to see it as her home, and themselves as honored guests in it. The thought was complete before she realized how out of character it was for her to think it.

Nathaniel arrived first, dressed in black slacks and a soft

black shirt, which made his eyes even bluer than usual. He handed Kelly a bottle of chilled Moselle—"For later"—and his eyes softened as he gazed at her. "You look beautiful," he said simply, as if he were evaluating a work of art.

Kelly felt herself blush to the roots of her hair. "Thanks," she muttered, taking the wine, so that her thanks could be construed as applying only to the gift.

The McCarthys arrived at that moment, much to Kelly's relief—Aidan in a suit, carrying his violin case, and Kiera in pale pink linen, pushing her grandmother in her chair. Eunice had on a black beaded mohair cardigan in honor of the occasion.

Behind them were Kyle and Mindy, with the baby asleep in a sling across Mindy's chest. "Hope you don't mind us bringing the little guy," Kyle said in a stage whisper. "I'll take him out if he makes a peep, but this time of the evening he usually sleeps like a log. And Mindy hasn't been out anywhere since he was born."

Kelly glanced at Mindy, whose smile seemed pasted over a rather frayed façade, then down again to the baby. "Of course, he's welcome. I'm happy to have you both. Besides, musical education can't start too young."

As she closed the door behind them and came into the living room, Kiera was maneuvering her grandmother's wheelchair into place next to the couch. "You look terrific!" she whispered to Kelly. "And so does the house. I think my domestication plan is beginning to work."

With a pang that was not wholly regretful, Kelly had to admit that it was.

MY OLD HOUSE HASN'T HEARD such music since June left. She was the one who used to play the piano, and once or twice Aidan came in to play duets with her. Father Aidan he was then, but it wasn't too long afterward he left the priesthood to get married. I always thought it was unhealthy the way the Catholics won't let their priests get married. That church they all go to now is much more sensible that way.

Eunice enjoyed the music, I could tell. It was good to see my old friend again, and it wouldn't surprise me if she knew I was there. Eunice always did have a kind of sensitivity that way—the Scots call it second sight. Why, I wouldn't even have known my June had passed on if it hadn't been for Eunice.

But back to the music. I have to admit, young Nathaniel plays even better than June did. It sounded to me—of course, what do I know—like he could be a professional. I guess Kelly thought so too, because she asked him afterward why he hadn't pursued a career in music.

They'd opened Nathaniel's Moselle, and Kiera'd brought over some of those chocolate-chip-peanut-butter cookies I used to make for her. Nathaniel finished a bite of cookie before he answered.

"It's kind of a gory story—sure you want to hear it?"

Kelly hesitated, then nodded. Misery loves company, I guess.

"I started playing very young. I loved it, took to it like a chisel to a block of wood. I guess I was doing pretty well, because my parents started pushing me to practice even more. They wanted to make a child prodigy of me.

"I was playing with the local symphony at age twelve, and at sixteen they took me to New York, to Juilliard. My parents were determined I would be the next Horowitz. But the pressure was too much for me. I only wanted to play—I didn't want to compete, to claw my way to the top. Halfway through Juilliard, I cracked."

Oh, those pushy parents—I hate them even more because I used to be one of them.

"Cracked?" Kelly said.

"I had a breakdown. They shipped me off to a 'rest home' in the Catskills. It took me six months to recover to the point I could function, and then I just said no. No to my parents, no to a career in music. At that point I thought I never wanted to see a piano again.

"I came out here on a whim. A friend got me a job with Aidan as an apprentice carpenter. Aidan helped me put my life back together and get trained as a cabinetmaker. After a while I found I missed the piano and started playing again, but only for myself and the occasional friend. I never want to get back on that crazy treadmill."

Kelly gazed at him with her head cocked on one side. I could see a little bit of Victor in that pose. "And you're not bitter?"

"What's to be bitter about? I'm happy being a cabinetmaker. It gives me the chance to strive for perfection without having to compete against other people, and that's what I love. And it's a living, which music never could have been for me since I couldn't take the pressure."

"But your parents. You're not bitter toward them for what they did to you?"

He stared into space for a minute, his eyes clouding. Kelly watched him as a cat watches a stranger, waiting to see if he's safe before venturing out for a pat.

"I was bitter at first. I thought they'd ruined my life. But Aidan helped me see they'd only done what they thought was best for me, and my life was my own to make of what I would."

Kelly's eyes grew round, then drifted in Aidan's direction. I could see her readjusting her opinion of him.

Nathaniel sipped his wine, looking at her over the brim of one of my Waterford glasses. I saw her color under his gaze and duck her head. He said, "I could ask you the same question, you know. Your technique isn't fully developed, but your musicality is pretty impressive. You and Aidan have something of the same feeling for the music, it seems to me."

"You know, I think you're right. The three of us played amazingly well together for our first time. It's like we were all in sync without even thinking about it." She looked at Aidan for a minute, then came back to Nathaniel. "But I never considered a career in music. Music wasn't valued in my family—I was a fluke. I knew from a very young age I wanted to study architecture and design."

"What did your father do?"

Her face hardened. "He was a builder. A developer. Completely without conscience—it was all about the money for him. I went into building in spite of him, not because of him. When he died, I made it my business to counteract his influence in the world wherever I could."

Nathaniel's face grew thoughtful. "I see," he said softly, and I believe in that moment he really did see—a great many things.

CHAPTER 9

NEXT DAY THE framing of the addition began. Kelly was not a carpenter, but she always liked to drive a few nails in the initial framing of a project. It gave her a sense of ownership, as well as a sense of reality—this addition was actually being built. She was putting her stamp on this house, Perkinses notwithstanding.

Aidan came over to inspect her work. "You drive a good straight nail, for—"

She bristled. "For a girl?"

"I was going to say, for an architect. Most architects I know are hopeless at anything practical. And just try explaining to them why what they've put on paper can't be built! But you have a real hands-on approach. I like that."

Kelly's offense evaporated. This man kept surprising her. "And I like that you like that. I've worked with some contractors who wanted me miles away."

They looked at each other for a moment, then both burst out laughing. Aidan put his long arm around her shoulders and squeezed. Kelly tensed involuntarily, and he dropped his arm as if her shoulders were white-hot.

"Sorry. Don't mean to be inappropriate. For a minute there I thought you were Kiera."

Kelly shook her head briskly, lower lip clamped painfully between her teeth, and mumbled, "It's okay. For a minute there I wished I was."

HER TOKEN CARPENTRY ACCOMPLISHED, KELLY moved into the library, which was next in line to have its woodwork restored. She would have to take all the books off the shelves, but first she wanted to plan how to expand the electrical supply to accommodate a computer setup.

She stood in the middle of the floor and pivoted by degrees. Bookshelves lined all four walls, interrupted only by doorways and windows, with a broad seat under the front window that faced the porch. A huge oak desk—either original Stickley or an excellent imitation—stood out in the center of the room, facing that window. A couple of old but comfortable leather armchairs sat between the desk and the window seat.

The only way to put a desk against the wall, where a computer desk would normally be, was to take out either the window seat or a significant portion of shelving. Not the window seat, she decided instantly. But perhaps some of the shelves could go. They were full now, but she herself didn't possess enough books to fill a fraction of them—nor, she reminded herself, would most potential buyers.

She began to skim the shelves. The two inner walls contained an impressive collection of classic literature—everything from Homer to Nabokov, from Wodehouse to Winnie the Pooh. Directly behind the desk were dictionaries, thesauruses, The Elements of Style. On the outer walls she found history, theology, and several oversized shelves devoted to art and architecture. All told, there might be one shelf of books she could let go without a pang. Victor Hansen must have been a well-read, thoughtful, and interesting man.

In pursuit more of his character than of her plan for the room, Kelly sat in the oak armchair and pulled out the drawers of the desk. One shallow drawer released a ghost of ancient pipe tobacco as she opened it. The large file drawer beneath it yielded all the usual household categories of bills, tax returns, and medical records, plus a bulging file labeled "June's Artwork."

Kelly maneuvered the artwork file out of the drawer and opened it on the desktop. At the front were the typical crayon scrawls and finger-paintings of a preschooler. These gave way to crayon or tempera renderings of stick people, stick pets, and square houses with triangular roofs. A folded construction-paper card showed a happy-faced girl with scarlet crayon ringlets holding a bouquet of round-petaled flowers under the scrawled words, "Happy Father's Day."

Once, at age six, Kelly had brought home a Father's Day card she had painstakingly made at school, covering every inch with houses and golf clubs and smiling little red-headed girls. When the day came, she gave it to Howard, who happened to be at home for a week or two. He glanced at it and made a harrumphing sound, and she saw it later that day in the kitchen garbage, stained with ketchup and hamburger grease.

She turned the card over and went on. The drawings and paintings began to reveal a developing and considerable skill. There were recognizable charcoal portraits of Victor, Esther, and June herself, perhaps in her early teens.

Toward the back of the folder, Kelly found a pastel sketch of a cartoon-style bear with crossed eyes, a goofy smile, and his tongue hanging out of his mouth. Kelly smiled. "It's Gladly the Cross-Eyed Bear," she said to herself.

Then she froze. "Wait—how did I know what to call him?" The lower half of the paper was covered by a smaller sheet. She pulled it free and read, "Gladly the Cross-Eyed Bear. June Rose Hansen, August 1975."

The drawing fell from her fingers and she slumped back in the chair. Then she was standing in her crib, reaching insufficient fingers toward a fuzzy brown puppet that stuck up above the bars. The bear waggled its head, its tongue hanging out from a goofy smile, and said in a falsely gruff voice, "Hi there. I'm Gladly the Cross-Eyed Bear."

The little Kelly clapped and squealed. "Do 'gain, Mommy! Do 'gain!" The laugh she heard in response could never have issued from Miriam Mason's throat.

KIERA AND NATHANIEL CAME IN a few minutes later to help pack up books and found Kelly staring into space with a haunted look. I hate for her to be so uncomfortable, but there doesn't seem to be any other way for her to learn the truth.

"Kelly, what's wrong?" Kiera rushed over and knelt by the chair.

Kelly blinked and slowly shook her head. "I . . . I think I'm going crazy."

Nathaniel squatted at her other side and laid a hand on her arm. "What happened?"

His touch seemed to break through her confusion. "It's this house," she said, looking around the room as if she expected something to jump out at her from behind the curtains or slip through a secret passageway behind the shelves. "I keep having these—flashes—I don't know if they're memories or what, but they seem to be from when I was very small. And what I'm remembering is a woman—a young girl, really—who seems to be my mother, but she looks just like June Hansen. And that's impossible. My mother is Miriam Mason. And I keep finding things that seem to link me to this house. Like this drawing."

She waved her hand toward the drawing of the goofy bear on the desk in front of her. I remember June making up that bear—she got his name from a hymn I used to sing around the house. "I knew the minute I saw it, when the name was still covered up, that it was Gladly the Cross-Eyed Bear. How did I know that? And there was the plate, and the window, and the recipe, and the bath salts, and the puzzle in the living room—I had that same picture on my wall when I was little. Of course it could be mere coincidence, but all those things together? It's uncanny."

"Let's go to the window seat where we can all sit down." Nathaniel took Kelly's elbow and led her around the desk as if she were an invalid. She didn't seem to mind. I don't think she would have been quite steady on her feet without that touch.

Kelly sat in the middle, Kiera holding her hand. "Now," said Nathaniel, "tell me about all those discoveries you mentioned."

Kelly told him, with Kiera filling in the details she knew. He thought for a while, rubbing his chin. "No, I don't think all those things together could be mere coincidence. There has to be a connection, an explanation somewhere."

"There's one possible explanation I don't even want to think about." Kelly paused, twisting her fingers together. "Sometimes, when I'm here alone at night . . . sometimes I feel as if I'm not alone."

Ah, so I am getting through to her. That's a comfort.

Nathaniel looked at her sharply. "You mean someone's getting into the house at night?"

95

"No, not that. I don't hear noises or anything—at least, nothing Ginger wouldn't account for. It's a different kind of presence. It's sort of—all around me. In the air, in the walls even. It's as if the house itself is alive—and trying to tell me something."

"Are you trying to say you think the house is haunted?"

She grimaced. "Now you'll really think I'm crazy."

"I didn't say that. There are more things in heaven and earth, Horatio, and all that. This presence you feel—does it seem hostile, benign, or neutral?"

"Not hostile. It sort of creeps me out, but only because I can't explain it. I think—it isn't trying to push me away. It's more like it's drawing me in . . . I think it's benign. Sometimes—like in the moments before I fall asleep—it's even kind of comforting."

That's me bending over her to say goodnight. I'd brush my lips against her forehead if I still had lips to brush.

"I wonder . . ." Kiera said. "I wonder if Esther could still be here, somehow. Not as a ghost, exactly. I just can't imagine Esther as a ghost; she was so completely down to earth. But her spirit sort of hanging around, waiting to see how things turn out . . ." She laughed. "Esther never was one to let things take their course without her help. She must have had a reason for leaving you this house—I bet she's staying to see how it works out. And help it along if things don't seem to be going her way."

Oh, that Kiera—she's onto me. She's got my number.

"But why?" Kelly wailed. "Why did she leave me this house? What does she want from me?"

Nathaniel rubbed his chin again. "Maybe it isn't what she wants from you. Maybe it's what she wants for you."

I do like that young man, more and more. He's got an open line to the invisible.

Kelly looked up at him. "What do you mean?"

96

"I'm not sure what I mean—it's just a feeling I have." He shrugged. "Maybe if you tell us more about yourself, we'll be able to find some connection."

Kelly gave a sigh that seemed to come from the tips of her toes. "All right. Here goes. I was born in San Francisco in 1978. My parents were Howard and Miriam Mason. They were in their forties when I was born—I'm an only child. Howard died when I was in college. Miriam developed Alzheimer's about the same time; she's in a rest home in Marin."

"No possibility you were adopted?" Nathaniel put in. Getting warmer . . .

"I don't see how. They certainly never said anything to that effect, and Miriam had pictures of me right back to newborn. I guess they could have adopted me at birth, but that wouldn't explain those weird memory flashes, would it?"

She looked at the others; they shook their heads.

"It's funny, though, I always used to imagine I was adopted. I felt like such an alien in that family—if you can call it a family. Howard was hardly ever around, gone for months at a time with his developments all over the world. We never went with him. And Miriam—well, she was peculiar. She showered me with every material thing you can imagine, and sometimes she'd be all over me with affection; but then she'd go back to her bridge parties and fashion shows and leave me with the housekeeper. I was like a doll she'd play with for a while and then forget about. Then when I got too old to play with, she didn't know what to do with me at all. She treated me like a guest who'd overstayed her welcome but whom she was too polite to throw out."

Kiera was cut as deep by that as I was. She hugged Kelly's waist. "No wonder," she said, and I think Kelly knew what she meant.

Nathaniel's eyes grew harder as she told her story, and his jaw clenched. "People like that should not be allowed to raise children." He took a breath and seemed to will himself to exhale his anger. "Kiera, what do you know about the Hansens?"

She pursed up her lips in that pretty way of hers that makes her look like a china doll. "Well, I know June was an only child too, born when Esther and Victor were around forty. But they were good parents, I'm sure, though Esther was maybe just a bit controlling."

Oh, sweetheart, you give me too much credit. Just a *lot* controlling is more like it.

"All I know about June is that she disappeared when she was seventeen, about six months after Victor died. There was some mystery about it that neither Pops nor Esther would ever explain."

"Do you know what year that was?"

"Mmm . . . I think it was seventy-seven or seventy-eight."

"Is it possible she was pregnant when she left?" Nathaniel asked.

What did I say about an open line to the invisible? But really, the peculiar thing is that nobody seems to have thought of it before.

"Nobody's ever said so, but it does seem a likely explanation." Kiera's eyes lit up and she turned toward Kelly. "Kelly, you could be—"

"No." Kelly had been growing more and more agitated as the two of them spoke, and now she stood abruptly and faced them with an expression I recognized—from my own mirror. "No. What you're thinking is impossible. I'm Kelly Mason, for better or worse. I'm thirty years old, I've been a virtual orphan all my life, and not one single thing I truly wanted has ever happened for me. I'm not going to start wishing for a family now—especially not a dead one." She turned and stalked out of the room.

I never thought she'd take it that way. I do still have my work cut out, indeed.

Nathaniel watched her go, then turned to look at Kiera. "I'm certain of it. Not in my head, but in my heart. What about you?"

"Me too. I just don't see how it could be any other way. And somehow Esther knew."

"We've got to prove it to her. If we can give her the gift of a family, maybe—"

"I know. Maybe she'll be open to love as well."

NOW THAT KELLY HAD VOICED her feelings about the spirit of the house, her awe in the face of it intensified. She almost feared being alone in the house that evening and kept Nathaniel working with her in the library well past quitting time just to postpone that hour. "I'd like to get these shelves finished so they can dry overnight and we can put the books back up tomorrow," she said, trying to keep the pleading out of her voice.

He made no objection, but simply nodded in his serene manner and continued polishing. But when the shelves were finished, he wiped his hands on a rag and said, "I caught a seaperch at the wharf yesterday that's too big for me to eat by myself. I'd hate to freeze it. Want to help me eat it?"

He said it so casually, it didn't sound like a date, and Kelly opened her mouth to accept. But then it occurred to her that she would be alone with him, on his home turf, with no employer/employee relationship to keep the proper distance between them. No telling what might happen.

"Thanks, but I . . ." She cast about for an excuse. She didn't want to hurt his feelings, after all. "I'm allergic to fish." It was a lame excuse, and not entirely true—she'd had a bad reaction to some tuna once, but it was probably the mayonnaise it was mixed with that did the mischief. She looked away, but the feeling of his eyes on her drew her back.

Disappointment tinged his fjord-grey eyes—not for himself, but for her. The quirk at one corner of his mouth told her he knew she was fibbing but would let her get away with it this time. "Well, perhaps another time I'll catch a nice steak instead. Unless you're allergic to beef too?"

She shook her head and dropped her eyes, feeling the blood in her cheeks. Why couldn't she let go and allow this relationship to take its course? But then, letting go had never been her strong point.

She walked him to the vestibule, as if that would somehow compensate for her rejection. As he donned his jacket, she half wished he'd renew the invitation so she could gracefully change her mind; but he only said "Good night," opened the outer door, and left. She stood in the doorway and watched him walk down the driveway until his figure was swallowed in the dusk.

She microwaved a frozen dinner, played through Bach's second cello suite, then chose a mystery from Esther's shelves to occupy her mind until bedtime. But she chose badly for her purposes—*Busman's Honeymoon* by Dorothy L. Sayers. Early in the book Lord Peter Wimsey took his new bride, Harriet, to Duke's Denver, where she met the family ghost—a nice old gentleman who spent all his time in the vast and ancient library.

Kelly shivered as she read the scene and looked up from her chair in the living room. Just beyond the sheltering circle of light from the reading lamp, she sensed that thickness in the air, that vibration she could neither hear nor truly feel, but which alerted her to the presence of some consciousness.

Ginger, who had been snoozing on her lap, lifted his head

and pricked his ears, then started to purr. "You feel it too, don't you, boy? But you're purring, so it must be friendly. Is it really Esther, then?" The cat turned its yellow eyes to hers and blinked, as if to say, "Well, duh!"

"What do you want from me?" Kelly whispered to the presence. "Have I done something wrong? Have I offended you? Don't you like what I'm doing to the house? Do you want me to leave?"

She felt the presence shimmer and move closer to her, enclosing her in warmth and an odd kind of peace. No, it didn't want her to leave; it wasn't rebuking her. She closed her eyes and leaned back her head, and felt herself gently swaying as if she were an infant being rocked in her mother's arms. She gave herself up to the motion, and soon her cheeks were wet with tears; and then she slept.

CHAPTER 10

WHEN THE ADDITION was framed, they had to call for an inspection. And of course, who should show up but that Perkins again. I wonder if he's reporting to the county or directly to Imogene.

Kelly and Nathaniel were working on the paneling in the front hall, so Kelly had to let Perkins in. But as soon as he flashed her his oily smile, Nathaniel was there at her shoulder, looming over Perkins and freezing him with a glance. Kelly couldn't see that glance; she probably thought her own chipped-ice demeanor was what wiped the smile off Perkins' face.

They passed Perkins through to the back of the house where the work was being done. Nathaniel frowned after him. "I don't like that man."

Kelly gave a little laugh. "Who could?"

"I mean I don't like the way he looks at you."

A flush crept up Kelly's neck. She bent over her work. "Oh, I can handle him. I've handled plenty of jerks in my life."

"I'm sure you have, but even so, I think you'd do well to avoid being alone with him."

Did I say how much I like that young man?

That nervous laugh again. "You don't seriously think he's dangerous?"

"Physically, no, he looks pretty soft. But he has a position of power, and I'm betting he wouldn't hesitate to abuse it." His tone softened and he put a cautious hand to her shoulder. "Please, Kelly, be careful."

She turned her head toward him, and I watched resentment lose out to gratification in her face. "All right. I will."

Meanwhile, out back, Perkins peered and measured and thumped and consulted his code book while Aidan leaned back against the wall, his eyes dancing. Finally, Perkins had to give up.

"Well, Inspector? Do we meet your most exacting standards?"

"It'll pass so far, I guess. But you better watch your step, McCarthy. I'm going to be watching you like a hulk."

"I think you mean a hawk, Inspector."

Perkins' eyes bulged even farther than usual. "Whatever. You just watch it, that's all." He stomped down the new back steps and around the house to his truck.

Next door, Imogene stood at her upstairs window, sniffing.

WITH THE FRAMING INSPECTION COMPLETE, it was time to roof the addition. Aidan's plan was to rebuild the chimney and then reroof the entire house at the same time.

Kyle came upstairs to examine what was left of the chimney below the roofline, where it came up through the undereave storage area. His gargantuan frame seemed to fill the cramped space to capacity.

He ran his large square fingers over the joins between the bricks. "This looks pretty sound. We'll have to cut out the roof patch and rebuild the top of the chimney, but it'll be easier from the roof side." He grinned at Kelly. "Lucky you—you won't have me tromping up your pretty stairs with a load of bricks and mud."

"Good thing, since Nathaniel and I were planning to start work on the stairwell today."

Kyle whistled. "Better you than me. There's a heckuva lot of wood on those stairs."

"We enjoy it. Just like you enjoy masonry. You'd never catch me up on that roof messing around with a lot of mud."

He shot her a sidelong glance, his hands still busy on the brickwork. "You and Nathaniel seem to have a lot in common."

She felt a flush creeping up her neck. "Music and wood. You call that a lot?"

"When those are some of the most important things in your lives, yeah, I call that a lot. And I bet there's more, if you'd give yourself the chance to find out."

Kelly squinted at a brick that seemed a fraction out of alignment. "How well do you know Nathaniel?"

"I've known him—oh, ten years or so. Worked with him, gone to church with him. We're not buddy-buddies—don't think he has buddies like that—but I know he's solid all through. No nasty surprises under the woodwork with him. He's good, he's true, and he's got your back." Kyle pulled a bandana from his back pocket and wiped his hands. "I'd let him marry my sister if he wanted to, and that's saying a lot."

"Has he ever been interested in Kiera?" Kelly's response was quicker, sharper than she intended, and she caught the smirk in Kyle's eyes.

"Nah, he seems to think she's like a cute little puppy or something. They're friends and all, but they wouldn't be right for each other." He grinned. "You, on the other hand . . ."

"I think it's time we both got to work."

LATER THAT AFTERNOON, KYLE CALLED down through the stairwell window, "Hey, Kelly, come out here a minute, wouldja?"

She set down her bucket and sponge with a sigh and went out the back door.

"Where are you?"

"Over here." His head appeared over the peak of the roof to her left.

She skirted the house, passing between the side wall and the oak tree, whose shriveled brown leaves still clung to its branches. This was not the natural death of autumn; this tree was dying of oak blight. Ginger, who had left the house at her heels, spotted a squirrel scampering up the trunk and sped up after it.

When she reached the front of the house and looked up, Kyle said, "See my problem?"

She did indeed. One main branch of the oak hung over the roof, low enough that a man nailing shingles could easily hit his head on it if he wasn't paying attention. The squirrel dashed to the end of the branch and sat there scolding at Ginger, who stopped halfway out, the branch sagging slightly under his weight.

"We gotta get this branch out of here," Kyle said. "I know a good tree man you could call."

Kelly sighed. It would only mean a day's delay, but she grudged even that. "Yeah, all right. What's his number?"

Kyle didn't have the number on him, but he gave her the name and she looked them up.

"Arthur's Tree Service, can I help you?"

"Yes, I've got an overhanging branch that needs trimming. Can you take care of it?"

"Sure thing. Let's see . . . We can fit you in here two or three weeks from now."

"Two or three weeks! We're working on the roof now. The branch is in the way."

"Sorry, ma'am, we're all booked up. This is pruning season. You won't find a tree man in the county with any space right now."

"Oh, all right, put me down for the first open slot."

She gave him her name and address, then flipped through the Yellow Pages and called some other companies. But the guy at Arthur's was right—everyone was booked. She went back out to tell Kyle.

"The tree service is all booked up. Can you work around it?"

"Sure we can, but it's kind of a safety issue. Not so much for us, but for you. This branch is dead—it could fall any time."

"Well, it's been there for years and it hasn't fallen yet. We'll just have to take our chances."

Kyle shrugged. "It's your funeral."

BY THE END OF THE week the roof and chimney were finished. Saturday dawned balmy and fine, the kind of late Indian summer day that draws people outdoors. Aidan said, "We've got everything sealed up now, so we're good if the rains come early. This might be the last warm weather we'll have for a while. Let's go to the beach."

Kelly herself was feeling rather claustrophobic by this time, so she readily agreed. All the McCarthys, from Eunice down to the baby, piled into a van along with umbrellas, coolers, and blankets. Nathaniel, somewhat tentatively, offered to drive Kelly in his truck, as she didn't know the way. She took a firm grip on herself and accepted; it would have been churlish not to.

They took a road Kelly hadn't driven before that climbed over the ridge of the coastal mountains and joined the coast highway north of Santa Cruz. Conversation seemed superfluous in the face of the scenery they were passing—deep forests that changed from redwood on the inland side of the ridge to pine on the seaward side, finally parting as they descended to afford a glimpse of deep blue water and an endless sky. Kelly caught her breath, transfixed; she'd been away from the ocean too long.

Aidan had chosen a beach that was too far from town to be overcrowded but had easy access for Eunice's sake. As Kelly and Nathaniel pulled into the parking lot, Aidan and Kyle were helping Eunice out of the van and making a chair with their arms to carry her down to the sand. Kelly and Nathaniel loaded themselves with baggage and set off after them.

"It's awfully sweet of them to bring Eunice," Kelly said, too low for the others to hear. "Most people wouldn't bother on a trek like this."

"That's the kind of people they are. They actually think about what it must be like to be confined to a wheelchair, stuck inside most of the time. They take every opportunity to get her out of the house."

"She must have been a good woman, for them to take care of her that way."

"I believe she was. Is. But I think they'd treat her the same no matter what."

Something gnawed at Kelly's vitals. Miriam Mason was confined to a wheelchair in a posh rest home in Marin County, where Kelly visited only once or twice a year. But Miriam was well cared for—her money saw to that—with as much in the way of outings as her advanced dementia allowed her to enjoy. And she hadn't recognized Kelly for some time, so she could hardly be missing her. Yet still that something gnawed, and Kelly resolved to make her next visit as soon as the house was finished.

They settled Eunice in a chair under the umbrella, with Mindy and the baby beside her. The others sprawled on blankets to either side. Kelly slathered sunscreen on her fair skin and added a wide-brimmed straw hat for good measure.

For half an hour they all absorbed the sun, the view, and the lulling crash of the waves. Mindy fed the baby, and he went back to sleep in her arms.

Then Kyle suggested a game of Frisbee, and Kiera and Nathaniel jumped up in agreement. Kelly stood to join them, then glanced down at Mindy, whose wistful gaze traveled from her husband to the baby sleeping in her arms.

"Why don't you go play?" Kelly said to Mindy. "I'll watch the baby."

Mindy's face lit up. "Really? Are you sure you don't mind?"

"Are you kidding? I can play Frisbee whenever I want, but I don't get to hold a baby every day."

Mindy stood and with great care transferred her bundle to Kelly's arms, waiting to be sure Kelly had the approved hold, with the baby's head well supported, before letting go. "You'll call me if he fusses?"

"You just relax and have a good time. We'll be fine."

"Okay. Thanks." She plodded through the deep sand to join the others at the water's edge.

Kelly saw Nathaniel greet Mindy, then turn back to look at her. It was hard to tell at this distance, with the sun in her eyes, but she thought she saw him nod. She flushed and looked down at the baby.

With the sun on her legs, feet buried in the warm sand, a gentle salt breeze on her face and a sleeping infant in her arms,

Kelly found it impossible to hold onto the tension she'd been living with for the past weeks—and indeed, for most of her life. It all drained out of her, and she imagined it flowing out through her feet, rippling through the sand to the water line, then surfacing to be washed away into the endless ocean, where all the tumult that seemed so overwhelming to her would be nothing but one tiny wavelet in the midst of the great, ever-seething sea.

She looked on indulgently as the others ran and leapt and shouted, feeling no more impulse to join them than did the old woman dozing beside her. Her eyes roved over the scene but always came back to Nathaniel, who moved with the grace and speed of a cheetah and rarely missed a catch. He was beautiful to her as that cheetah would be beautiful, as the sea and the sky and the baby in her arms were beautiful—as an expression of the deep beauty that underlay all things and shone forth wherever humans had not corrupted it. And in that moment, the seed that had been planted in her heart at their first meeting broke through the crusted soil and sent its first tentative green shoot up toward the sunlight.

Aidan returned, wheezing, and plopped onto the blanket next to her chair. When he had his breath, he said, "Go play a while, Kelly. I'll take the little guy."

Reluctantly she handed over her charge, but as soon as she stood, she felt life flowing in her veins, demanding movement. She ran to join the game. Nathaniel threw the Frisbee to her, and she leapt like a dancer to catch it, then returned it in one smooth motion. She laughed with the sheer joy of it, unable to remember when she had felt so alive.

When everyone tired and returned to the blankets to eat, Kelly and Nathaniel lingered behind. He scrutinized her with his head on one side, and she met his gaze without flinching.

"There's something different about you," he said at last.

"Yes." She spread her arms in a great circle. "I think I'm finally learning how to live."

CHAPTER 11

WISH I COULD have seen what happened at that picnic, because Kelly came home looking like a different woman. She had such a peace about her, she almost glowed. But Monday morning they started on the remodeling upstairs, which meant ripping out the bathroom fixtures as well as part of a wall in my old room. The noise was something fierce, and it wasn't long before I saw the lines of tension start to creep back into Kelly's face.

With all the dust and debris, the second story looked like being pretty unlivable for the next little while, so Kiera made another foray in her mission to domesticate Kelly. With all the determination her little frame can hold—and that's plenty—she stood before her, arms akimbo, and said, "Now, Kelly, surely even you can see you can't go on living here without a bathroom, with the whole second floor torn up till who knows when. You're simply going to have to come and live with us. We've got plenty of space—you can have Kyle's old room. I promise I cleaned out the cooties after he moved out."

I held my breath—figuratively speaking. I want Kelly to get domesticated too, but if she goes and stays with them I won't be able to see her any of the time she's over there. My dispensation extends only to the boundaries of this property.

Kelly just smiled down at her. "Sorry, Kiera, but no. My bedroom won't be affected; I can shut the door and everything'll be fine. Besides, Ginger would miss me." She bent down to scratch his head. I swear, that animal follows her around like a puppy. I've never seen anything like it.

"But the bathroom! You have the powder room downstairs, but where are you going to shower?"

Kelly clucked her tongue. "You got me there. I'll tell you what—I'll sleep here and come over to your house to shower. Okay?"

Kiera crossed her arms and tapped her foot. "Well . . . okay. On one condition: you have to stay for breakfast."

Kelly laughed. "It's a deal."

A good deal—for both of us.

THE NEXT MORNING, KELLY DRESSED, grabbed her toiletry bag and towel, and ducked through a gap in the hedge to the back door of the McCarthys' house, hoping this route was sheltered from the view of Mrs. Perkins' upstairs window. Lord only knew what she'd think if she saw Kelly going over there this early in the morning.

Kiera had told her to use Eunice's bathroom on the ground floor; Eunice would be up and dressed before she got there. But even knowing the old woman was out of the way, Kelly felt like a trespasser going through her bedroom and into the handicapped-accessible bath, both of which smelled faintly of urine, baby powder, and old age. She showered and dressed as quickly as possible, trying not to touch anything more than was necessary.

On a whim, she used the blow dryer hanging in the bathroom to fluff out her hair, which was getting longer than she knew what to do with but not yet long enough to tie back. Pleased with the result, she emerged into the kitchen, where Kiera was frying bacon while Aidan fed Eunice some Cream of Wheat.

Aidan glanced up. "Morning, Kelly." Then he took a closer look. "Your hair looks nice."

"Thanks," she mumbled, sitting across from him. "I had to do something with it. I'm overdue for a trim."

"Oh, don't cut it, Kel," Kiera put in, setting a mug of coffee in front of her. "Let it grow. It's such a lovely color, and it does look nice this way."

Kelly addressed herself to her coffee and did not respond.

Aidan finished spooning the cereal into Eunice's mouth and moved to the sink to rinse out the bowl. Kelly looked up to see Eunice's watery eyes staring intently into hers. The old woman's mouth worked, but only a faint groaning sound came out.

Kelly leaned across the table. "What is it, Mrs. McCarthy? Do you want to tell me something?"

Eunice's jaw pumped, and like a trickle of rusty water from an old well, speech-like sounds began to emerge. "Oo . . . my me . . . Es-er," Kelly made out.

Aidan had turned from the sink and was watching his mother. He mouthed her sounds over to himself. "She reminds you of Esther?"

The ancient head wobbled forward so abruptly Kelly almost feared it would fall off.

Aidan's gaze shifted to Kelly. "Hmm . . . I see what you mean, Mother. You have her bone structure, Kelly, and—I think something of her personality as well. What an interesting coincidence."

Kiera brought the frying pan to the table and began to dish out the bacon. With a sidelong glance at Kelly, she said, "Pops . . . We were wondering the other day—Kelly keeps finding stuff that seems to link her to that house, and Nathaniel and I were wondering if it might be more than coincidence. What I mean is—well, is there any chance June could have been pregnant when she disappeared?"

Kelly stiffened, ready to protest, but her words were arrested by the others' reactions. Eunice grew agitated, her head wobbling alarmingly, but this time her grunts were completely unintelligible. Aidan, on the other hand, went rigid. "No," he said in a strangled voice. "No. That isn't possible."

His Adam's apple bobbed, and he spoke again, almost normally. "Really, it's impossible. I was her priest, and she was very devout. I would have known."

"You—you were a priest?" Kelly was as shocked as if he'd said he'd been in prison, but why exactly, she couldn't say.

Aidan gave a shaky smile. "For a short time. I realized pretty quickly I wasn't cut out for it and asked to be released."

She gave a sympathetic grimace. "The celibacy thing?"

His eyes went hard and he dropped words like stones. "Yes. I wanted to marry. And now I think we'd all better eat our breakfast and get to work."

BY THE TIME HE CALLED Kelly into Esther's bedroom later that morning, Aidan was his usual self again; but his normally smooth brow was furrowed. "We've got a problem here."

He shined a flashlight on a section of wall from which the lath and plaster had been stripped away. The light glinted off a glass knob with wires emerging from it.

"Knob-and-tube wiring," Kelly groaned. "I should have known."

"This bit here's in good shape—the insulation on the wires is still intact. Chances are good the wiring through the whole house is perfectly safe. But this is an area that idiot inspector is likely to jump on. It can legally be grandfathered in, but it's at the discretion of the inspector—if he wanted to make trouble, he could require us to replace the wiring all through the house."

"Oh, Lord. And making trouble seems to be what he lives for."

Aidan nodded, frowning.

Kelly drummed her fingers on the framing as she looked around the room. "All this original plaster . . . all that gorgeous woodwork downstairs. I just can't see ripping it all out. It'd be next to impossible to replace." She turned to Aidan. "What do you think?"

"I think we should redo the kitchen wiring, since we're tearing that room up anyway and it's a big electrical load. And you'll need the library upgraded to take a computer system, right? But we can do that with a new circuit and bring it in through the floor; we don't have to rip anything out. For the rest of the house, I'm with you—I don't see the point of demolishing everything to fix what ain't broke."

Kelly nodded slowly, her tongue between her teeth, then straightened with her hands on her hips. "Right. Then you're willing to take on Perkins and all his fury?"

Aidan grinned. "There's nothing I like better than a nice little fight with the county. I'm game."

"And we don't have to call him in again until the plumbing and electrical are finished, right? So maybe he won't even have to know."

Aidan reached out and thumped Kelly's shoulder. "That's my kind of thinking, girl."

BUT PERKINS SEEMED TO HAVE his own timetable. He showed up, unscheduled and unannounced, the next day, when the kitchen walls stood naked, all their outdated wiring exposed. Kelly stayed out of the way while he was doing his inspection, but afterward he cornered her in the library, where she was sorting books on her own. Nathaniel had gone back to his workshop to finish building the kitchen cabinets.

She could barely control a shudder looking at Perkins. Something about him—the combover perhaps, or the attitude—reminded her of Howard Mason. Ginger, who had been serenely cleaning himself on the desk, sat up and glared at the intruder, his tail twitching.

At sight of Kelly, a leer crept into Perkins' eyes while the rest of his face remained fixed in a belligerent frown.

"You've got a bad situation with that old knob-and-tube wiring. You know we can't just let a thing like that slide." A grotesque simper distorted his already unattractive face. "It'd be an awful shame if a pretty little lady like yourself got into trouble with the law."

Kelly drew herself up to her full five-foot-ten, a good six inches taller than Perkins. "I am not a little lady, Mr. Perkins, and neither am I in violation of the building code, let alone the law. As I'm sure Mr. McCarthy explained to you, we're replacing all that knob-and-tube in the kitchen and the attic. If you had waited until we called you, you'd have seen the most up-to-date wiring even you could ask for."

Perkins came closer until her nostrils were filled with his

disgusting smell—sweat and cigarette smoke overlaid with musk. "Now, now, you can't pull the wood over my eyes that easy. I know perfectly well the rest of the house is all knob-and-tube too, and I don't see you making any plans to replace it."

"I believe the code allows that to be grandfathered."

He wagged a finger in her face—a none-too-clean finger with ragged cuticle and bitten nail. "That's at my discretion, missy. Completely at my discretion."

His leer intensified, spreading into a repulsive grin. "And after all, I'm a reasonable man. I'm sure we can come to some kind of . . . arrangement." He lowered his repellent finger and ran it down the outside of her sleeve.

Ginger leapt onto a shelf next to them and growled at Perkins, lashing the offending hand with his claws. Perkins jerked his arm away, cursing. "That's no cat, that's a demon! You're arboring a dangerous animal—I'll get you for that too!"

Then Aidan was in the archway. "What seems to be the problem here?"

Kelly hugged Ginger to her chest, shuddering.

Perkins rounded on Aidan, the red flush spreading up his neck again. "You know damn well what the problem is! You've got wiring all through this house that's in clear violation of the building code!" He pulled a handkerchief from his pocket and pressed it to his bleeding hand. "Besides, that damned demon cat tried to kill me!"

Aidan raised his eyebrows. "Please, Mr. Perkins, there's a lady present! Yes, you and I discussed the wiring a few minutes ago. But I don't see any reason for you to pester Miss Mason about it."

Glowering, Perkins pushed past Aidan toward the front door. Then he turned and shook his code book at them, looking so like a villain in an old melodrama that Kelly almost laughed.

"You walk your step, McCarthy, or you'll be getting a red tag for this!"

Aidan watched him out, shaking his head, then turned to Kelly. After a glance at her face, he was beside her in one stride. "Kelly, you're white as new plaster! What happened?"

He led her to the front window, where she sank gratefully onto the seat and propped her head in her hands, willing her pulse to return to its normal pace.

"He . . . he hinted I might be able to buy him off."

"That disgusting flea. You won't do it, will you?"

She couldn't stop shaking. "I don't think . . . he meant money."

Aidan sprang to his feet, a fierce flame in his eyes. "Fleas can be squashed."

"No—he's not worth it. Please. There's no point in antagonizing him even further."

He hesitated, the flame softening into concern. He sat beside her again and put his arm around her quivering shoulders. "All right. But don't let him get another chance to harass you. Let me deal with him from now on."

She nodded, relaxing under his arm. Maybe this was what it was like to have a father—a real father, that is. One who cared.

WORK PROCEEDED IN SPITE OF Perkins' threats. The new breakfast nook was a solid structure now, impervious to the elements, so the crew tore out the section of exterior wall that separated it from the kitchen.

Kelly watched this work with mixed emotions. Up until this moment, she'd been able to tell herself she was just fixing up a house that really belonged to someone else—doing what the Hansens themselves might have done had they lived and had the money for it. But as the Skilsaws sliced through what had been the outside wall, violating the very skin of the house in order to graft a foreign body onto it, she felt with a wrench that for good or ill, she had now taken the house for her own. She hoped its spirit, which she felt so thick in the air all around her, would not regard this as a rape, but as the act of love she meant it to be.

"Ready to pack china?" said a voice at her shoulder.

"Kiera! You startled me. I was watching all this and thinking, it's so . . . irrevocable. It's like a commitment."

"Well, it's time you had some commitment in your life. People weren't made to float around the way you've been doing. You need roots."

Kelly rotated one shoulder, as if adjusting an uncomfortable coat. "I always thought I'd put down roots someday—years from now—but I expected to choose carefully where I would do it. This I just fell into, with no warning."

"That's the way it works. Does a seed choose where it gets blown to? It falls in some random spot, and that's where it roots. But you didn't fall here randomly. You belong here, Kelly. You may as well get used to it."

OF COURSE, I WAS DELIGHTED that Kelly was beginning to feel a sense of possession for my house; I didn't much care what it took for her to get there. And I think that breakfast nook will be real nice, all light and cheerful, facing southeast as it does: the perfect place to sip a cup of coffee and plan out the day.

But as they say, you can't make an omelet without breaking eggs, and in this case, the eggs were Imogene Perkins' eardrums. She came stalking up the front walk halfway through the morning, while the chainsaws were whining and the sledgehammers pounding in the back. She did ring the bell—I'll give her that—but of course no one could hear it with all the noise, so after a minute she just marched right in.

She poked her pink nose into the kitchen first, then drew back, her ever-present tissue over her nose and mouth. I'm sure her pristine nature was deeply offended by the chaos, and anyway Kelly wasn't there. She crossed the hall to the dining room and hit the jackpot. Kelly and Kiera were in there boxing up the Spode from the plate rail so the wood finish could be cleaned up. And I must say, I couldn't have handled it more carefully myself. It was gratifying to see how Kelly cherished that china that had meant so much to me—and to June.

The girls didn't hear Imogene come in, of course, nor see her at first, as they were on step stools taking the plates and platters down. Ginger saw her and hightailed it out of there. But then Kelly turned to come down and there she was, her ferrety nose sniffing in every direction.

"Mrs. Perkins!" I could see it was on the tip of Kelly's tongue to say, "What are you doing here?" but she caught herself and changed it to, "Is there something I can do for you?"

Imogene came close and turned up her face to peer at Kelly. "There certainly is. You can stop all this horrible noise. Why, I can't even hear myself think in my own home."

Kelly set the platter she was holding on the table. "I'm very sorry about the noise, Mrs. Perkins. I know it's especially bad today, but this won't last long. They'll have that section of wall out by the end of the day, and then things will go back to normal." Imogene's eyebrows rose to her sprayed-helmet hairline. "Well, normal for a remodeling job at any rate. And in the meantime, I'd be happy to lend you some noise-canceling headphones."

Imogene drew herself up with a mighty sniff. "I'd like to see myself with those horrible-looking things on my head! Why, they'd crush my coiffure." She gave her hair a reverent pat. Coiffure, indeed. Imogene doesn't even go to the beauty parlor. She could afford it, but she's too cheap.

"Well, suit yourself. But in any case, as I say, it's just for today. And I'm sure it's a lot less noisy at your house with the windows closed than it is in here."

Of course, that was a diplomatic way to say we'd rather have your room than your company. But Imogene, as I've had many occasions to notice, is completely immune to hints.

She peered around the room at the china. Now, in general, Imogene's taste and mine are as much at odds as a man and his mother-in-law, but there was one thing of mine she always coveted, and that was my Spode. I'd been collecting for a long time and had pieces that hadn't been available for years. She was forever hinting around that she'd like to buy my collection, but I'd sooner have given it to a careless family with ten children than sell it to her.

So now she started in on Kelly. "I see you're packing up the Spode, dear. Of course, you wouldn't have any use for it, would you? I'd be happy to take it off your hands, you know. Dear Esther wouldn't part with it for sentimental reasons, but those don't apply to you, do they? You don't want a bunch of old china cluttering up your attic."

Kelly's eyes turned to daggers of ice. "On the contrary, Mrs. Perkins, we're only getting it out of the way temporarily so we can work on the paneling. This china is every bit as precious to me as it was to Esther, and as soon as the work in here is done, it's going back on the plate rail. Why, I may even give a dinner party for my friends just so I can use it." She laid a little extra emphasis on "friends."

Imogene dabbed at her pink nose. "Well, you'll suit yourself, of course. But if you ever change your mind, I'm right next door." She turned and walked out of the room without even saying goodbye.

Kelly followed her to the hall door and caught her with her foot on the bottom stair. That woman meant to sneak upstairs and snoop around without even a by-your-leave! Kelly said in a voice like a Minnesota winter, "Your nephew has already inspected the work upstairs, Mrs. Perkins. There's no need for you to do it again."

Imogene sputtered. "I . . . I was just admiring the work you've done on this staircase." She ran her hand over the newel. "This wood looks almost as good as new. Of course, all this elaborate woodwork is so difficult to care for properly. I'm surprised you don't take it all out and put in wallboard and carpeting—it would be a tremendous improvement, and so much easier to keep clean." She looked brightly at Kelly, whose face was still several degrees below zero. "Well, I can't stand around here chatting all day. So much to do! I have to clean two or three times a day now, what with all the dust coming over from this place."

She lifted her chin, turned, and minced down the hall. Kelly watched her out the door to be sure she really did leave the house. Then she stalked back to her step stool, still seething. "The nerve of that woman! You know, I think she actually expected me to just *give* her all this china. Even if I wanted to get rid of it, it's worth a small fortune."

Kiera laughed. "That's Mrs. Perkins for you. She'll pinch a penny till it bleeds. When Kyle and I were little, we were convinced she had piles of gold buried under her artificial turf. We figured she couldn't grow real grass because there was no dirt under there, only treasure. In fact, I'm still not entirely convinced that's not true. If she ever dies—which I wouldn't count on, she's so full of preservatives—I might buy her house just so I can rip up the turf and see."

By the end of this flight of fancy, Kelly's anger had left her and she was laughing along with Kiera. Thank the Lord for Kiera—I doubt my plan would succeed without her.

CHAPTER 12

ONCE THE DINING room was cleared, Nathaniel came in to work on the paneling and the built-in sideboard. Kelly gave him a smile that tried to say she was happy to see him and ready to accept him on a deeper level than before.

They worked quietly but comfortably together through the afternoon. As they were cleaning up, he turned to her and gazed into her in his usual disconcerting way. This time she did not attempt to close the door against him.

"I have a couple of nice juicy T-bones at home, and a pumpkin pie that began its life in my garden. Can I tempt you?"

Kelly stared at him. "You actually made a pumpkin pie? Completely from scratch?"

"Absolutely. With eggs from my own chickens. And I plan to whip the cream by hand, too." He grinned. "Then after dinner, I'll build a fire and we can watch a movie on my steam-powered television."

She gaped a moment, then burst into laughter. "This I have to see. Just give me a minute to clean up."

She washed quickly in the powder room, then raced upstairs and rifled through her closet for something appropriate to wear—something feminine, but still casual. She had to settle for a plain but decent sweater in a flattering pumpkin color—that was appropriate, at any rate—and a clean pair of jeans that fit her well. She took a moment to fluff out her hair before heading downstairs.

Nathaniel smiled when he saw her. "You look like the spirit of autumn. I've always wanted to meet her. She does a great job, don't you think?"

"She's my favorite, for sure."

At the door he paused and said, "I just live around the corner. Do you mind walking? I'll make sure you get home safely."

Not for the first time, Kelly was touched by his concern for her. Where once she might have resented such solicitude—after all, she'd been taking care of herself for most of her life—now it felt like a great embracing chair into which she could relax with gratitude.

"No problem, I love to walk in the gloaming."

"That's a great word, 'gloaming.' A poetic word for a poetic time of day. Way better than 'crepuscule.' You know that Thelonious Monk tune, 'Crepuscule with Nellie'? It sounds like a medical condition. And a nasty one at that."

She laughed. "I know. It's almost enough to put one off of Monk. But then there's 'Round Midnight.' The world would be poorer without that tune."

"Yeah. Good thing he didn't write 'Round Crepuscule.'"

They both laughed as they walked. Kelly's balance faltered a moment, and she bumped against Nathaniel's arm. When she recovered, she found their hands were joined. Her first impulse was to snatch her hand away, but it felt good sheltered within his long, gentle fingers. She avoided looking at him, pretending she hadn't noticed.

The evening was fine and brisk, and they scuffed through small clumps of leaves gathered at the side of the road. Nathaniel told her little stories about the people who lived in the houses they passed. Either he was much more involved in the community than she'd suspected, or he had a vivid imagination; either would be a point in his favor.

"Tell me about the log cabin," she said on a whim. She was curious whether the story she'd invented about that one when she first came to the neighborhood bore any relation to the truth.

"That? Oh, no one lives there now. It has a history, though." He paused, and she had the sense he was traveling in his mind back to the time when the cabin was built.

"Tom and Eliza Morency built that cabin in 1854. They came all the way from the East Coast because Morency was hungry for gold. Crossing the plains nearly did them in; their only child died, and Eliza lost the baby she was carrying. They settled in Placerville, and Morency staked a mining claim, but he never found a single ounce of gold. When they were down to the clothes on their backs, Eliza put her foot down and insisted he find some way to support them. She missed the ocean, and there was logging in this area, so they headed west. They got to this spot and the wagon broke down. Tom was going to fix it and go on, but Eliza said no, it was a sign from God they were meant to stop right here. So he cleared the land and built the cabin, then went to work as a lumberjack. But the very first week, a tree fell on him and he was killed."

"Oh!" Kelly's triumph at having guessed partly right evaporated. "What a sad story! I'm sorry I asked."

He squeezed her hand. "Believe it or not, the story has a happy ending—for Eliza at least. Tom wasn't that great of a husband anyway, and when the foreman, Riggs, came to give Eliza the news, they were rather taken with each other. They ended up getting married and raising the first half-dozen of their ten children in that little cabin. After a while Riggs started his own logging company and got rich, and built this house we're coming to now—on Riggs Street."

He stopped in front of a large early-Victorian house Kelly had admired in her comings and goings through the neighborhood. "Well, here we are."

She stared at him. "You live *here?*" The house was easily big enough for a family of twelve.

"Not exactly. I live in the carriage house around back."

He led her down the gravel driveway to a two-story garage. Next to it was an area enclosed in a tall redwood fence. "That's my apartment," he said, pointing to the second story of the garage, "and this is my garden." He opened a gate in the fence and stood aside to let her in.

It was the neatest, homiest garden Kelly had ever seen, with a cheery row of ripe pumpkins down one side and a wire enclosure with a sturdy little chicken coop at the far end. Half-a-dozen chickens of every color and stripe strutted around the enclosure, pecking at bugs. "Natural pest control," Nathaniel said with a grin. "If you'll excuse me, I need to get these ladies settled for the night before we eat." He opened the coop door, and the hens filed in.

He latched the coop door shut and closed the wire gate after him. Then he bent over a row of vegetables, pushed aside the huge low leaves, and stood, holding a large green squash in both hands. "The last of the crop. I hope you like zucchini?"

"Sure. Especially when it's fresh from the garden."

"Oh, good. I always end up with more of these than we can use."

Kelly got a sudden hollow feeling in her stomach. "We?" She'd always assumed he lived alone.

He waved toward the big house. "The Riggs. I give them some of the produce in exchange for the right to use the garden. They're happy to have me do it—they don't care for gardening themselves."

Her stomach relaxed. What had she been afraid of—a secret wife and children? Kyle had said Nathaniel was transparent, and she could sense that herself, if her fear wouldn't keep arguing with her better judgment.

He led her out of the garden and up the stairs at the side of the garage, then turned the handle of the apartment door and held it open for her.

"You don't lock your door?"

"You are a city girl, aren't you? This is a very small town. The most excitement our sheriffs get is the occasional home-grown marijuana bust. Besides, if anyone is poor enough to need my stuff, he's welcome to it."

Kelly shook her head, still feeling bemused, and entered the apartment. She saw a single room, as compact and well-fitted as a ship's cabin, the walls lined with built-in shelves, cabinets, and benches. The small kitchen occupied the end nearer the street; at the opposite end, in an alcove next to the bathroom, was a curtained box bed that looked like something out of a Carl Larsson painting. Every piece was expertly crafted, with small, intricate carvings of birds, flowers, vines, and animals along the upper trim.

She turned to him in wonder. "You built all this, didn't you?"

He nodded.

"And you're only renting here?"

He shrugged. "If I ever have to move, I'll do it over again

in my new place. It's the work I love as much as the finished product."

She turned and scanned the room again. In truth, his movable possessions seemed to contain little that would tempt a thief. She saw plenty of books, but a notable lack of techno-toys—no computer, only a small television and VCR, and an inexpensive boombox. "I'm surprised you don't have a high-end stereo system—you being a musician, I mean."

"It's precisely because I'm a musician that I don't. To me, recorded music is so far from the real thing, it isn't worth the money to strive for the best possible sound. If I want real music, I go to a concert or play it myself."

"But—I don't see a piano? There's hardly room for one in here."

He grinned. "The piano is in the music room. I'll show you after dinner—I'm starved!"

He moved around the tiny kitchen with a precision that reminded her of Gene Kelly in the opening scene of *An American in Paris*. She made a tentative offer to help, but he just smiled. "Thanks, but there's not much to do, and I've got it down to a science." Between the lines she read, *You'd only be in the way.*

She sat in the small dining booth, similar to her own planned breakfast nook, and divided her time between watching Nathaniel and admiring his handiwork at close range. Here, on a border above the tops of the benches, he'd carved a small frieze in which alternated a sheaf of wheat, a bunch of grapes, a chalice, and a small round loaf of bread. The detail was astonishing for so small a scale; the chalice was intricately wrought, and she could make out an elaborate pattern stamped into the surface of the bread.

"This is incredible," she said, tracing the outlines of the

frieze with her fingers. "Will you do something like this in my breakfast nook?"

He hesitated, chopping knife poised over a zucchini. "I could carve you some kind of design, certainly."

"But I love this one. Are you the kind of artist who refuses to repeat himself? I can respect that, don't get me wrong, but this is so beautiful."

"It isn't that, exactly." He laid down the knife and came to sit opposite her. "This frieze isn't mere decoration, Kelly. The bread and wine represent the Eucharist, the central sacrament of the Orthodox Christian faith. Because I'm a Christian, every time I sit down to eat a meal here, it's a small reflection of that sacrament. But for someone who doesn't believe—well, it wouldn't mean the same thing." He touched his long fingers to the back of her hand. "How about just the wheat and the grapes? I could throw in a cow and a chicken, and then you'd have a balanced diet."

His eyes sparkled at this, but she couldn't raise a smile. She was absurdly hurt that he didn't consider her worthy of the full eucharistic pattern. She would have liked to believe in God— there was a kind of emptiness at the back of her world that she suspected God might fill—but if the Christians' heavenly Father was anything like her own earthly father, she wanted nothing to do with him.

She could not say this to Nathaniel, nor even raise her filling eyes from the table where his hand still lay against hers. After a minute he rose and went back to his cooking.

She shifted her scrutiny to the wall of bookshelves opposite the booth, where a small framed picture interrupted the books at eye level. She rose and went to look at it more closely.

The black-and-white photograph showed a boy in his late

teens dressed in white tie and tails, seated at a grand piano. His features seemed vaguely familiar, but they were blurred and obscured by the superfluous flesh of the jowls. The boy's neck bulged out from his collar; rolls of flesh marred the smooth front of his tucked shirt and strained the black-ribboned seams of his trousers.

"Who is this?" she said, moving to the counter and showing the picture to Nathaniel. "Did you have a brother who was a pianist too?"

He grimaced at the yams he was mashing and his cheeks went red. "I'm an only child. That's me."

Her eyes widened with the effort to take this in. She looked from the picture to the lean, muscular figure before her. "I don't believe it."

"It's true. I told you I couldn't take the pressure of competition. The way I dealt with it was to eat. I spent so many hours practicing, I never got any other exercise, and by the time I had my breakdown I looked like that." His mouth quirked. "The months in the hospital took some of it off, and Aidan worked off the rest. After a year with him my own parents didn't recognize me."

She looked back at the picture and shook her head. "Why do you keep this around? I'd think you'd want to forget all that."

"I can't forget." His voice tightened. "When I look in the mirror, I still see that boy. I mean, I see the way I look now, but it doesn't feel real to me. I keep thinking Fat Boy is the real me and this body is just an impostor."

Kelly watched him for a moment, his face red as he bent over his work, the sinews standing out taut in his forearms. Her hand ached to reach out and brush her fingertips against his cheek. She tightened her grip on the picture, but when she spoke, her voice betrayed her.

"Nat," she said gently, "believe me, when I look at you, I don't see the person in this picture. I see—" She swallowed. She wasn't ready to tell him exactly what she saw. "I don't see an ounce of fat on your body, but there's more to it than that. There's a change inside you—a big change. You could never go back to being Fat Boy, as you call him, because you could never go back to forcing yourself into a life that isn't right for you. You're past that—you're a grown-up now."

He laid down his potato masher and wiped his hands on a towel. "Thank you, Kelly. I knew that, really, but I needed to hear it—from you."

Now it was her turn to redden. She dropped her eyes and fumbled with the picture frame. "If I were you, I'd get rid of this. Forget the past and move on."

He braced his hands against the counter and leaned toward her. "Forgetting is not the way to move on. You have to take everything you are, everything that's happened to you, the good and the bad, and let God work with it like clay, mashing and pulling and pounding it until it takes a new shape—the shape of the person you were meant to be. I keep that picture because the person I was is part of the person I am now."

She stared at him, dumbfounded, unable to comprehend more than a fraction of what he was saying—but something in her knew it for truth, all the same.

Trembling, she replaced the photo and returned to her seat in the booth. Soon dinner was on the table.

She recovered herself after a few bites of tender, juicy steak, buttery zucchini, and cinnamon-spiced mashed yams, with a local vintage Merlot to wash it down. "Mmm. This is fabulous. Can I hire you as a cook as well as a carpenter?"

He gave her a small smile. "I'm not for hire, but you're welcome to join me for dinner here as often as you like. And I mean that."

She did not doubt it. And strangely, she sensed no agenda behind the invitation. She did not fear she would ever be asked to pay for his home-cooked meals in any kind whatsoever; yet at the same time she felt equally certain that his interest in her was more than platonic. He was a puzzlement, indeed—transparent and yet infinitely complex.

When they had finished dinner, he said, "Pie now or later?"

She leaned back in her seat. "Later, please. I'm stuffed."

"Would you like to see the music room, then?"

"Absolutely. I can't imagine where you've hidden it. I'm pretty sure there are no secret passages behind this paneling—I'd swear on my architect's license the inside is as big as the outside."

He laughed. "It's not quite as mysterious as all that."

He led her out the door, down the stairs, and around to the back of the building, where he opened an inconspicuous door. Now she found herself in another small room lined with shelves and cabinets, but these held mostly music books. Almost the entire floor space was occupied by a grand piano.

"If I ever do move, this piano is going to be the real problem. We had to move it in through the garage door, and I put that wall up after it was in." He pointed toward the front of the building. "On the other side is my workshop. I'd have to tear that wall down again to get the piano out."

Kelly turned slowly in place, shaking her head. "You amaze me, Nathaniel. I don't see how you do it. You're so rooted here, with your garden and your built-ins and this piano. And yet you're only renting, you have so little, and you hold it all with an open hand. I understand the few-possessions part—everything I own fits in the back of my truck. It's the rootedness combined with it that baffles me."

He gave her that small smile again, then pulled a chair from a corner for her and sat backward on the piano bench. "Well—I don't know if you can understand this, Kelly, but I'll try to explain it. Within my faith there's an ideal some people try to follow of really living out the commands of the Gospel. Most of these people are monks or nuns. At one time I thought I might be meant for that life myself, but Aidan helped me see that I wanted it for the wrong reasons—I wanted to run away from the world, rather than running toward God. But still, as far as I can, I embrace the monastic ideals: poverty, chastity, and stability.

"For me the poverty and stability come almost naturally. It's a very free way to live, paradoxical as that might sound. But the celibacy I'm hoping won't be permanent."

He said this with no trace of embarrassment or flirtation, but Kelly felt herself flush from her neck to the roots of her hair. She dropped her eyes and said, "Would you play something for me?"

"Certainly. Anything in particular you'd like?"

"How about some Bach?"

He didn't answer, but flexed his fingers, played a couple of warm-up scales, and launched into a two-part invention. Kelly sat back in her chair, closed her eyes, and let the master's music wash through her, its brilliant order creating simplicity out of complexity, both in the notes and in her soul.

When the last notes died away, she woke not from sleep but from a trance-like state to see Nathaniel gazing at her with an expression part tenderness, part longing, part almost a detached appraisal. He stood and offered her his hands to help her rise.

They stood face to face with only inches between them, and she felt sure he was about to kiss her. She gazed at him with a kind of entreaty, whether a plea for love or for clemency she could not be certain.

They stood that way for an eternal moment, then he dropped her hands and stepped back. "Ready for that pie?"

She took a gasping breath as if she'd surfaced after a deep dive. What was happening to her? Why would he take her to the brink and leave her there? Maybe he sensed her fear was still too strong.

She collected herself and said, "Sure."

The pie was probably the best she'd ever tasted, but she ate it in a daze, responding mechanically to his attempts at conversation. When they'd finished, he offered to walk her home. Feeling incapable of navigating even that short distance in her present condition, she accepted, and walked the whole way leaning on his arm.

When they reached her doorstep, she turned to him, both hoping and fearing another charged moment. "Thank you for a lovely evening," she said, trying to infuse the trite words with all the strange mixture of emotions she truly felt.

He took her hand from his arm and raised it to his lips. "I hope it will be the first of many."

She nodded, opened the door and entered the vestibule, then turned back to say good night. The porch light haloed his head so she could not see his features, but his "good night" said everything she hoped to hear.

CHAPTER 13

WHEN KELLY CAME back from that evening with Nathaniel, I wished once again I could have seen what had happened while she was gone. That hard shell of hers was all peeling off, the soft, tender underside showing through. Thank God for Nathaniel; I don't know another man who could have such an effect on her.

My, what a flurry of work began once that section of wall was out! Aidan brought in more men, and they had one crew putting up wallboard in the breakfast nook, one refinishing the floors in the front rooms, and another installing new fixtures in the bathroom. We always thought clawfoot tubs and pedestal sinks were old-fashioned, but I have to say when the new ones went into that bathroom they just looked *right*.

Kelly and Nathaniel finished up the woodwork in the dining room, and the floor men got started in there. Nathaniel began his main job of building all the kitchen cabinetry and the benches in the breakfast nook. Kelly couldn't put a foot downstairs without being in somebody's way, so she and Kiera started in on the bedrooms.

"Let's do June's room first," Kelly said. "They'll want to get started on that linen closet soon." The linen closet was to be cut out of one corner of June's room. I wish I'd thought of doing that years ago.

But like I said, I never could bring myself to touch a thing in June's room, except to straighten it up at first and then keep it dusted. I guess I felt deep down that if I left her room alone, she might come back to it. It's hard to accept a person's death when you don't see them dead; all I ever had was Eunice's word that June had passed on, and Eunice knew it with her second sight. She said June's spirit had said goodbye to her on its way to heaven. I couldn't understand why she wouldn't say goodbye to me as well, me her own mother, and I know she'd forgiven me by then; but Eunice said I wouldn't have been able to hear her because my spirit was deaf and dumb.

Well, that hurt, but it's true, we Lutherans don't go in for second sight. So although I did believe Eunice, there was always a little part of me that hoped she was wrong, and someday my little girl would walk back in the door and up the stairs; and I wanted her to find her room just as she'd left it when she did.

Kelly and Kiera looked around the room, which held every single thing June had collected in seventeen years, and the air went out of them like a punctured tire.

Kiera recovered first. "Well, we've got to start somewhere. How about the dolls and stuffed animals? Those are an easy thrift store call, right?"

Kelly nodded slowly. "I guess so." She walked over to the bed, where Ginger had curled up next to the doll that lay in the center of the pillow. The doll's arm lay across his neck and her orange yarn hair matched his fur. "This one seems kind of special, though."

That girl has good instincts. She'd picked out the Anne of Green Gables doll I made for June when she was about six, along with a whole wardrobe. She loved that thing to pieces, literally; I had to repair it I don't know how many times. "Mommy," she'd say to me, "Annie needs to go to the hospital again," and I'd suture an arm or a leg or reattach a button eye. Long past the age when she was through with dolls in general, June would take that one to bed with her, and change its clothes to match the seasons.

"I think I'll keep this one," Kelly said, and set it aside.

They got down to work after that and bagged up all the other dolls and animals, saving a couple of the smaller ones for Kyle's boy. They boxed up some of the books, too, but Kelly pulled out a few favorites to keep—*Winnie the Pooh, Stuart Little, Wind in the Willows*. And Virginia Lee Burton's picture book, *The Little House*. Kelly exclaimed when she got to that one. She sat on the floor and paged through it.

"This is my very favorite book ever," she said with a catch in her voice. "It sounds weird, but I so identified with the Little House. I hated the city; I always wanted to live on a hill with apple trees all around. I can't even think about this book without crying."

"Don't you already have a copy, then?"

Kelly looked up, her eyes bleak. "My mother gave it away. Along with practically everything else I owned. I came back after my first semester of college and didn't even recognize my room. She'd given all my old clothes, the few toys I'd saved, and all my children's books to charity. She figured I was grown up and didn't need them anymore."

Kiera's "oh!" was a cry of real pain. She knelt by Kelly and put her arms around her. "What a horrible woman! She couldn't have been your real mother. No real mother would do such a thing."

Certainly not—not even a failure of a mother like me.

Kelly's voice and touch were gentle as she put her hands on Kiera's shoulders and pulled back to look her in the face. "Kiera, please. Don't go there. No false hopes, remember?"

Kiera bit her lip. "All right, if you insist. But you can't stop me thinking it."

Kelly's mouth twitched as she added the book to her "keeper" pile. "I very much doubt I could stop you doing anything you really wanted to do. We're rather alike that way, you and I."

She ended up saving quite a few things—a lot of June's artwork and art supplies, and even a few pieces of clothing: a big floppy straw hat, a shawl that June had crocheted herself, a patchwork skirt she'd made with scraps of all the dresses I'd sewn for her since she was little.

They piled all the keepers on the bed, then turned to look at the walls.

"All these posters will have to come down, won't they?" asked Kiera.

"Definitely. And the wallpaper too."

Goodness, I don't blame her for that; it was the strangest wallpaper I'd ever seen, shiny black with neon-colored squiggles all over it. I'd never have let June put it up if Victor hadn't said in his quiet way, "Now, Esther, let her have it if she wants it. It's just a phase. If we humor her in the little things, she won't want to rebel in the things that matter." He was right, of course, as he generally was, though I would never admit it without a fight. But after he was gone, everything changed; she wasn't the same girl anymore.

Kelly and Kiera pulled the furniture away from the walls; Ginger awoke and leapt off the bed in a huff. They ripped down the posters, then Kelly got a stool and pulled on a loose top corner of wallpaper. It came away easily, being that cheap prepasted stuff, and underneath was the paper I'd put up when June was little: many-colored carousel horses all decked out in fancy bridles and saddles with ribbons braided into their manes and tails.

Kelly froze with the black paper in her hand. She sang in a broken whisper, "All the pretty little horses . . ."

"What was that?" asked Kiera.

"It's a lullaby my mother used to sing to me. 'Hushaby, don't you cry, go to sleep, my little baby. When you wake, you shall have all the pretty little horses.'"

I remember singing that song to June every night when she was little. It was her favorite—and the reason we bought that wallpaper.

"Your mother sang you lullabies? She doesn't sound like the type."

"No." Kelly shook her head slowly and spoke as if in a trance. "No, it must have been my other mother. She had a lovely voice."

Kiera came over and touched Kelly's hand. "There, you see? You said it yourself. You had another mother."

Kelly looked down at her and a cloud cleared from her eyes. She shook her head briskly. "No. There has to be some other explanation. Maybe I had a nanny I was super attached to. That would make sense—I can't imagine Miriam actually caring for an infant."

Kiera raised one eyebrow. "Hm. Well, my lips are sealed, but you know what I think of that theory." She turned toward the wall behind the bed and froze. "Kelly, look at this."

Ginger had found a place where a corner of wallpaper was loose. He stood up on his hind legs like a meerkat and fussed at it until it came away. Kelly went closer to investigate. Cut into the old wallpaper and the plaster beneath it, just behind where the headboard had been, was a shallow rectangular hole, and in the hole a small book bound in green leather.

Kelly reached in and carefully pried the book from the hole, handling it as if it were a thousand-year-old relic. She turned back the cover and read, "My Diary. June Rose Hansen, June 17, 1977."

It was the diary Victor had given her for her seventeenth birthday. When she left, I combed the room for it, thinking it might contain a clue to where she'd gone and why, but I never found it; I figured she must have taken it with her. But it was right there behind her headboard all along.

I never took June to be so secretive. I must have been an awfully nosy mother to make her go to such lengths to keep her privacy.

Kelly hesitated with her fingers poised to turn the next page.

"Aren't you going to read it?" Kiera said. "It's not really invasion of privacy, since she's dead. And it could tell us something—interesting."

Kelly closed the book. "I'm going to read it—later. We've still got a lot of work to do."

I hope she doesn't wait too long. I need to see what's in that diary myself.

THAT NIGHT, KELLY BEGGED OFF of dinner with Nathaniel so she could read June's diary.

"You understand, don't you? I'd be no company if I did come—I can't get that thing off my mind."

"Of course. I'm dying to know what it says myself—but I know you have to read it alone." He took her hands for a moment. "But if you need to, call me when you're done—even if it's three AM."

She nuked a frozen dinner and carried it into the inglenook, grateful the chimney had been repaired and cleaned so she could build a fire. Then she settled down to read.

The first few entries were typical teenage fare—friends, clothes, outings, a few flutters over a boy designated as "B," all in a self-consciously elaborated upright script. Kelly paged through them quickly, feeling not like a trespasser but like an alien—this land of carefree adolescence was one she'd never visited.

Then she turned to a page dated August 17 and found a black border inked in around the two-page spread. The writing was shaky and the purple ink blurred in spots where the paper had once been wet.

THE DIARY OF JUNE ROSE HANSEN

August 17, 1977.

Daddy died today.

There, I've written it, but I still can't believe it. My own sweet
Daddy, with the biggest, warmest, tenderest heart in the whole
wide world. How could that heart just stop?

The entry ended there; the rest of the left-hand page was blank.
Then on the next page:

August 20.

The funeral is over and everyone is gone. They were all so kind,
I couldn't bear it. I wanted to howl like a banshee when they
lowered him into the ground, but I couldn't do it with all those
kind faces looking on. I've read about cultures where women wail
and tear their hair when someone dies; I think they've got the
right idea. Only Father Aidan seemed to understand. His voice
kept breaking as he read the prayers, and I had the feeling if I had
howled he would have howled along with me.

August 23.

I saw B today when I went for a walk. He wouldn't look me in the
eye, but mumbled something about being sorry. I felt sorry for

him, he was so awkward. It's hard to believe that only a week ago my heart went pitter-pat whenever he looked at me. He seems like a child to me now. And I feel about a thousand years old.

I went on to the church and had a talk with Father Aidan. He always looks me in the eye and treats me like a grownup, like a human being. And even though he doesn't know what to say to me either, it's comforting just to be with him. His own father died last year, so he <u>knows</u>.

You'd think Mother and I would be able to comfort each other, but I can't get through to her <u>at all</u>. She doesn't act like a woman who's just lost her beloved husband. She acts like—I don't know, like Vice President Johnson taking over after President Kennedy was shot. All worry and responsibility, all uptight. I not only can't cry <u>with</u> her, I can't even cry in front of her. And I still feel like crying almost all the time.

August 28.
School starts tomorrow, and I don't think I can stand it. The thought of being surrounded by all those people all day long makes me ill. And then to have to think, to concentrate. I can't even draw, let alone tackle a math problem. And it's Calculus this year! Why don't they have sabbaticals for students?

August 30.
The first full day of school, and it was every bit as bad as I thought it would be. Maybe worse. Multiply B by 150 and you have everyone in my class. Even Genevieve doesn't know how to talk to me. And I can't help them out one bit. It's too exhausting. At lunch I took refuge in Mr. Mulligan's room. Hard to imagine I could think of anything connected with math as a refuge! But he invited me to stay there after third period, and since he was the first person to look me in the eye all day, I decided I would. He has nice eyes—I had him all last year and never noticed. When I was a kid, he was just a teacher, but now that I'm a thousand years old, he's turned into a fellow human being. He sat at his desk

and graded papers while I picked at my lunch and stared out the window. It was very companionable in a standoffish kind of way, and just what I needed right then.

September 4.
After Mass Father Aidan invited me for a walk. We went down by the river where I used to go with Daddy, and I was able to really talk about him for the first time—about Daddy himself, I mean, not about how it feels to lose him. Little things, like the gift he had of getting butterflies to come to him. He would stand very still, so still he hardly seemed to be breathing but not stiff like when you hold your breath, and butterflies would come and land on his shoulder or the top of his head, as if he were a flower. Once a monarch landed on his nose, and he managed to stay still for about five seconds before his nose twitched and it flew away. I told that to Father Aidan and we actually laughed—the first time I've laughed since Daddy died. Then I felt terrible, like I'd betrayed him or betrayed my own grief, but Father Aidan said no, it was good to laugh. He said Daddy's joyful in heaven and he would want me to be joyful on earth. I said what about purgatory, and he said he couldn't imagine Victor Hansen had any sins to expiate. Well, maybe, but one laugh doesn't make joy. I think joy is still a long way off.

September 8.
I've been spending all my lunches in Mr. Mulligan's room. We actually talk a bit now. He told me his mother died when he was in high school, so he knows how I feel. How I can't talk to kids my own age any more. But we talk about other stuff too, like art and music. How a math teacher knows about art and music I don't know, but he likes a lot of the same stuff I like, so it's cool. Grownups can be pretty interesting when you get to know them.

September 11.
This afternoon Father Aidan came over and we played duets. It's

the first time I've played seriously since it happened, so I was a little rusty, but I guess we did okay. Mother stood in the archway and listened for a while, and when we were finished, she had tears running down her cheeks. I started to go to her, but she turned and hurried back into the library to pay some more bills.

I stood there looking after her and crying, and Father Aidan came up behind me and put his hands on my shoulders. I never noticed before what nice hands he has, firm and strong but not overbearing—kind of like Daddy. He told me to give her time and let her work through things in her own way. I wish she would talk to him like I do, but she's a Lutheran; she doesn't believe in priests, and her minister is a man nobody could talk to about anything. I'd probably go crazy if I didn't have Father Aidan.

September 15.
The other kids are starting to notice how much time I spend in Mr. Mulligan's room. Genevieve got on my case about it today. She said B was getting jealous, of all things. As if I cared; I'm way past that now. I'm past caring what Genevieve thinks, too. They just don't get it. I have to spend time with people who understand me, who don't treat me like something in a freak show, or I'll go nuts. Talking with Mr. Mulligan makes me feel like a mature human being, one who might someday have something to offer the world besides a tear-stained face and a broken soul. I have to go on reaching for that.

After this came a gap of several pages, and the next entry was dated October 20.

I had to leave that gap because since I last wrote, my life has changed completely and forever. Something has been happening that I hardly dare to write about. But now it's gotten to the point that if I don't write it I think I'm going to explode.

I'm falling in love.

There. I've written it. I've made it real.

Falling in love is supposed to be wonderful. So they say. But I don't feel wonderful. I feel confused and scared and tied up in knots and—well, yes, occasionally wonderful, when he looks in my eyes and I think maybe he loves me too. But the next minute I tell myself to shut up and not be ridiculous. He's a grown man, thirty at least, what could he possibly see in a kid like me? Because now I feel like a kid again, only not the kid I was before. A thousand-year-old kid.

And even if he did love me, what good would it do? It's impossible. In his position, he'd be in so much trouble I can't even begin to think about it. So much I don't even dare to write his name here, although I've made a great little hiding place for this diary that it would take Sherlock Holmes himself to find. But I have to call him something besides "him," so I guess I'll call him M. M for Man. M for Marvelous. M for wish-he-were-Mine. And of course, if you want to get prosaic, M for . . . the name I can't write. Or speak. To anyone. Ever.

I didn't mean to fall in love with him. Does anyone ever mean to fall in love? When it's real, that is. I "fell in love" with B pretty much on purpose, but that wasn't love at all. Too bad, because it would have been so much easier. Love is when the other person becomes everything in the world to you, so that nothing matters except being with him. Unless, that is, being with him means he could lose his job, his career, his whole life. He would have to love me as much as I love him to sacrifice that.

I'm jealous of his job, even though that's what brought us together in the first place. If he hadn't been so kind to me, spent so many hours talking with me or letting me talk, I never would have seen him as anything but just another grownup. It's his kindness that I mostly love, but there's something more as well— for others have been kind to me too. With M there's something that seems to draw us together, something I can never explain—I guess that's how it is with love.

October 28.

HE LOVES ME!!!

Oh, I never thought it possible that I could be so happy. And so miserable at the same time.

I'd better explain.

For a long time we'd never been really alone. Oh, we might be the only two people in a room, but there was always a chance someone else would walk in, so it didn't count. But this afternoon I stayed late, till no one else was around, and then he got up and locked the door. He came over and sat down beside me and took both my hands. I thought I would die just from the wonder of touching him.

He looked in my eyes and said, "Rose" (he's taken to calling me Rose, and I love it), "Rose, there's something I have to say to you. I've resisted saying it for a long time because I thought it couldn't do any good, and I wasn't sure . . . Well, I'm still not sure, but it seems . . . Rose, do you—care for me at all? I don't mean as a friend, I mean . . ."

I did something terribly bold at that point. I put up my hand to touch his lips, and oh, they were soft and trembling.

"Yes," I whispered. "Yes. I love you."

He kind of sagged at that point, as though he'd been holding a lot of tension and now it was released. He closed his eyes and took a long, kind of shuddery breath. Then he looked at me as if he could never get enough of looking, and he said, "My darling Rose" —oh, how those words thrilled through me— "I love you too. There, I've said it—but I must never say it again. You know why. It's wrong for me to love you. Nothing good can come of it. I've done you wrong, spoiled your youth, betrayed your trust, and I have nothing to offer you in exchange."

I said, "You've just given me everything I wanted. You love me—that's enough."

He shook his head. "No, no, it isn't enough, it isn't anything at all because I can't act on it. I should never have let it happen. I could have stopped it, early on, if I'd been honest with myself and admitted that I saw it coming. But I pretended it was all harmless, that you saw me as a father-figure, that I was helping you and being kind to you. Kind!" Here he gave what I think is meant by "a hollow laugh." It was a dreadful thing to hear—the hollowness went all the way down.

I couldn't bear to see him suffer so. I put up my hand again and stroked his cheek. He caught my palm and kissed it, almost crushed it, then put it from him and stood up. "You've got to go now, Rose. I'm sorry, but it's best if we don't see each other alone any more. I—I can't answer for my actions if we do."

I did leave, but it was the hardest thing I've ever done. Even harder than saying goodbye to Daddy. I left my heart behind in that room.

So this is what love really means. To break your heart for the sake of not destroying someone else, even though his heart is breaking too.

November 4.
I meant to stay away, tried to stay away, but in the end my feet seemed to go there of their own accord. I knew I shouldn't, <u>mustn't</u> go, but how can you keep apart from your own heart? And so what happened was clearly entirely my fault.

I waited until no one else was around, then I went in and locked the door behind me. He whipped around to face me as if a thief had entered with a gun. That's almost what I felt like.

He looked so fierce I only took one faltering step into the room, and I couldn't open my mouth to speak. He hung there for a moment, full of a taut energy like a cat about to spring; and then in two bounds he crossed the room and snatched me into his arms.

What happened after that I couldn't write even if I wanted to. It had a kind of horror and a kind of holiness, too. I know that's a funny word to use in the circumstances—a blasphemous word, even; but that's the way it felt to me, as if we were transgressing on something too holy to touch. Once it took hold of us, no power on earth could have stopped it. Maybe a heavenly power could, but we were in no state to call on such help.

And now—now I am really a woman, and if possible an even more heartbroken one than before, because I know I can never be with him again. He told me as much, afterward, when we were clinging to each other and crying. "I've failed," he said over and over. "I'm unworthy. I can't stay here, it's clear now I can't resist you. I'll have to go away."

And I knew he was right, and it was all my fault for tempting him, and I would have to let him go.

Only—there's just one little thing. How am I to go on living without him?

November 7.
M is gone. A leave of absence, they said. They sent another man to take his place. And I am the only one who knows that his place can never, ever be filled. It will be an emptiness inside me for the rest of my life.

At this point Kelly stopped reading, blinded by tears. She stared a while at the dying fire, then got up to stoke it. Her tea had gone cold as well, so she went into the dining room to make a fresh cup.

She looked around her. Here, within these walls, this lovely and innocent young girl—for Kelly could not but see her as innocent despite her "fall"—had suffered an anguish that a grown woman would need all her resources to survive. She ran her fingertips over the paneling, imagining she could feel that anguish, as well as the years of happiness that preceded it, embedded in the grain.

"For you, Rose," she whispered, not knowing exactly what she meant. But all she could do for Rose now was to care for the house that had sheltered her pain.

She went back to the inglenook and read on.

December 7.
I'm beginning to think I may not always be empty after all. M
is still gone and my heart is still empty, but I suspect my womb
may not be. My period is two weeks late.

I ought to be terrified—and I suppose on some level I am—but
a crazy joy keeps leaping up inside me. If I cannot have M, perhaps I can have his child, and that would be some compensation.

December 15.
I threw up this morning. I don't think Mother noticed. I begged
off of breakfast, saying I was late for school. Later in the day I
felt fine, so it isn't the flu. I think I must really be pregnant. And
now the terror is beginning to stir, because what on earth will I
do? The mere thought of telling Mother makes me feel ill again.
And I'll be showing long before school is out, so no graduation
for me. And I was in the running for valedictorian. If only Nana
were still alive, I could go stay with her—she would take me in
no matter what I'd done. Mormor is a different story, and anyway
she's not well enough. There's no one else, no one I can even tell,
let alone who would help me. And how can I dare to pray for help,
when it was a mortal sin that got me into this fix—a sin I haven't
even been able to confess?

December 22.
I've thrown up every morning this week, and Mother finally
noticed. She really looked at me for the first time in months and
said, "You're looking awfully peaky, dear. I think you'd better stay
in bed today."

Fine with me. There's nothing out there that holds any appeal
for me anyway. But if this keeps up, eventually she'll realize I'm
not sick, and then . . .

December 25.
This was the most miserable Christmas I have ever spent. Mother
and I were both too exhausted to make any preparations; since

school let out I've hardly gotten out of bed. Usually Christmas is my favorite time, but it was always a time I shared with Daddy. He and I would buy the tree and decorate the house and sing carols while Mother holed up in the kitchen, baking every Christmas goodie known to man. My physical state aside, I just can't imagine doing all that without him.

Finally last night Mother said, "We <u>have</u> to have a tree," and she went out and got one for nothing because they were closing down the lot. It's a pretty pitiful tree, short and crooked and mangy-looking, a real Charlie Brown kind of tree. But when we got some ornaments on it, it didn't magically transform into a full symmetrical tree like Charlie Brown's did. It only looked more pitiful.

We went to Mass, like we always do on Christmas, and even that was miserable because of the weight on my heart. All I could think of was how much I miss M, and then I felt guilty for thinking of him when I should have been thinking about Christ's Birth. Afterward Mother and I managed a few little presents for each other, but Mother has always been so terribly practical when it comes to choosing gifts. The fun, delightful, surprising things—the I-didn't-know-it-till-I-saw-it-but-this-is-exactly-what-I've-always-wanted things—always came from Daddy.

And I need Daddy now for so much more than gifts. I need him to stand between me and Mother when she figures out what's wrong with me. It can't be far off now.

December 28.
Today Mother caught me throwing up again—I hadn't for a couple days—and said, "That does it. I'm taking you to the doctor." I tried to put her off, telling her I felt fine, really, I must have eaten something that disagreed with me, but she was adamant. And Mother adamant could give the dictionary a whole new meaning for the word.

Of course she came into the examining room with me, as she always does, as if I were still a child. But after the doctor had peered and poked and prodded and listened and questioned and frowned, he sent Mother out of the room (which was the medical feat of the century in itself). Then he asked me, "Young lady, is there any possibility you could be pregnant?"

I wanted to deny it, but the tears started to my eyes and gave me away. The doctor was very kind, very gentle. He had me pee in a cup for the test to confirm it, although he said he was pretty sure, and I told him I was too. He asked me if I'd been forced or coerced, and I said no. Then he asked me if there was anything he could do to help me. I shook my head. What is there that anyone could do?

He told Mother to bring me back in a week to get the results of "the lab work," as he called it, so as not to give her any ideas. I was grateful for the week's reprieve, but in a way it would almost have been better just to get it over with. I'll be living this week like a prisoner in the Tower awaiting the block.

January 3, 1978.

I asked someone today when M was coming back. I've been torn between thinking he ought to know and thinking I ought to spare him this ultimate nail in the coffin of his career. But it looks as though I may not have the opportunity to choose. They told me he isn't coming back, and they don't even know where to reach him. Oh, my love, my own, this is the most unkindest cut of all. I can live without you if I must, I can bear your child and raise it on my own, somehow—but never to hear from you again, never even to know where you are—how can I bear that? Was my sin so great that I deserve this punishment? My sin was only that I loved not wisely, but too well.

January 4.

Today was my Waterloo, my Pearl Harbor, my day of infamy. We went back to the doctor. He took us both into his office and gave Mother the news. (The test was positive, of course.) She blustered at first that it was impossible, that I was a mere child, a virgin, didn't even have a boyfriend. She's always been so sure she knew everything about me, but in the last five months she's known nothing at all.

When she'd wound down, the doctor simply repeated the test results, then added quietly that he'd confirmed with me that it was possible. Then she looked at me for the first time, and this expression came over her face as if she'd never seen me before, had no idea who was this stranger masquerading as her daughter.

That passed in a moment, and then she was fierce. "Who did this to you?" she demanded. "I'll have the law on him. He can't get away with ruining my baby's life."

The doctor cleared his throat. "Mrs. Hansen, may I point out that your daughter is over the age of consent? And I've seen no evidence that this was a case of rape. The fellow may be at fault, I dare say he is, but I don't think you'd have any legal recourse against him."

Mother stared at him as if he'd spoken in Chinese, then turned back to me. "Who did this to you?"

I only shook my head. I will never tell, her or anyone. If M is to suffer, it won't be because of me.

She took me home after that and started the barrage afresh. She went on and on at me—I can't write it all. First she called him every name in the book, and when I defended him she started in on me. I always thought she loved me, in her overprotective, controlling way; but now that love is beginning to look like hate.

January 5.

Mother was calmer today, but she hasn't given up the battle; she only changed her tactics. She cooked my favorite breakfast of French toast and sausage, which I couldn't eat more than a few bites of, and told me she wanted me to stay home from school so I could rest. I thought for a few minutes that maybe she would leave me in peace about the baby's father and magically transform into the tender, supportive mother I need right now.

Then she started talking about the responsibility of raising a child, how hard it is for a woman to do it on her own. She went on about how a man has a responsibility for a child he's created, even if it was by accident, and how we needed to persuade the father of my child to marry me. I took this for a while, then I lost my patience and said, "He can't marry me."

Immediately I was sorry. I hadn't meant to say so much. She leapt out of her chair and said, "You don't mean to tell me he's married already?" But I had my guard back up by that time. I stared out the window and didn't say another word.

It was back to yelling and name-calling then, and I just got up and left the room. I've never dared to walk out on her in a tirade before, but it doesn't seem to matter now. What more can she do to me than has already been done? What more could I suffer than I've suffered already?

(Later.)
I came up here and pushed a chair against the door—she's never let me have a lock, of course—and wrote that first part. After a while she came and knocked on the door and asked in a very quiet and (for her) humble voice if she could talk to me, so I put this diary back in its hiding place and let her in.

She sat on the bed and spoke, quite calmly and reasonably, the words that would destroy me. "June, I've been thinking," she said. "We're in a very difficult situation. Your father is gone, and I have all I can do just to keep a roof over our heads. I'm almost sixty, June. I'm too old to raise another child, and you're too young—you need to finish high school, go to college, make a life for yourself. We can't let this baby get in the way of all that."

I stared at her. I tried to swallow, but there was a lump the size of an egg in my throat. "You don't mean . . . you want me to have . . ." I could hardly even speak the word. ". . . an abortion?"

I've already imperiled my immortal soul by fornication. I'm not going to put myself beyond the reach of pardon by killing my child. M's child. Even if it weren't a mortal sin, I could never kill his child; it's all I have left of him.

But Mother shook her head. "No, no, I would never think of that. I want you to go to Minnesota and stay with Aunt Ingrid for a while. I'll give you my wedding band, and you can say your husband's in the military overseas. Then when the baby's born we'll put it up for adoption. You can study on your own and get your GED, and then you can come home and start college next fall."

Her words fell on me like stones. Put my baby up for adoption? M's baby? "I can't do that."

Her face went dark. "What do you mean, you can't do that? I've just told you, that's what we're going to do."

I shook my head. It took an enormous effort to move it from side to side. "This is my baby, Mother. I'm the one who's responsible for it, and I have to decide what to do. I'm going to keep the baby and raise it. If you won't help me, I'll do it by myself, but I will do it."

She got up from the bed, her face white, quaking all over. I've seen her angry before, but this was something beyond—this was a woman I didn't know. She frightened me, but not enough to make me change my mind.

She spoke with a voice I didn't recognize, low and controlled but pulsing with fury. "You will not raise your little bastard in my house." Then she turned on her heel and left the room.

I could forgive her anger toward me, her rejection of me. But I can't forgive the name she called my child.

So now my course is clear. I will have to leave. I don't know where I'll go or what I'll do, who I'll find to help me, because I will need help, I know. But I have a little money saved, enough to keep me going for a month or two. Maybe I can find a commune that will take me in.

(Later.)

It's late. Mother's gone to bed. I've packed a few things in a backpack, just as much as I can carry. I would take this diary except I see I've gotten to the last page. I can't afford to take one extra thing.

It's strange to look around my bedroom, this room where I spent my whole childhood, and think this is the last night I will ever sleep in it. And yet it seems fitting somehow. I left my childhood behind the day I became M's lover; I'm a stranger to this room now. It's time to find another place for myself in the world.

Tomorrow I'll get on the Metro bus to go to school and just keep going. I'll have a whole day's start before she'll realize I'm gone. The only thing that hurts is that I won't be able to say goodbye. I can say goodbye to this diary, though. You've been my faithful friend through the most tumultuous months of my life, and I'm going to miss you. I'll put you back in your hiding place, and maybe someday, years from now, Mother will decide to tear down this wallpaper she's always hated and she'll find you. But maybe by that time all will be forgiven. I'll visit Mother with my little girl—I'm sure somehow that it's a girl—and we'll read this diary and cry a little, but then we'll hug and laugh and put the past behind us forever.

Goodbye, diary—goodbye, childhood—goodbye, my old life. Mother, if you ever find this, I forgive you.

CHAPTER 14

I READ THE WHOLE thing over Kelly's shoulder. What a mercy I never found it—my heart would have broken in so many pieces I never could have gathered them up again. Now I'm in a place where there are no more tears. I've done my penance, and I know June is in the Presence, all joy. It's only Kelly who still bears the hurt.

We think we know ourselves, and all the time there's a dragon coiled inside us. He flicks his snaky tongue out now and then, but it takes something like I went through thirty years ago—Victor's death, trying desperately to make ends meet, then June's pregnancy—to let him reveal himself in all his hideousness. And then he breathes a fire that can scorch everyone for miles around.

It was only the next day that I repented of those words the dragon had spoken to June. But she was up and out of the house so quietly I didn't have a chance to apologize—and then she never came back. I called the police, of course, but it was clear she'd run away of her own volition, and a runaway seventeen-year-old wasn't going to be top priority with them. I had no money to hire a detective, and for my own part, once I'd contacted everyone she knew and no one had news of her, I didn't know what else to do.

I certainly did the only thing I could do, which was pray. I even went into the Catholic church and did the whole candles and kneeling bit, just in case—June herself was a Catholic, so I thought maybe God would hear me better if I prayed from there. And all those prayers were well watered with tears upon tears, but still they didn't bear fruit—or at least not the fruit I was looking for. I know better now: I know that the fruits of prayer sometimes grow so slowly that a lifetime is not enough to see them ripen. I'm watching that final ripening now, that softening and sweetening and bursting into color that comes just before the fruit is ready to pick. And I think the harvest will be rich beyond my dreams.

KELLY CLOSED THE JOURNAL WITH swimming eyes, feeling as if her soul had been through the wringer—as if she herself had lived Rose's heartache and were now venturing into the world, unprotected and alone.

She looked at the small, humble book in her hands, turned it over and back again. "Where's the sequel?" she said to Ginger, who was snoozing on her lap. "Where's the happily ever after?" She felt she would not be able to rest until she knew what had become of Rose and her baby girl (for Kelly was as certain as Rose herself the baby had been a girl). Yet there seemed no possibility of finding out—Esther herself apparently had never known, and now the trail was thirty years cold.

She flipped through the journal again, and her anger mounted against Esther and against the unknown "M" who had abandoned Rose to her fate. It must be the teacher, she thought, Mulligan—the older man who was "kind" to her. Kind but a coward. He'd left before he could even have known about Rose's pregnancy. It was possible Rose had found him after she left home, but Kelly doubted it; she'd never expressed that intention.

Somewhere in the world was a man who didn't know he had a daughter. If he had known, would he have cared? Would he have sacrificed everything to save the two of them from their lonely fate? Would he have been the kind of father who would cherish a handmade Father's Day card until his death?

She toyed with the idea of trying to find Mulligan. It might be possible; the local high school would have records that would show his first name and perhaps where he'd gone when he left here. But until she knew what had happened to Rose and her baby, what would be the point? You don't show up on a man's doorstep and tell him, "You have a child," without being able to tell him who and where that child is. Besides, she couldn't be positive Mulligan was even the man. "M" could be some other perfidious person Rose hadn't even mentioned in the diary before she recorded falling in love with him.

"Men!" she said to Ginger, who blinked up at her and yawned in response. "Cowards, cads, and creeps, the lot of them. Except for you, of course, Ginger." And except for Victor—a girl couldn't ask for a better father than he, and surely a better husband than Esther deserved. And there were Aidan, Kyle, Nathaniel. None of them would act as "M" had acted. Especially not Nathaniel, her rational mind insisted.

But somewhere deep inside her wounded heart a tiny, frightened child's voice whispered, *Would he?*

CHAPTER 15

THE NEXT MORNING Kelly was in the kitchen, surrounded by the forlorn shells of half-finished cabinets, when Kiera and Nathaniel came in. The rest of the crew was upstairs working on that laundry room I wish I could have had.

"Well, did you read it?" Kiera demanded.

Kelly nodded. "It was heartbreaking. She *was* pregnant when she left. Esther as good as kicked her out. And the father ran off before he even knew about the baby."

Kiera uttered a strangled "Oh!" I hated to have her think ill of me, hated even more to hear Kelly speak of me with such indignation. How can I ever make her understand?

Nathaniel shook his head in sorrow. "Did she say who the father was?"

"No, only that he was older and his career would have been endangered if anyone found out. She called him 'M.' I think it may have been a teacher she mentioned earlier, a Mr. Mulligan. He befriended her after her father died."

"I can't believe Esther would kick her out," Kiera protested. Oh, thank you for that vote of confidence, sweetheart. "She was a strong woman, kind of bossy, but she had such a warm heart.

How could she kick out her own pregnant daughter?"

"Well, she didn't *exactly*." Kelly explained the situation. "So Rose—sorry, I think of her as Rose now—felt like her only choice was to leave."

Her voice wavered on that last phrase. It stabbed me to see her hurt so much for June Rose. But maybe I should be glad for it—maybe that's the soft spot in her that will grow into forgiveness in the end. If only that end comes before she leaves my house.

Nathaniel turned a close eye on her, then put an arm around her shoulders. "The story really got to you, didn't it?"

She nodded, biting her lip. "I feel—so connected to her somehow. As if I have a responsibility to find out what happened to Rose and her baby. Maybe even find the father, if he's still alive."

I caught a significant glance between Kiera and Nathaniel. I could see Kelly caught it too. The thought she'd forbidden them to voice was written all over their faces.

"I know what you two are thinking. And—well, I'm not going to fight it any more. But neither am I going to believe it without some hard evidence. I can't do much while the house is in process, but when we're finished here, I'm going to do some research. If I am Esther's granddaughter, it can't be coincidence that she left the house to me. Somebody must have been able to trace the connection, and that means I can trace it too."

Yes! Praise the Lord, at least she doesn't hate me so much that she doesn't *want* to find the connection.

Kiera hugged her. "I knew it! I knew it must be true. And there could be more evidence right in this house. We still haven't sorted through Esther's bedroom, you know."

And it's perfect they've left that room for last. I bet Raphael had something to do with that.

"That's true. But we can't do it right now, we'd only be in the way while they're working on the laundry room. As soon as the crew is finished up there, we'll turn that room inside out."

"Then I'd better get moving with these cabinets," said Nathaniel. "I want to be in on the search."

THE WORK ON THE LAUNDRY room seemed to take forever, though in fact it was only a few days. The plumbing and electrical had been finished earlier, and all that remained for now was the drywall and painting; Nathaniel would put in the cabinets later. Kelly and Kiera decided to spend the time moving things back into the front downstairs rooms now that the refinished floors were ready for use.

But when Kelly looked from the empty living room, its oak floors and redwood paneling softly gleaming in the morning light, to the pile of overstuffed chintz in the hall, something in her revolted. While the furniture had all stood in its age-old places, she had not had the heart to disturb it; but now the spell was broken. Why should she live with all the belongings of a woman she had come almost to hate for the way she had treated her daughter? The happiness of this home had been shattered years ago, with Victor's death and all that came after. If it was to be happy again, Kelly would have to rebuild that happiness from scratch.

She turned to Kiera. "I don't think I want to put all this back. Most of it doesn't even fit the style of the house. Let's go shopping."

Kiera grinned broadly. "It's working."

"What's working?"

"My plan. To domesticate you."

"No, it isn't that—" Kelly bridled automatically, then thought

163

again. She had certainly made a decision about furniture based on an unconsidered, unconscious assumption that she was in the house to stay. Apparently her heart had decided the issue while her head was otherwise engaged.

"Well, maybe it is. It's worth a try, anyway."

Kiera bounced on her toes, clearly restraining herself with difficulty from an all-out victory dance. "So, where shall we go? New or old?"

"Mission style. Stickley, if it's to be had. Old is best, but authentic reproduction will do."

"I know just the place. Come on."

They took Kelly's truck and headed to Santa Cruz, where Kiera had her eye on one particular store on Mission Street. "It's called Mission Furniture, but it's not because of the street. It's because they specialize in Mission style, old and new."

The store was narrow; the light from the front windows penetrated only a few feet into an interior that was not otherwise lit and seemed to dissolve into infinite depths. As the two women stood blinking in the front of the shop, an absurdly tall, emaciated figure emerged from those depths, his stork-like limbs moving jerkily. He came within a few feet of them and stopped, putting up a weathered brown claw to adjust round wire-rimmed glasses on a hawk's-beak nose. Black hair streaked with white stood out from his head in every direction. Kelly felt as if she'd stumbled into a scene by Dickens. The birdman's quite ordinary clothing—T-shirt and jeans blotched with shades of reddish-brown—only added to his surreal appearance; if he'd been wearing a frock coat, she would have known where she was.

"Well, what do you want then?" he said in a high, cracked voice with a whistle at the back of it.

Kelly was tempted to answer, "Nothing at all, and do forgive us for disturbing you." But Kiera elbowed her and said, "Please, Mr. Herron, my friend is looking for some real Stickley, if you happen to have any on hand. We're restoring her Stickley house up in the Valley."

The grey eyes behind the spectacles flashed into life. "Stickley, eh?" he wheezed. "What room?"

Kelly cleared her throat, which seemed to have been paralyzed since Herron's appearance. "Living room, to begin with."

He rubbed his clawlike hands together and emitted a high-pitched cackle. "Oh yes, living room, oh yes. This way, ladies, this way."

He led them through a maze of tables, beds, and sofas— which Kelly could see, now that her eyes had adjusted, were all of modern manufacture—and through a low door at the back. There she stood blinking again, this time because the room was flooded with light from a bay window that took up the entire back wall. In the bay stood a sofa table with a bottle of alcohol and a pad of superfine steel wool resting on its surface. The design on its two pedestal legs echoed the pattern in the stained glass in Kelly's front door.

"That table." She pointed. "And anything you have that matches it. That's exactly the pattern of my stained glass."

Herron cackled again. "Oh, that's a nice one, that is. Just finished fixing it up. And the rest of the family here too, all cleaned up and ready to go. Have to keep them all together, you know. Have to make sure they go to a good home." He picked his way around to the far corner, where a sofa and two armchairs clustered around a square coffee table. All the pieces had the same design worked into the legs and sides.

Kelly examined them, and she and Kiera sat on the sofa and chairs. The leather seats were sturdy and comfortable, and the wood looked better than new—it had the character of age without the obvious damage one would expect after a century's use.

"I'll take the lot. How much?"

Herron's eyes narrowed and his head nearly disappeared between his hunched shoulders. "Now just a minute, young lady, not so fast, not so fast. Need some credentials. Can't let my darlings go to just anyone, you know."

Kelly boggled. She'd never expected to meet a dealer who treated his wares like children up for adoption.

"What sort of credentials? I'm an architect, I restore old houses. I've loved Stickley for years, and finally I inherited this Stickley house up in the Valley, so I'm restoring it. The furniture that came with the house was inappropriate, and I want to replace it with something that belongs."

Herron's head jerked to one side. "Pictures? Got to see this house for myself, you know. Might not be right."

Kelly turned to Kiera with a hopeless gesture. Kiera grinned. "I took a few with my cell phone before we left." Clearly Kiera had dealt with Herron before.

She held up the phone for him to see and clicked through the photographs. He bobbed his head with a gleam in his eyes. "Not bad, not bad. Fine work, nicely cleaned up. You did this?" He glanced sharply at Kelly.

"With a friend, yes. Nathaniel Erikson is helping me."

Kelly wasn't sure what had prompted her to mention Nathaniel's name—other than the fact that it was always at the forefront of her mind—but apparently it was the right thing to do. Herron's head came out from his shoulders and he pranced in a circle, flapping his arms. "Nathaniel! Should've said so in the first place!" He skittered over to a high desk near the door and scribbled for a moment, then turned to Kelly and announced a figure that seemed to her absurdly low. "All five pieces, now. Have to take all five."

"Yes, of course. You're sure that's all you want for them?"

He waved one claw. "Money doesn't matter. Where they go matters. Nathaniel, best in the business. He'll take good care of them."

Kelly's face went hot, and she opened her mouth to say that Nathaniel would not always be around to do so; but at a look from Kiera she closed it again. Instead, she smiled acquiescence and got out her checkbook. Something told her Herron would not know what to do with a credit card.

With great ceremony and a quantity of ropes and blankets, the three of them loaded the furniture into Kelly's truck. Herron patted each piece, his eyes moist. "Nathaniel will take care of my babies." He peered intently at Kelly, then nodded. "And you'll take care of him."

Once again, Kelly opened her mouth to protest, but then her mind filled with a vision of Nathaniel taking his ease in one of the armchairs and herself bending over him, handing him a cup of tea. It was such an alluring vision that the protest died unspoken.

INFECTED WITH HERRON'S SOLICITUDE, KELLY nursed the truck back up the winding road through the valley with ridiculous care. Nathaniel and Aidan came out to help unload, and Kelly told them the story of her acquisition—omitting the old man's strange, prophetic parting words.

Nathaniel laughed softly. "Old Herron. What a treat. Wish I'd known you were going there—I would've liked to come along. He taught me most of what I know about cabinetmaking.

Lucky you thought to mention my name, or he might never have sold to you. He hates to let go of anything good."

They carried the furniture in and arranged it in the living room, where it looked as if it had stood since the house was built. Ginger hopped up on the couch, padded in a tight circle, then settled down for a nap. Kiera laughed. "It's got Ginger's seal of approval."

Nathaniel said, "May I?" and sat in an armchair, and he looked as if he belonged there too. Kelly had to bite her tongue to keep herself from offering him a cup of tea.

But Nathaniel had already had his morning break. "I could sit here forever, but duty calls," he said with a wink at Kelly. "If I keep going I can finish the breakfast nook today."

He went out, and at a look from Aidan, Kiera also evaporated. Aidan turned to Kelly. "Can we have a word? There're a few issues I'd like to discuss."

"Sure." She waved him to the chair Nathaniel had vacated and sat on the couch next to Ginger.

Aidan settled himself in the chair with an appreciative sigh. "This is one fine piece of furniture. Good choice, Kelly." Then he sat forward and impaled her with his gaze. "You have good judgment, you know. About a lot of things. You should trust it more."

"What do you mean? I do trust it. You haven't heard me second-guessing myself about the house, have you?"

"Not the house, no." He looked at her as if he were trying to read her soul. "I'm talking about people."

"People?" Her voice grew small and wavery.

"People. Kiera's told me a little about your background. I can understand you would have a hard time trusting people, especially men. But Kelly, there are good men in the world, and Nathaniel is one of them. I've seen what's starting to develop between you two, and I've also seen you holding back. I just want to encourage you to let go. There are no obstacles between the two of you except what you put up for yourselves—no great difference in age, no prior commitments. Let him into your heart. He won't let you down."

Kelly broke from his gaze, understanding for the first time what had made this man become a priest—he had a gift for eliciting confessions. "I'm trying, Aidan. Truly I am. But—being in this house—it's doing something to me. It's changing me. I don't quite know who I am anymore. And in the midst of that to try to build a relationship—to learn to . . ."

"To love, Kelly? Don't be afraid of the word. There's no life without it. It can be painful, yes, it can be dangerous; nobody knows that better than I. But think of the alternative—to go through life with a heart like a dried-up peach pit? That's not your destiny, Kelly. You were born to love."

She swallowed painfully. "I have to find out . . ." He didn't know yet about June's journal, and she wasn't sure she wanted to tell him; the subject of June seemed to be a painful one for him. No doubt if he knew the truth he would feel he had failed her as her priest. "I have to find out why I'm here. Why Esther brought me here. It could affect—the rest of my life. I won't feel free until I know."

She looked up at him, blinking the mist from her eyes. "But after that, I promise you I'll try. I'll give it my best shot. That is, assuming Nathaniel really wants me to."

Aidan gave a small, wry smile. "That much I think you can count on."

CHAPTER 16

OH, IT'S BEEN hard to see Kelly harden her heart against me—even against my furniture!—although I surely deserve it. Winning her forgiveness won't be easy now she knows the truth of what I did; but then her forgiveness wouldn't be worth much if she didn't know.

All the heavy work on the laundry room is done now, so they're going to start cleaning out my room, and no doubt they'll find June's letters. Will that help or hinder my cause? I don't know.

Of course, there's a deal of just plain junk they'll have to wade through first. When I look at it now, I can't fathom what possessed me to hang onto all that stuff—drawers full of worn-out underwear, torn stockings I thought I might use to stuff a pillow, old clothes I meant to cut up for quilt scraps, spare buttons for garments I hadn't worn since the sixties. Why do we burden ourselves with all these useless things? I guess subconsciously we see them as some kind of hedge against an uncertain future. But the only certain future is death, and all the buttons in the world won't keep your soul fastened to your body when it's time for it to go.

I did feel sorry for the three of them, sitting on the floor surrounded by all my junk. They didn't want to throw it all out wholesale since they hoped to find something meaningful, something that would give them a clue. If I only could have pointed them in the right direction, I could have saved them a lot of time.

But at last, when the bureau and the chifforobe and the closet had been emptied and bags and bags of stuff filled for the trash or the thrift store, someone thought to look in the nightstands. Victor's was still full of his litter of pipe cleaners, loose change, fingernail clippers, and so on; Kiera picked out the change and dumped the rest in the trash, and rightly so. But then Kelly started on mine.

The front of the drawer held the usual things—lotions, hairnets, a little notebook I kept to write down things that occurred to me at night that I knew I'd forget by morning. Kelly flipped through that, but all it said was things like "call doctor" and "butter, eggs, bread." There was one note to "Look into will" that caught her attention, but she looked forward and back from there and nothing more was said about it, so at last she set the notebook aside. I kind of wish now I'd been the type to keep a journal or at least a regular sort of planner, because it would have helped her more; but I was always a great one for trying to keep everything in my head. That little notebook was my only concession to the weakness of age. Lord, forgive my foolish pride!

Underneath that was an article I'd clipped from the San Francisco newspaper about Kelly and the work she did with old houses. Of course I didn't know for sure then she was *my* Kelly. But the article had a color picture of her, so I could see the coloring was right, and I thought her face looked kind of familiar, as if she belonged in our family. That picture was what gave me the idea of leaving the house to her—I figured it would give the lawyers something to go on to find her, and they might be able to figure out if she was really my Kelly or not.

"Well," she said when she'd looked at the clipping for a bit, "I guess this explains the will, at any rate. Sort of."

The drawer looked empty now, but I knew it wasn't. It had been warped for some years and wouldn't pull out all the way, so Kelly would have to put her hand back into its dark depths to find what she was looking for. But of course she didn't know that, and she started to close the drawer. That's when I called out to Ginger with all my spirit, and thank the Lord—clever cat that he is, he heard me. He hopped up on the bed with a mighty yowl and started pawing at the drawer.

"What is it, Ginger? You smell a mouse in there?"

She put her head down and peered in, then felt around in it with splayed fingers. "No mouse here, Ginger."

Ginger got up on the nightstand and twisted himself half into the drawer, reaching one paw way into the back. His claw caught on a bit of ribbon, and he pulled the packet of letters out into the light.

Kelly picked up the packet and gave Ginger an absentminded scratch on the head. He mewed as if to say, "You're welcome, you poor clueless, clawless human, and where would you be without me?" then curled up inside the empty drawer for a well-deserved nap. Oh, what a priceless cat!

There were only three letters—two slender envelopes and a postcard tied together with a black ribbon. Black for my grief, black for my sin, black for my heart that drove my baby away.

Kelly took them in trembling fingers and pulled the ribbon off. She looked for a return address, but there was none, not on the front or back of either of the envelopes or the card. "It's Rose's writing, though. And the postmarks are from seventy-eight and seventy-nine—after she left."

She sat on the bed, and Kiera and Nathaniel came to sit on

either side of her. She read the postcard first. It was one of those blank pre-stamped ones, and it started cold with no greeting. Kelly read it aloud, her voice shaking.

I am safe and well, in case you care. Don't try to trace me by the postmark because I'm sending this through a friend. You don't know her and she doesn't know where I am. I will let you know when the baby is born. June.

That postcard tore my heart out when I first got it. "In case you care"! When my heart was bleeding for what I'd done, and all I wanted was to find her and tell her I was sorry, and she could stay with me and we'd raise her baby together, and I'd be proud to claim my grandchild before the world. But she hadn't given me any clues, and it was months before I got the first real letter.

"Dear Mother," it began, and that was such a comfort I can't begin to tell you.

I am safe and well, and you have a beautiful baby granddaughter who is now a month old. I wish you could see her, I really think she would melt your heart. I don't have a camera or I'd send you a picture. She has pure white skin and a full head of red hair, just like Daddy's and mine.

Kelly's fingers strayed to her hair as she read this.

She doesn't do much yet besides sleep, which is a good thing because I'm pretty busy. I have a job as a live-in maid for a rich couple. When I first left home, I stayed in a commune for a while. The people were nice enough, but it wasn't my scene—drugs and stuff, you know. Then about a month before I was due I met this woman by accident, and she offered me a job. She said the baby would be no problem; she loved babies and couldn't have any of her own. She said she was lonely rattling around in a big house, all by herself most of the time because her husband was away on business a lot. He's away now, in fact; I haven't met him yet. I hope he won't be too surprised when he comes home and finds us here.

So now I'm living in this big posh house, and baby and I have a room of our own—a nice room with a private bath, not like a maid's room at all. Oh, I forgot to tell you, I named the baby Kelly.

At this, Kelly's voice broke and her hands shook so much she could hardly hold the letter. She raised haunted eyes to Nathaniel. He put his arm around her shoulders, took the letter in his other hand, and started reading where she'd left off.

The work isn't too bad because there's only the one woman, and the house is very modern and easy to clean. I don't have to cook every night; she goes out a lot with her bridge club friends. She likes my baking, though. I made Crustimony Proseedcake for her and she loved it. I hope you don't mind that I wrote down the recipe for her.

I could see Kelly's shoulders quiver under Nathaniel's hand.

I want you to know I've forgiven you, Mother. I hope someday we can be friends again. But I can't risk coming home or letting you know where I am until I've saved enough to be independent. I hope you understand. Being Kelly's mommy is the most important thing in the world to me, and I won't let you or anyone take that away from me.

I'll write again sometime.

Love, June.

Nathaniel put the letter down and looked at Kelly, who was almost as white as my body was, lying in the coffin. "Are you okay? We don't have to go on with this."

174

She took a deep breath and clenched her shaking hands in her lap. "I'm fine. Go on."

He looked at the third letter. "This one's postmarked December of seventy-nine. Quite a gap."

He slid the letter out of the envelope and unfolded it, then returned his arm to Kelly's shoulders.

Dear Mother,

I know it's been a long time since I wrote. I'm still doing the same maid job, but these days I'm run off my feet between work and taking care of Kelly. She's at that age where she has maximum mobility with minimum judgment, so I have to watch her every minute. Yesterday I turned my back for ten seconds and she started eating shoe polish! Fortunately she didn't get enough to hurt her. The woman I work for plays with Kelly every once in a while, but as soon as there's any kind of trouble—a whine, a dirty diaper, a mess to clean up—she hands her back to me.

The man of the house is home now, too, and that makes a lot more work. He's the kind who never picks up a single solitary thing. When he's done with anything—jackets, magazines, even his pipe—he drops it wherever he happens to be, but if it's still there next time he walks that way, too bad for me. I have to run behind him picking up his trail all the time he's home—which, fortunately, is only an hour or two a day.

But being behind him is a lot better than being in front of him, because when I'm in his line of vision, the way he looks at me gives me the creeps. He hasn't done anything, but he's always making suggestive remarks. I'm afraid if I put him in his place the way I'd like to, I'll lose my job. I try to avoid being alone in a room with him.

The fact is, Mother, I'm sick of this place and I'd like to come home. I miss my old room, my art, my piano, my special thinking spot down by the creek. And I miss you. I wonder if you've mellowed by now. I just know if you could be with Kelly for even a

*minute, you'd want to keep her. I borrowed my employer's Polaroid
camera and took a picture of her; I'm putting it in with this letter.*

Kelly sat upright at this and looked urgently at Nathaniel. He
set the letter down and peered inside the envelope. The picture
was face down against the back. He drew it out, turned it over,
and handed it to Kelly.

There she was, the sweetest little thing you ever saw, with
bright copper curls and a sunny smile that showed her little pearly
teeth. Well, of course I fell in love with her the first time I saw that
picture.

When Kelly looked at it, I thought she was going to faint. She
stared at it for a minute, gripping it so tightly I thought it would
tear in two. "That's me," she said. "It looks just like my baby pictures. And those people she's describing sound just like my parents—I mean the Masons. Oh my God, it must be true! They're
not my parents after all!" She stared at the picture a minute longer, then turned to Nathaniel. "But what happened to her? June, I
mean. Why didn't she come home?"

"There's a little more of the letter. Let's see."

*If you are willing to take Kelly and me back and let us live with
you—you won't have to take care of her, I promise, I'll do that
myself, and I've got a fair bit of money saved too—write to me
care of general delivery in Seattle and my friend will send the
letter on. Oh, Mother, I do hope you say yes, because this place
has become like a prison camp to me. I don't want Kelly to grow
up with these people.*

Please write soon.

Love, June.

Kelly stared open-mouthed from Nathaniel to Kiera. "Is it

176

possible Esther never wrote to her? That she wasn't willing to take them—I guess I should say *us*—back?"

Kiera shook her head. "No. I'm sure she would have written. I knew Esther, and really she had a very soft heart, if maybe a bit of a temper. I'm positive she'd repented long before she got this letter. She would have jumped at the chance to get you and June back."

"Then what happened? Why didn't we come home? Why did she—my *mother*—leave me there with *them?*" Kelly's voice escalated to the wail of an abandoned child.

Nathaniel gathered her into his arms and rocked her with her head against his chest. "I don't know what happened, but we'll find out. Somehow or other, we'll find out."

I COULD HAVE TOLD THEM what happened, up to a point. I wrote to her—of course I wrote, the minute I finished crying over the letter, and mailed my letter the very same day. But I never got an answer. I thought the letter might have gone astray, so I wrote again. Nothing.

Then one day Eunice came to see me—this was before she had her first stroke—and sat me down and talked to me so gently that I knew something was terribly wrong. "Esther," she said to me, "I think June's dead."

And then she told me how June's spirit had come to her in the night, on its way from the body to begin its journey with the angels. "Tell Mother," June had said; "she won't be able to hear me herself."

And she was right, of course. I heard the words coming from Eunice's mouth, but they wouldn't penetrate my heart. I just couldn't believe my baby was dead.

I went to the police, but what could I tell them? I didn't know what city she'd been living in or what name she'd been going by. My only evidence she might have died was a couple of unanswered letters and the word of what they would have called a crazy person, though a saner woman than Eunice McCarthy I could never hope to know. They humored me, but it was clear they weren't going to put themselves out.

Time went by, and I gradually came to accept that June had been taken away from me for good. Once I let that thought into my heart, I knew it was true. From that moment I had nothing left to live for except to try to atone for what I'd done.

But I never did find out how she died. She didn't bother to tell Eunice that little detail. It doesn't much matter to me now, though for years I thought it might have been some comfort if I'd known. But I know Kelly won't rest until the mystery is solved.

KELLY CAME TO HERSELF IN stages—from the abandonment of shock and grief she passed to an awareness of being sheltered in Nathaniel's arms, and a great peace stole over her. But eventually that passed as well, and she grew embarrassed to be lingering in that sweet embrace. She freed herself, sat up, and used the tissue Kiera handed her to dry her eyes.

"So this is partly good news, right?" Kiera ventured. "I mean, you know now those horrible people weren't your real parents. You don't have to feel guilty for what they did."

Kelly looked at her and said patiently, "That's true, Kiera. But now I'm a double orphan. I've lost the people I thought were my parents, and I have no one to put in their place. I don't know who my father is, whether he's even alive or would want anything to do with me if he were; and as far as I can tell, my mother must be dead. On balance I don't find it extremely comforting."

"No, of course not. Sorry. Just trying to find the silver lining."

The bent brown head looked so pitiful, Kelly immediately regretted her words. She squeezed Kiera's shoulders. "I know. And no doubt after a while I'll be able to see it shine. Just not yet."

She looked from Kiera to Nathaniel. "I really appreciate both of you being with me through this, but now I think I need some time alone to process it all."

"Of course." Nathaniel stood and checked his watch. "We've got a couple hours to go before quitting time. I might as well start on the laundry room cabinets, if I won't be disturbing you."

"Fine. I'll go to my room and lie down for a while. This has all been kind of exhausting."

Kelly stood to leave the room, but Kiera stood before her, toeing the carpet like a child caught in mischief. "Kelly, do you mind if I tell Pops about this? I know he's wondered all these years about what happened to June. Even though we don't have all the answers yet, I think he'd like to know what we've found out—and he might even be able to add a piece to the puzzle." She looked up. "Unless you'd like to tell him yourself, that is."

The weariness that had been hovering around Kelly engulfed her at that thought. Aidan did have some right to know, she could see that; but to rehearse all their discoveries for a third person was quite beyond her strength. "Go ahead, Kiera, whatever you think best."

She dragged herself down the hall to her room, where she fell onto the bed and into a troubled sleep.

CHAPTER 17

TOWARD QUITTING TIME that afternoon, while Kelly was still sleeping, Perkins showed up again. This time Aidan was ready for him: the kitchen and back porch practically finished except for the flooring and appliances, bathroom done, laundry room just getting the finishing touches. The new linen closet still needed shelves and doors, but Perkins couldn't find anything to complain about there. He huffed and grumped his way through the house, getting redder in the face every minute, till I expected to see steam coming out his ears because he couldn't find one little code violation to hang his red tag on.

But when they came to the library, he perked up. Kelly wanted wiring in there that would take a computer system, and rather than tear out the plaster or the paneling, Aidan had the electrician put in a new circuit and run a line to a four-hole plug in the floor under the desk. Perkins saw that plug and rounded on Aidan.

"You didn't replace that knob-and-tube wiring, did you? You put in this floor plug so you could bypass it."

Aidan kept his cool. "That's correct. The wiring was in good shape and perfectly safe for the load it carried, but the owner wanted to hook up a computer in here, so we added a circuit."

"I told you that wiring had to be replaced."

"And I know it's perfectly legal for knob-and-tube to be grandfathered in. You have no good grounds for insisting we replace it."

Here came the steam out the ears. "I want to see the owner."

"Then you'll have to come back tomorrow. She's indisposed right now and not to be disturbed." Kiera had given him that tip, though she was saving her full revelation for later in the evening.

Perkins made a great effort and pulled the steam back in. "All right. But you haven't heard the past of me, McCarthy." With a flourish of his clipboard he stalked out. I heard his tires squeal as he drove away.

Aidan and the crew finished up for the day and left. After they were gone, a truck pulled up on the street outside the hedge and stopped. Then I saw Perkins creep up the driveway, keeping flat against the hedge on Imogene's side like he was in a spy movie, and slip in the front door.

KELLY AWOKE AT DUSK, HER consciousness emerging from deep sleep while her body remained inert, as if paralyzed. She had no desire to rise but lay still, hoping sleep would return and carry her back to blessed oblivion. After a few minutes, though, it became apparent her bladder would not allow that to happen.

She dragged herself up and stumbled into the bathroom, grateful it was finished and she didn't have to go downstairs. The sight of the pristine white period fixtures harmonizing with the seawater effect of the green and blue tiles brought her a small measure of the peace beauty always imparted to her soul. But she still felt slightly drugged when she emerged from the bathroom onto the landing.

When her eyes focused on the sight before her, she thought

181

she must still be dreaming. Coming up the last few steps was a short, dumpy figure with a few strands of black hair pasted across its shiny skull.

"Mr. Perkins? What are you doing here at this hour? Where's Aidan?"

A grin spread across his oily face, revealing chipped and discolored front teeth. "He's gone. They've all gone home, little lady. Now we can have our little discussion, just you and me."

Kelly froze. "You can't possibly have anything to say to me that couldn't be better said to Mr. McCarthy."

He came up close to her, backing her against the railing over the stairwell. If she put up her hands to push him away, he might send her right over.

She edged along the railing, but he sidled with her. His breath in her face made her want to retch. "Well, now, that's where you're wrong, little lady. McCarthy's got nothing to do with what I want to discuss with you."

Kelly cowered, frozen in horror, as he traced a stubby finger up her throat. "Wouldn't it be a terrible shame if a pretty lady like you got a red tag on her house? And that's just what's going to happen unless you and I can make a deal. You give me what I want, and I'll sign off on your outdated wiring. Otherwise—" He shrugged. "I'll have no choice but to shut you down."

She willed her hand to come up and slap him, but it would not relinquish its death grip on the railing. She willed her voice to repel him, but it would not pass the dry obstruction in her throat. She ducked aside but could not escape before his arm went round her waist and his flabby lips came within an inch of her own.

Those flabby lips—that reek of cigarettes—the sound of his breathing, ragged with lust—

Kelly was no longer the woman struggling to release herself from the hated embrace. It was another woman, smaller but with hair to her waist, as vivid copper as Kelly's own; and the man was tall, towering over her. He was the evil ogre trying to carry off the princess, her mother, and Kelly was so small, so helpless inside her crib, gripping the bars as she peered through them onto the landing. The ogre pressed the princess back over the railing, his mouth coming down on hers, but with a deft movement she twisted free of him right at the edge. She turned to run down the stairs, he grabbed for her, she lost her balance, and then . . . "Mommy!" the little Kelly screamed as the princess tumbled over and over down the long stairway to rest at last at the bottom. Atop a contorted pile of limbs, her white face stared unseeing amid the halo of her gleaming hair, while a dark red stain seeped outward through its auburn rays.

THE BLACKNESS INSIDE KELLY'S HEAD gave way to a blur of color, which resolved into a man's face bending close to hers. She screamed and lashed out, but it was Nathaniel's voice that came soft to her ear. "Hush now, you're all right. It's over. I'm here."

She blinked him into focus. Yes, it was Nathaniel's dear, ascetic face, smooth-skinned and fine-boned, not that horrid excrescence that had confronted her a moment ago. But was it a moment? Behind Nathaniel's head she could see the walnut posts of her own bed, and under her hand she felt the stitching of the quilted coverlet. And Ginger was beside her, butting his nose against her cheek.

"What happened? The last thing I remember . . ." Her mouth grew round with horror as that last memory resurfaced.

A gentle hand touched her lips. "Shh, it's all right. He's gone.

You fainted. I was cleaning up in the laundry room when I heard a terrific yowl from Ginger. I got there just as you hit the floor—it's a miracle you didn't fall down the stairs." A blue fire lit his eyes. "Ginger and I got rid of that animal Perkins. I very much doubt he'll be back."

His eyes softened again. "And then I brought you in here and revived you. It took a while—you had me worried." He chafed her hands between his own, and she noticed that hers were still like ice.

"Oh . . . Nat . . . it was horrible. I wanted to fight him off but . . . I couldn't move, or talk, or anything. And then . . ." A deep shudder shook her whole frame.

He lay down beside her and gathered her into his arms. Gradually the shaking subsided.

"Then what, Kelly?" he said. "Was there something more?"

"I had a . . . I guess you'd call it a flashback. Nat—I think I saw my mother's death. She was as good as murdered." Haltingly she told him what she'd seen.

He stroked her back. "The man—the ogre—was it Mason? Your adoptive father?"

She nodded against his chest.

"That's so bizarre. What kind of people would keep you after a thing like that? You'd think they would have tried to find June's family. And why didn't he go to prison, for manslaughter at least?"

"You can't expect reasonable behavior where Howard and Miriam are concerned. He probably bought his way out. And I expect she wanted to keep me as her little toy."

"Is there any way you can find out? Verify your own memory and find out what happened afterward?"

"I don't see how. Howard is dead, and Miriam's senile. I

guess I could try to track down police records or something, but I really wouldn't know where to start."

"Esther's lawyers found you with very little to go on. Maybe they could help."

"Maybe." Her voice was thick with exhaustion.

He clucked his tongue. "Shame on me, you need to rest and I'm pestering you with questions. I'll go now and let you get some sleep."

He started to pull away, but she gripped his arm. The horror was still too close—without his shelter it would engulf her. "Don't leave me, Nat. Please."

He put out a hand to stroke her hair, pulled her head close and kissed her forehead. "All right. I'll stay." He kicked off his shoes and pulled the spare blanket up over them both. She laid her head on his chest and drifted into oblivion.

WHEN THAT PERKINS WENT AFTER my Kelly, that's when I wished I'd been granted some kind of power to interfere with things on earth. But I guess it's a good thing I couldn't interfere too soon, or she would never have remembered how my poor sweet June died.

It's a good thing I didn't know about that at the time, because I would have gone after Mason with a shotgun. But everything looks different from up here, and the pains that break your heart on earth are tempered by the knowledge—not just the belief, but the *knowledge*—that God works all things together for good.

At any rate, Kelly had her protectors: Ginger did a flying leap and dug his claws into Perkins' back just as Nathaniel came rushing out. My, but that boy has a strong right hook! There is some Viking in him, along with the saint. Perkins will be nursing his jaw for some time, I imagine. He won't be back. He's the type to press charges for battery, but then it would come out what he did to provoke the attack; so I think we're safe on that score.

Now Kelly's asleep, and Nathaniel's lying there with his arms around her, staring into the darkness, with only Ginger for a chaperone. That can't be easy for him, loving her the way he does; but he's far too good a man to ever think of taking advantage of her weakened state. Still, I'd like to see them married, or engaged at least, before I go on home. I won't feel quite easy about Kelly's future until I know she's learned how to love.

CHAPTER 18

WHEN KELLY AWOKE at daybreak, she was first aware of the soft fuzz of Nathaniel's flannel shirt beneath her cheek and hand. This confused her, as her sheets were smooth percale. Then she opened her eyes and saw him, and the memory of the previous evening overwhelmed her.

Her first impulse was to jerk away from his embrace. The thought of the weakness and vulnerability she'd betrayed to him appalled her. Distance must be reestablished at all costs.

But then she looked at his face, and tenderness overcame her at the calm of his sleeping eyelids, the gentle curve of his breath. What would it cost her, after all, to be vulnerable to such a man, to accept his care and protection, which she was almost sure he would be happy to extend indefinitely? Only her hard shell, only her independence, which had been shattered by last night's events. She tried to pull the shards of it around her and found it could not be done. The rents were too deep and too gaping.

So she lay still and watched him sleep, and a feeling grew in her that she was all but a stranger to—a feeling that it would be good to be united to this man, in body and soul together. Indeed, in this new emotion she felt for the first time how impossible it was that body and soul should be separated. She had scarcely acknowledged before that she had a soul, but now she felt it stirring, unfurling its wings and blinking in the sunlight, calling to Nathaniel's soul as deep calls to deep. Still she lay unmoving, but all within her leapt and danced and strained toward him, beckoning him to share her joy.

Such a call could not be resisted. His eyelids fluttered open. He blinked, then focused on her face, and his own was transformed by what he saw there. In his eyes she saw reflected the awe and joy that possessed her, and for a long moment it flowed between them. Then he put a hand behind her head and drew her face to his, and their lips met in a communion so sweet Kelly thought she would burst with joy.

When she could breathe again, he said, "I think we'd better get out of this bed before we do something we'll both regret."

That was hardly the reaction she'd expected. She raised a hand to smooth his disheveled hair. "What's to regret?"

He sat up and drew her to sit on the edge of the bed beside him. "You've been through a lot in the past twenty-four hours. You're vulnerable. I'm thrilled to my toes that you've opened up to me, but I don't want to push you too fast. Let's just take it slow and let things take their course. All right?"

She thought "letting things take their course" would have led the opposite direction. But he was probably right. What did she know of love, after all, she who had never allowed herself so much as to think the word until this morning?

She put up a hand to stroke his face, feeling the smooth skin over his cheekbone give way to rough stubble on his jaw. "All right. If you say so."

He took her hand and kissed the fingertips. "Now I'm going to go and get us some breakfast. In case you didn't notice, we both missed dinner last night, and I for one am starved."

Now that he mentioned it, Kelly felt a gnawing emptiness in her stomach as well. "Good. I'll make coffee." Other than Crustimony Proseedcake, coffee was the sole culinary art she'd perfected.

He kissed her again, then put on his shoes and left, whistling a Bach partita. Kelly showered, and by the time she had the coffee ready he had returned, bearing a hearty takeout breakfast from the local diner.

They ate in the finished breakfast nook, where the morning sun flowed gently through the windows in the east and south walls. "This is exactly the way I envisioned it would be," she said. "I think all the time I was planning this nook, I had in mind someone to share it with, though I didn't know that at the time." She smiled shyly up at him.

"I knew when I built it that I was building it for two. Not that I was being presumptuous," he added quickly as her eyebrows rose. "I just knew somehow that it was a space to be shared. Eating is a sacramental act, you know, and sacraments are always communal affairs."

She remembered their first dinner at his apartment. "You never did carve me a frieze for this nook."

"No." His face clouded.

She reached across the narrow table to lay a hand on his arm. "Tell me about this faith of yours."

The cloud dispersed, but he hesitated. "It isn't so much a thing you can tell," he said at last. "It's more a thing you experience. Why don't you come to church with me, and then we can talk about it. Would you do that? Tomorrow?"

Fear rose in her throat, but she forced it down. "All right."

At that moment Aidan walked into the kitchen. That was the

189

trouble with living in a house under construction; no one ever bothered to ring the bell.

He came far enough into the room to take in the two of them seated there, hands clasped over the remains of their breakfast, Nathaniel still unshaven in yesterday's rumpled clothes. Aidan stopped short, staring at the two of them.

"I know I encouraged your relationship, you two, but this isn't exactly what I had in mind."

Kelly snatched back her hand, feeling her face go hot. But Nathaniel looked Aidan in the eye with perfect composure. "It isn't what it looks like, Aidan. Kelly had a very rough evening, and I couldn't leave her alone. We did *sleep* together, literally, but that's all."

Aidan examined Nathaniel's face through narrowed eyes, then slowly nodded. "Right."

Kelly watched this interchange with a mixture of confusion and indignation. "Of course Nathaniel's telling you the truth, Aidan, but just why is it your business what we did last night?"

Aidan started, but before he could reply, Nathaniel answered low, "He's my godfather. It is his business to help keep me from grave sin."

This reply only confused Kelly further, but before she could ask him to explain, Aidan said, "I have a stake in you, too, Kelly—as a friend, but more than that. That's what I came over here on a Saturday morning to talk to you about." He looked significantly at Nathaniel.

"You want this to be a private discussion?"

"I'd rather it were, if you don't mind."

Kelly reached for Nathaniel's hand. "Don't go. Please. Whatever concerns me concerns you."

He covered her hand with his own. "It's all right, love. I

won't be gone long. I'll just run home and shower, and then I'll be back."

She sighed, marveling at how necessary he had become to her in so short a time. "All right."

She walked him to the front door so they could share a kiss in private, then returned to the kitchen, where Aidan was clearing the table. Her heart revolted against the idea of sitting there with him for this mysterious discussion; the nook was now sacred to the new entity that was herself and Nathaniel.

"Let's go into the living room," she said, and led the way out before Aidan could protest.

She sat in the armchair she now thought of as Nathaniel's, to prevent Aidan from sitting there. She detected in herself a feeling toward Aidan that was almost hostility, when only yesterday she had regarded him as a valued friend. Only his suspicion regarding her night with Nathaniel could explain this shift, and that suspicion was entirely natural, not even so far from being justified. She gave her shoulders a shrug as if she could thus shake off this unwelcome attitude.

"So. What's all this about?"

Aidan lowered himself to the couch as if feeling his years for a change. He blew out a long breath and ran his hand over his thick, grizzled hair. "This isn't going to be easy, Kelly. Please be patient with me."

He linked his fingers and stretched his hands out in front of him, then brought them back to his lap. "Kiera told me about the journal and the letters." He leaned toward her. "Kelly, you have to believe me—I never knew Rose was pregnant. I never had a clue what happened to her after she left here."

"You told me that before. But that's not your fault—she chose not to confess to you. That's not so surprising. You were friends—she wouldn't want to disappoint you."

He shook his head, his face contorted. Then it struck her. "Wait a minute—you called her Rose just now. Do you mean to say—oh my God, 'M' for McCarthy. Is that it? It was you?"

He nodded dumbly, head cradled in his hands.

She leapt to her feet. "How could you? You—a priest—seduce a young girl? And then desert her!" She paced a circle around the group of couch and chairs. "Do you have any idea what that led to? Do you know how she died?"

"No. I know nothing beyond that last letter."

She stopped in front of him, hands on hips, a fiery energy coursing through her. "Well, I'll tell you. I remembered it last night, because of—well, that doesn't matter. The point is, she was murdered. Or as good as. Howard Mason made a pass at her, and she tried to get away and fell down a flight of stairs. I guess she hit her head—there was blood—" She shuddered, then clenched her fists, willing herself to stay upright. "And I watched the whole thing. From my crib. I couldn't have been more than two. That's what you did, *Father* Aidan McCarthy."

She paced on, then a new twist hit her. "And you have the nerve to come in here and accuse Nathaniel and me! Two consenting adults with no other ties—so what if we had made love? On top of everything else, you're a hypocrite!"

Aidan made a strangled noise, and she turned to look at him. His face was buried in his hands, and his shoulders heaved. She was confounded. She couldn't remember ever having seen a man of his age cry.

An impulse to comfort him rose within her, but her fury shouted it down. He was her father—he was the one who ought to be comforting her.

Her *father*. In her rage of indignation over the injustice done to her mother, she had glanced over that implication. Rose's lover was Kelly's father.

Something in her head exploded at that moment. This man she had grown to trust, even—she choked on the word—almost to love, had betrayed her from the moment of her conception. She looked at him, sobbing on her couch, and the bile rose in her throat. She had to get away.

She whirled out of the room and out of the house, slowing only to grab her jacket and keys from the vestibule. On the porch she nearly collided with Nathaniel. "Kelly, what—" he started, but she shook her head, brushed past him, and climbed into her truck. Moments later she was on the highway, heading north.

WELL, YOU COULD HAVE BLOWN me down with a sneeze when I heard what Aidan had to say. If I'd heard his story when I was still alive, I might have been just as mad as Kelly. But I'm as much to blame as he is. What a judgment on my foolish pride, keeping June's pregnancy a secret all those years. Aidan and I between us certainly do have a lot to account for.

But even so, he's a good man and he's led a good life. He may have helped me partly out of guilt all those years, but I'm not the only one he's helped. He's always been there when anyone in the neighborhood needed a hand, or an ear, or a few dollars to get them through a tight spot. He's done his penance many times over, and now he's got to do it all over again with Kelly.

Nathaniel came in, bewildered, to find Aidan crouched on the floor. He got him up, sat him on the couch, and got the whole story out of him.

"She won't forgive me," Aidan croaked, head in his hands. "She took off, and God knows if she's ever coming back."

Nathaniel rubbed Aidan's shoulder. "I think she'll be back. She's had a very emotional twenty-four hours. First finding those letters, and then—did she tell you about Perkins?"

Aidan jerked his head around. "What about Perkins?"

Nathaniel told him all about it, including Kelly's flashback. A fire lit in Aidan's eyes and his fists clenched. "Never mind, Aidan, I dealt with Perkins. And Mason's been dead for years."

Aidan's fists relaxed, but I could see the tension still in his jaw. Nathaniel went on. "I told you I stayed with her—she was too cut up to be alone. And this morning when we woke—well, some kind of barrier finally came down between us. But she was still weak and vulnerable, and I wouldn't count on that wall staying down if I'm not there to remove each brick as she puts it up."

He raised a hand and let it fall. "And then on top of that, to find out about you. Someone she'd allowed herself to trust, and now she feels you betrayed her. I think it was just one too many for her. She needs some time alone to sort things out. By God's grace it'll all come right in the end."

Aidan turned a ravaged face toward him. "But what if it doesn't? What if she doesn't come back?"

Oh, my gracious Lord, *what* if she doesn't come back? I'll be alone in the Vestibule for all eternity.

"If she's not back by nightfall, I'll go after her."

"But where? We don't know where she's gone."

"I'll find her, Aidan. She's part of me now."

194

CHAPTER 19

KELLY WAS HALFWAY to San Francisco before she thought consciously about where she was going—or about anything else. She drove furiously, hounded by a foaming brew of so many emotions she didn't bother to try to identify them. One thought dominated— despite all the evidence, there was still room for a tiny whiff of doubt that she was Rose and Aidan's daughter. She had to be completely sure, and there was only one living person who could provide that last link.

She drove on through the city, across the Golden Gate, and westward up into the Marin hills. At the end of a long, curving driveway, on a prime piece of real estate at the top of a cliff with a view that swept from bay to ocean, she came to the locked gates of Seaside Rest. She announced herself and was buzzed in.

After parking her truck between a Jaguar and a Porsche, she checked in at the reception desk. A starched white nurse escorted her down the hall to Miriam's suite.

At the door her momentum ran out. She hesitated with her knuckles raised to knock. What was the point? She hadn't caught Miriam in a lucid moment in the last three years, and Miriam with her mind wandering was a sight between piteous and repulsive.

But the nurse was already unlocking the door, calling out, "Mrs. Mason? Your daughter's here to see you, now isn't that nice?"

The old woman sat in an armchair in front of the television, her back to the door. She did not respond to the nurse's announcement.

The nurse turned off the TV and beckoned Kelly around to face Miriam. "Here's your daughter, Mrs. Mason," she said again.

The lumpy figure had been neatly dressed in slacks and a sweater, the sparse gray hair curled and combed, and the drooping, wrinkled face made up with mascara and rouge. But the vacant eyes that peered through the curled lashes turned that brave shell into a mocking mask. Kelly felt if she were to touch that shell it would crumble instantly to reveal a tiny, blackened walnut of a soul.

She suppressed a shudder and forced her voice from her throat. "Miriam? It's Kelly."

Some flicker of recognition came into the vacant eyes as they focused on Kelly's face. "Kelly," she mumbled.

"There now, she knows you!" the nurse said. "It must be one of her good days. I'll just leave you two to visit." She rustled out, closing the door behind her.

"Miriam?" Kelly squatted before the old woman. "Do you know me?"

"Know you . . . Kelly . . ."

"Miriam, I need to talk to you. I need you to tell me—the truth. About myself. Where I came from."

The watery eyes met hers for a moment, then drifted away. The head wobbled, and one withered hand plucked at the blanket that covered her lap.

Kelly steeled herself, then took Miriam's head between her hands and held it upright. "Stay with me, Miriam. I have to know. I'm not really your daughter, am I? You adopted me. Is that right?"

"Right . . ." the shrunken lips mumbled, but whether in agreement or mere echo, Kelly couldn't be sure.

"Miriam, listen. Who was my real mother? What was her name?" The mouth worked, but no sound emerged. Kelly suppressed the urge to supply the name; if Miriam repeated it after her she would never know whether that repetition held any meaning.

"What—was—her—name?" she repeated, involuntarily giving the old woman's head a tiny shake.

"Name . . ." The vacant gaze drifted past Kelly's head. She followed its path to a vase of roses on a table next to the TV. "Rose." The word came out decisively. "Name . . . Rose."

Kelly blew out a long breath, and with it the tension that had sustained her to this point. She dropped her hands from Miriam's head and sat back on her heels. "What happened to Rose, Miriam? Why did you adopt me?"

The eyes kindled with a mixture of fear and cunning. "No . . . can't tell you . . ."

Kelly gripped the arms of the chair and leaned forward. "Miriam, I have to know!"

One claw lifted from the blanket and waved toward a desk at the other side of the room. "Letter . . . read . . . can't tell you . . ." The faint spark that had lit the eyes died, and they were vacant once more.

Kelly pushed herself up and went to the desk. It was an elaborate roll-top affair with what seemed dozens of cubbyholes, cupboards, and doors, all stuffed with odd objects, from candy wrappers to spoons to, in one tiny cupboard, a large sapphire ring. She shook her head in frustration and opened the shallow drawer just under the desktop. There, alone in the center of the otherwise empty drawer, lay a fat pale blue envelope with "Kelly" printed on it in a shaky hand.

She sank into the desk chair and stared at the envelope for a minute, then turned it over and slid a trembling finger under the flap.

The letter she unfolded was dated five years before and began with no greeting.

I've heard adopted children always figure it out in the end and want to know who their real parents were. I'm surprised you haven't got there yet, but since you haven't, and I can feel my mind starting to go, I'm going to write it down now so when you do get around to asking you'll have an answer. If nothing else, you can read this when I'm dead. I'm not going to tell you before I have to because you might decide you don't have to take care of me, and I'm going to be needing some care.

I don't know who your father is; I might as well tell you that up front. But I don't suppose a lot of adopted kids get to know who their fathers are, being bastards and all. For that matter, I could never be sure your mother gave me her right name. Chances are she didn't, since no one came forward to claim you, or her body, after she died. But the name she gave me was Rose McCarthy. She never told me anything about her family or where she came from, and I didn't ask.

I found Rose selling flowers on a street corner in San Francisco. She was "great with child," as the good book says, and no wedding ring. I stopped to chat, being always interested in pregnant women because I so longed to be one myself and never could. Well, it came out that she had no people and not much of a place to go. I'd just lost my live-in maid, so I offered her the job. I figured if I couldn't have a child of my own, at least I could have one in the house. I'd tried to get Howard to agree to adopt, but he flat-out refused. He said kids were nothing but trouble, and unless he could have a son

198

of his blood to pass on the business to, he couldn't be bothered.

After a month or so you came along. We had an unregistered midwife come to the house to deliver you because Rose didn't want any hospital records. You were a sweet little doll of a baby, I will say that. I just adored you. It was kind of like being a grandmother, I guess, because I could hold you and play with you, but the minute you fussed or made a mess I could hand you back to your mother. She was happy, I didn't make her work too hard, and we three got along fine.

Then Howard came home. He'd been back for a couple days here and there, but this time he came home for a good stretch. He had a project going out in Walnut Creek. I saw trouble coming from the start, because Rose was such a pretty girl. Howard never could resist a pretty girl. It was no skin off my nose if he wanted to fool around; I was pretty well used to it, and he hadn't seen the inside of my bedroom for years, not since we found out I could never have a child. But he was making Rose unhappy, and I was afraid she'd leave and take you with her.

She managed to stay out of his way for a while, but one night I was out late at a bridge party and when I came home, oh lord what a sight. There she lay at the bottom of the stairs, all over blood, and Howard sitting on the bottom step blubbering like a baby. And you up in your crib screaming your head off. I finally got it out of Howard what had happened. He'd been pestering her up on the landing, and she tried to get away and fell down the stairs. And you'd apparently seen the whole thing.

That was when I saw my chance. I told Howard I'd help him cover it up if he'd agree to let me adopt you. He was horrified at first at the thought of always having you around to remind him, but I made him see that if you were going to remember anything about what happened—have nightmares about it, say, after you were old enough to talk better—we'd only be safe if you were here with us.

So we worked it all out, and then I called the police and told them Rose had had an accident. I told them I'd witnessed it all, that she'd been carrying a load of laundry and lost her footing and fell. Later, when it looked like they might be inclined to ask awkward questions, I slipped a nice packet to the police commissioner and he called off his dogs.

The adoption was a little awkward since Rose had no formal identification and we didn't know who your father was. They made us wait a while to see if anyone would come forward to claim you. But of course no one did, and another nice packet smoothed over any little difficulties there might have been

You pretty much know the rest. At first I was tickled to have you to myself, but I soon found out being a mother was a lot more work than I'd imagined. You'd cry and I just flat wouldn't know what to do with you. You'd get this terrible, pitiful look in your eyes that made me feel like it was all my fault your real mother was gone, when in fact I had nothing at all to do with it. So I got a new maid, an older woman, and let her look after you most of the time. But it was still fun to buy you pretty clothes and dress you up and take you out for people to coo over. You were an awfully pretty child.

I guess that about says it. I suppose you think I was a poor mother to you, and maybe I was. Certainly Howard wasn't any kind of father. But we gave you everything you needed, a better start in life than most children get, and you seem to be doing pretty well for yourself, so I don't think you have anything to reproach me with. And now Howard's gone to his reward, which I expect will be a pretty fiery one, so there's not much point reproaching him either.

There the letter ended, as devoid of closing greeting as of opening. Kelly turned the last sheet over and back again, shook out the envelope, but found nothing more.

She folded the letter and put it in her purse, then stood and walked over to the wreck of humanity slumped in the easy chair. She raised her hand, and the old woman cowered as if she feared being struck. But Kelly merely took Miriam's chin in her hand so she could look directly in her eyes.

"Goodbye, Miriam. The trust will make sure you're taken care of, but I won't be back. You're no mother of mine, and I see no reason to torture us both by coming here. Do you understand?" The vacant eyes slid away from Kelly's as the chin wobbled in her fingers. Kelly dropped her hand, wiped it on her jeans, and turned the television back on. Then she walked out of the room, out of the building, out of every kind of life she'd ever known.

FOR SOME MINUTES SHE STOOD at the railing of the overlook between the parking lot and the edge of the cliff. Far out to sea a ship's whistle hooted. Above her head a gull squawked, and her eyes followed its looping flight down, down, a thousand feet or more, to where, in her imagination—far beyond her sight—the surf crashed against the rocks of the shore.

She swayed dizzily and put out a hand to steady herself against the railing. The edge of a cliff might not be the best place for her at this moment. She forced herself steady as she walked to the truck, and deliberately restrained her speed as she drove down the mountain—not back the way she'd come but continuing west along the shore till she came to the little town of Stinson Beach. A restaurant sign reminded her it was lunchtime. She bought coffee and a cardboard tray of fish and chips from an outdoor bar and took them to a picnic table in a park that bordered the beach.

The November wind was punishing, but it only bothered her because her hair was now long enough to blow into her mouth as she tried to eat. She welcomed the sting of the wind

201

on her face, its chill fingers penetrating her light jacket. Her mind was in a fever; she needed it cooled and swept clean so she could think.

Miriam's letter put the truth beyond reach of cavil: Kelly was the daughter of June Rose Hansen and Aidan McCarthy. A dead woman and a man she would never again be able to trust.

Her old life was meaningless now; she had no moral right to Howard Mason's money and no obligation to put right his wrongs. But the new life she'd begun to build looked empty too. She shuddered at the thought of returning to the Hansen house, which now seemed to her to be full of keening ghosts, all clutching at her, demanding that she fulfill their wasted or aborted lives. Nor could she simply flip a switch and join the close, affectionate McCarthy clan after a lifetime of lonely orphanhood. But if she wasn't a Mason, a Hansen, or a McCarthy, who was she? What could she possibly have to offer Nathaniel if she was no one?

The memory of those early-morning moments when she had believed herself happy stabbed through her heart with more power to wound than Miriam's letter, Aidan's revelations, or even the flashback of her mother's death. Those moments now seemed a lifetime ago. They belonged to another world, a world of fantasy where she had sojourned a brief and glorious while, but into which she would never again find the magic door.

What remained to her now? Only duty, the responsibility to finish what she had begun. And Ginger—he would miss her if she didn't return. She would see the work completed, pay off Aidan and his men, then put the house on the market and—what? She had no home to go to after that, no friends, no career to pick up where she'd left off.

"I'll think about that tomorrow," she said, with the only

flash of sympathy for Scarlett O'Hara she'd ever felt. "I won't think about that today."

KELLY ROSE, COLLECTED HER TRASH, and turned to leave the park. There before her stood a brown-haired, freckled young man, staring at her as his features worked. So great was her disorientation that it took her a long moment to recognize him as her former coworker, Jim Meriwether.

He was the first to speak. "Kelly?" he said, and his voice broke. He cleared his throat. "What are you doing here?"

How much to tell him? Her old habits of reticence won out. "I've been to see Miriam. And you?"

"Just finished up the Morgan job. Taking a drive around the point—for some R&R."

The edge in his voice reminded her of their last face-to-face conversation, and her stomach sank. Was that only three months ago? Three eons, more like. "Oh, yeah. How'd it go?"

"Pretty well. Squires isn't you, but it came out okay—you should go by and see it sometime. What about your job?"

"Good. Almost done. It's a Stickley house, really a gem of its kind. I wish you could see it." That last came out automatically, because she knew Jim was interested in Stickley. But his response made her wish she'd bitten her tongue.

His whole face brightened. "I'd love to come down and take a look. Where is it exactly?"

She groaned inwardly. She'd really put her foot in it now. But on the other hand, there was still work to be done, and if Jim were there he could act as a buffer between her and Aidan.

She gave him the address. "Actually, if you're free, I could use a little help wrapping things up. I had a—a bit of a falling out with the contractor."

Jim's smile twisted. "Really. Imagine that."

Kelly bridled, then sagged. His sarcasm was more than justified—the whole Bay Area was littered with contractors she'd fired because they wouldn't do everything her way. "It isn't like that this time. It's personal."

His face contorted in pain, and she remembered she'd effectively dismissed Jim himself for personal reasons. "And it's not like that, either. Look, I can't explain. It's just—different. The point is, I need some help. Do you want to come or not?"

She could read his struggle in his face—and his ultimate defeat. "Sure, I'll come. Tomorrow, or Monday?"

Then she knew what she had done, and was sorry. He would think she was leading him on. If she couldn't allow herself to love Nathaniel, she would certainly never love Jim or anyone else. But it was too late to take back her offer now.

"Tomorrow would be great."

SHE DROVE BACK ALONG THE coast, both to avoid the traffic and to delay her return until after nightfall. She hoped to arrive undetected and unchallenged. But when she pulled into her driveway, the porch light was on and Nathaniel was sitting on the steps.

She considered simply backing down the driveway again, but exhaustion washed over her at the thought of finding another place to spend the night. She dragged herself from the truck, and he rose to meet her.

The temptation was powerful to fall into the arms he held open to her, but she gathered her strength and pushed past him into the house. He stood in the living room archway and regarded her sprawled on the couch.

"Kelly, I can see you're exhausted, but can you tell me what's wrong? Whatever's happened, it can't have anything to do with—us."

Without opening her eyes, she groped in her purse. "I went to see Miriam. She gave me this." She held the letter out to him.

He crossed the room and took it from her; she heard the sigh of the leather as he sat in "his" chair. No, not his chair. Not her chair either. Nobody's chair, nobody's house. Leave it to the ghosts.

After a time he said, "Oh, Kelly. My poor love."

"I'm not your love. I'm nobody. Don't you see? It's all been pulled out from under me."

"I'm afraid I don't see. You know who you are now. You're Rose and Aidan's daughter. How is that 'nobody'?"

She sighed as if explaining to a two-year-old. "My mother is dead. My father is indirectly responsible for her death and for my being brought up by her murderer. Aidan was a man I thought I could trust—and now this."

Nathaniel came to kneel by her and took her hand. She tried to pull it away, but he held fast. "No, my love. Not 'now this.' Then this. All of that happened thirty years ago. Aidan made one mistake, and he's spent his lifetime trying to atone for it. Now he's found you, and he finally has the opportunity to really atone by being a father to you." He waited, but she did not respond. "He needs your forgiveness, Kelly. And you need to give it. It's the only way you can heal."

She turned her ravaged eyes to his. "How can I ever trust him again? How can I trust anyone after this? How can I know even you won't betray me?"

"Kelly, I love you as part of myself. As far as anyone can promise anything, I promise I will never betray you."

His grey-blue eyes were clear as the sky after rain; but what were eyes that she should trust in them?

"But trust isn't about knowing," he went on. "You can never know. Trust is about believing, and hoping, and seeing the best in people. And it's about being willing to take the consequences if the trust should be broken."

She shut down her face. She would not cry.

"It hurts when trust is broken. Of course it does. But that's part of being alive, Kelly. That's part of learning how to love."

She wrenched her hand away and stood. "Then I guess I flunk the test. I'm sorry, but the price is just too high." With her last iota of strength, she strode from the room and up the stairs. As she entered her bedroom, she heard the front door shut behind him.

She threw herself on the bed, which still held the depression of his body, and wept.

OH, HOW COULD EVERYTHING HAVE gone so completely and horribly wrong? Just when I thought it would all come out so right. Why, you'd think she'd be glad to have a father turn up right next door, someone she already knows and likes, with children who'd like nothing better than to claim her as a sister. But I guess the scars of her childhood cut too deep. You don't heal from something like that overnight. And then to push Nathaniel away from her too! She's gone back to square one and then some—she's fallen off the playing board onto the floor. She could be lost, or crushed.

But she's got to bounce back from this, she's simply got to. More fates than her own are riding on it. Raphael, I need your help again. It's going to take something big to bring her around.

CHAPTER 20

THE NEXT DAY was Sunday. Jim showed up early, and Kelly worked him and herself like furies through the day, finishing up as much as they could. They put the shelves and poles in the closets, screwed on all the switch plates, and laid the linoleum tile on the laundry room floor. The slate tile floor in the kitchen and mudroom had yet to be laid, and the appliances would be brought in after that; those things, regrettably, she would have to leave to others.

Ginger was skittish and whiny all day, as if he knew what was coming. Kelly was sorry, but she couldn't take the time to comfort him.

Nathaniel came to the door at twilight. Kelly peeked through the library window to see him on the porch. Her body yearned traitorously toward him, but she did not answer his ring.

Jim came up behind her and peered over her head. "Who's that? Why don't you let him in?"

She responded only with a tiny shiver as Nathaniel turned to leave.

"Is that your contractor? Is it so bad you don't even want to talk to him?"

"Not the contractor. He's the cabinetmaker. We're—friends. *Were* friends." She stopped because her voice was betraying her.

Jim put his hands on her shoulders and turned her to face him. He lifted her chin and studied her face for a moment, then dropped his hands and stood back.

"You're in love with him, aren't you." He made it sound like an accusation.

She nodded dumbly, too shaken to protest.

"I knew it would happen eventually. And I knew it wouldn't be me."

His voice was full of such pain that for a moment Kelly forgot her own. "Jim—I'm sorry. I should never have brought you here. I'm so sorry."

He paced the circuit of the library, then came back to face her. "What happened? If you love him, how come you're not with him? You didn't turn him away because I'm here, surely?"

"No, of course not. I just—can't face him. I can't do it, I can't go through with it, and I can't bear to look in his eyes." She covered her face and broke into dry, silent sobs.

Jim sat her down on the window seat. "I don't get it, Kelly. Of course you've always been as emotionally available as a porcupine, but I thought if you found the right guy it would have to be different. Are you really so far gone as to turn down a chance at love?"

"You don't understand. There's more to it than that."

"So tell me." When she did not respond, he said softer, "Don't you think you owe me that much? After all you've put me through?"

Yes, she did owe him that much. And perhaps it would even be good to talk about it to someone who wasn't in the midst of it all.

She made as short a story as she could of the last three

months, finishing with the same argument she'd used with Nathaniel the night before—that she was nobody now and thus could not belong to anyone.

Jim was silent so long she began to wonder if he was sleeping with his eyes open. But finally he spoke.

"You've got it all twisted, Kel. Here's everything you've ever wanted—a home, a family, a guy you love who's apparently crazy about you—all staring you in the face, and you're ready to throw it all away. You're worse off even than I thought."

Suddenly she was furious. She leapt from the seat and turned on him. "Who do you think you are to come into my house and judge me? Get out!"

He rose but did not move from the spot. "I thought I was your friend. Friends tell people the truth. But sometimes they're not ready to hear it." He moved into the hall and began to collect his tools.

Her fury vanished as quickly as it had come. She went after him. "Jim—don't go. I'm sorry. And I do need a friend right now. Just—don't push me. Please. I'm doing the best I can."

He regarded her for a long moment, then nodded. "All right. Let's go get some dinner, and then you can show me to the nearest motel."

GOODNESS, THIS IS A NEW development—this Jim person. I'm not sure what to make of him. But if he cares about Kelly enough to tell her the truth—and enough not to try to interfere between her and Nathaniel—then I guess he's on my side.

But I have to confess I came near to losing hope this morning when Kelly looked in the phone book, put her finger down on a real estate agent, and made an appointment for this afternoon. If she sells the house now, I'm done for. And more importantly, so is she. If she can't learn to open up here, she'll sure as taxes never do it anywhere else. Raphael, help!

Kyle showed up right at eight to put in the kitchen floor, and Jim wasn't far behind him. "Hey, sis," Kyle said with a shy grin. When Kelly froze, he put up his great paw and said, "I know you and Pops are on the outs, though I don't quite get why. I'm not gonna throw myself at you, but I just want you to know I'm stoked to have you for a sister. If you ever need me for anything, I'll be there, no questions asked. Okay?"

Now, if Kiera's a puppy, Kyle is a half-grown bear cub, and equally irresistible. My guess is Kelly had no intention of calling on him, but she couldn't stand to hurt his feelings by telling him so. She gave a brisk nod. "Okay."

He grinned widely. "I can handle the floor myself, but Pops wanted me to ask if you need any of the other guys today."

"No. I took care of all the odds and ends with Jim yesterday." Jim had followed Kyle as far as the porch but hung back until Kelly beckoned him in. "Kyle, this is Jim Meriwether. He's an old friend—we used to work together all the time. I ran into him over the weekend and he came down to help out. Jim, Kyle McCarthy."

Kyle looked from Jim to Kelly and back again, and I could see what he was thinking, because I'd thought the same thing myself the day before: *Who is this guy? Is he trying to cut out Nathaniel?* But Jim stuck out his hand with such a frank and easy "Pleased to meet you" that Kyle relaxed and gave his hand a good shake. To his credit, Jim didn't flinch, though Kyle's got a handshake that could crush a king crab.

"Ever laid any slate tile, Jim?"

"More'n I could shake a stick at."

"Well, if you're up for it, it'll go quicker with two. I'll give my pop a call and tell him we're good for today."

Kyle pulled out a cell phone and spoke briefly to Aidan, then said to Kelly, "Just want to check on the little guy real quick. He's not feeling too well this morning."

He spoke to Mindy, then put the phone away, shaking his head. "He's worse. His fever's up. She's gonna take him to the doctor."

A pang crossed Kelly's face. At least she still cares about her nephew; that's something. "Listen, Kyle, if you want to go with them, Jim and I can handle the floor."

He looked at her like a child let out of school, but then shook his head. "Nah. Thanks, but I'm better off working than worrying."

I guess Kelly had nothing else to do for the morning; she just watched the two of them work and shifted stacks of tiles as they needed them. The guys chatted and joked as they went along, and by lunchtime you would've thought they'd known each other for years.

At noon Kyle called Mindy again. When he hung up his face was ashen.

"The little guy's worse. The doctor says it's bronchitis."

Kelly grimaced. I'm sure she was feeling Kyle and Mindy's pain as well as the baby's. That girl has a great big soft heart in her chest if she'd only learn how to use it.

"Kyle, you'd better go home. There's not much left to do on the floor—Jim and I can finish it. Go."

"Thanks, Kel. You're a pal. A sister, in fact." He gathered her into a bear hug before she could protest, then sped out the door, leaving her with tears in her eyes.

She doesn't really want to go away and leave Kyle and Kiera—they're not to blame for what their father and I did, and they're her family. She just needs a little something more to tip her over

211

the edge and make her stay. Now then, Raphael, what have you got up your sleeve?

JIM HEADED BACK TO THE kitchen as Kyle leapt down the porch steps, nearly colliding with a woman coming up them. Kyle called "Sorry!" over his shoulder as he sprinted down the driveway.

Kelly leaned against the doorjamb, arms crossed, as the woman collected herself, her stringy brown hands plucking at the kaleidoscopic collection of shawls, scarves, and sarongs that enveloped her spare form. Kelly checked her watch: one o'clock, the time she'd arranged to meet the real estate agent. She hoped this woman, who was no doubt collecting for the Sierra Club or some such thing, would take herself off before the agent arrived. Ginger, prowling in the yard, took one look at the visitor and dove under the porch.

At last the fluttering hands stilled and the woman raised vague eyes to Kelly. "My dear, that man has completely disrupted my aura. Are you Kelly Mason?"

Kelly straightened and dropped her arms. She wasn't in the phone book—how did this collector know her name?

The woman came forward with outstretched hand. "I'm Genevieve Deeds, the realtor."

Kelly tried to keep her face neutral as she shifted mental gears. Well, this was Santa Cruz, after all.

She extended her hand, but instead of shaking it, Genevieve slid her fingertips along Kelly's palm, closing her eyes with a little shiver.

"Oh, my dear, what strong vibrations you have! You simply shake me to my core. Our karmas must be connected." Her eyes popped open, revealing irises of a blue so pale it was almost white. A shiver went up Kelly's spine at the sight of them. "I know—we must have known each other in a previous life!"

"I don't really think so. But please come in."

Genevieve shook her head. "There's *some* connection, I just know it." She stretched out her arms and rotated in a slow circle, then spun the last ninety degrees to face Kelly again.

"I've got it! I *knew* there was some reason the vibrations were so strong. This is where June Hansen used to live—my best friend from high school." She clapped her hands with a smile of triumph. "And you must be a relative!"

Ah yes, Kelly remembered the name Genevieve now—the friend from the journal who had been so clueless when Victor died. Though part of her itched to pump this woman for information about her mother, Kelly recoiled from the idea of the intimacy that would imply. "Yes, that's right. I'm Esther's heir."

Genevieve clutched her arm. "And you're selling the place? But you can't! It's just so obvious the universe has brought you here. You *belong!*"

She made the last word sound pregnant with mystical significance.

Kelly stepped back into the vestibule, disengaging herself from Genevieve's touch. "I'm afraid I can't just pick up and move here. My life is elsewhere." Kelly paused, but Genevieve did not appear to see this untruth reflected in her aura. "A house like this needs a full-time family, not someone who comes for a vacation a couple weeks out of the year."

Genevieve shook her head. "You're only fighting your destiny . . . But since I'm here, I may as well look around."

She stepped into the hall. As she took in the polished woodwork, the gleaming floors, the stained-glass window in the stairwell, her vague stare focused and kindled into avidity. Perhaps this aging flower child did know something about real estate after all.

"I'd forgotten what a lovely house this is." She stretched out her arms in front of her and swept them to each side, fingers twiddling. "Wonderful vibrations! And in such good condition for its age! Have you been doing some work here?"

"Yes, we've done quite a bit of restoration and a little remodeling. Come, I'll show you around."

Kelly led Genevieve through the house; each room seemed to impress her more than the last. In the kitchen, where Jim nodded to her and kept working, Genevieve gushed until Kelly began to feel as if she'd eaten too much sugar. When they returned to the hall, the realtor's gaze went misty again.

"This is no ordinary house. I think it must be sited right over a confluence of energies. It just seems to live, doesn't it? And I do think you're right, it's longing for a family. Just the right family, of course—one that will harmonize with its chi."

One that will pay top dollar, you mean, thought Kelly, then chided herself for her cynicism. Underneath all the layers of New Age nonsense, the woman might possibly be sincere.

"Of course, the market is rather depressed just now, but even so, a house like this is bound to attract the right people—the sensitive ones. Really, listing the house is a pure formality—its aura will just draw those whose spirits are open to its call."

Her wandering gaze drifted back to Kelly's face, which must have reflected some fraction of her skepticism. Genevieve gave a high, tittering laugh. "But of course we do have to observe these formalities, don't we? I'll just go back to my office and run some numbers and come up with a good listing price for you, and then we can sign a contract. All right?"

Kelly nodded, not trusting herself to speak. The thought

of having her house turned into some cross between a tourist attraction and a pagan shrine was making the bile rise in her throat. She ushered the agent out as quickly as possible, then ran back to the powder room and retched until her throat was raw.

At last she slumped on the cold tile floor, back against the wall. She had less invested in this powder room than in any other room of the house, and yet now that she had chosen to abandon it, every cranny and knickknack had become inexpressibly dear to her: the odd angles of the low ceiling where the stairway passed above it; the wallpaper with its delicate primrose design; the green ceramic soap dish in the shape of a bullfrog, the soap resting in its open mouth. She pictured strangers walking through the house, coldly evaluating every feature, deciding to keep this and sell that, or maybe tear out a bedroom and build a spa-like master suite. Her stomach heaved again at the thought, but it was beyond empty now.

Still, there was nothing for it. She could not stay in a house full of ghosts, next door to the father who'd betrayed her. What had happened to her? Once she'd had the skin of a rhinoceros; the transformation of her house into a commodity would have glanced off her hide like the lash of a wet noodle. But that was before she'd had a place she was tempted to call home.

OF ALL THE THINGS RAPHAEL could have pulled out of his hat, I never expected Genevieve Deeds. She might just do the trick.

I never did have any use for that girl. She was always a flake, right back to elementary school, and I never could tell what June saw in her. But I could kiss her now, just for being her own silly self and helping Kelly begin to see she'll never be able to part with my house.

Her house.

Our house.

SHAKILY, KELLY RETURNED TO THE kitchen. Jim said, "What was that all about?" then looked up and saw her face. "Kelly, what's wrong?"

She lowered herself to the floor, back against a cabinet. "That was the real estate agent. I don't know if I'm really going to sign with her, though. I may need to find someone more—normal."

He grinned. "Yeah, she looked like a real Santa Cruz type." Then his face grew serious. "Maybe it's a sign—you shouldn't sell the house at all."

She opened her mouth to protest, but just then the doorbell rang. She tried to push herself to her feet, then gave up. "See who it is, would you, Jim? But don't let anybody in. I can't face any more of the world today."

He shot her a skeptical look, then wiped his hands and went out. Seconds later, Kiera's voice snaked down the hall and into the kitchen and wrapped Kelly in a stranglehold. But she would not go to the door.

When far too many agonizing minutes had passed, Jim returned. "That was Kiera. Your—half-sister, right? Seems like a really sweet girl." He knelt to resume his work, then said as if to himself, "Easy on the eyes, too. Very easy."

"What did she want?"

"To talk to you. I told her you weren't ready yet, come back tomorrow."

Kelly groaned. "What'd you say that for?"

"Because you need to talk to her. And anyway, I wouldn't mind seeing her again myself."

Kelly hugged her knees and buried her face in them. Everyone was out to get her, even Jim. What an idiot she'd been to bring him here.

Later in the afternoon, as they were laying the last tile, Genevieve Deeds called. "Kelly, dear, I have your contract all ready, but my horoscope says I mustn't conclude any deals today—the stars are completely wrong for it. I'll come by tomorrow morning—the moon will be auspicious then. All right?"

Kelly agreed, wondering again if she should use the interval to find a different realtor. But after all, what did it matter? As soon as she'd signed the contract and seen the last of the work completed, she'd be able to leave; she wouldn't have to encounter Genevieve's aura in person again until she had a buyer ready to close.

Jim took off, saying he wanted to drive around and see the sights; but Kelly noticed he headed for the McCarthys' house rather than for his truck. Minutes later, Aidan walked in without warning and surprised her in the living room, where she was looking for a book to while away the evening with.

She froze, book in hand, the hairs on her arms bristling. "What are you doing here?"

He put out a supplicating hand. "Kelly, please—you didn't give me a chance to explain. Please let me explain."

"What is there to explain? You seduced and betrayed my mother and abandoned me. Those look like pretty clear facts to me."

He winced. "On the surface, yes. But those words don't show what was really going on underneath. I'm not trying to justify myself, Kelly—I was a rotten excuse for a priest, I let my passion for Rose take hold of me, and I destroyed her. But there is another side to the story—if you'd only let me tell it."

Kelly willed herself steady. In all justice she would have to listen to him. And somewhere underneath her rage and pain lurked a tiny bud of hope that he would say something that would enable her to forgive him.

"All right. Sit down."

She took the chair opposite to "Nathaniel's chair" and motioned Aidan toward the couch. He sat on the edge of the cushion, fingers pressed together between his knees, and took a long breath.

"I went into the priesthood because I loved God and wanted to serve Him, and I didn't know any other way to do that. I'd never been close to a girl and didn't really know what I was giving up on that score. I think now that if I'd been Orthodox at the time—Orthodox have married priests—I might have done all right. But when I fell in love with Rose . . . I just didn't know how to handle it."

Not knowing how to handle love . . . that was something she could relate to.

"We'd grown up together, sort of, living next door, although of course she was quite a bit younger; I used to babysit her when I was in high school. She was nothing but a nice kid to me until her father died. Then—well, you know from the diary, she started coming to me for counsel. It seemed like she had no one else to talk to, and counseling the grieving is part of a priest's job, after all. I shared with her my own grief at my father's death, and I guess that kind of opened things up. And she was such a lovely girl. She had a kind of ethereal beauty—well, you've seen pictures, but they don't fully capture that quality she had. Almost angelic, childlike, but at the same time so womanly. I've never known anyone like her."

The sweet voice, the loving face of her memories drifted

across Kelly's mind. She'd never known anyone like Rose either—and it was Aidan who had deprived her of that. She stirred in her chair, but he went on.

"Anyway, it happened so gradually, by the time I realized I was in danger it was too late, I was gone. Head over heels in love. I swear to you, Kelly, I never meant to seduce her. I tried to cut it off, but in the situation, it was impossible for us to avoid each other completely. Then she happened on me when I was alone, already torn to pieces, and something snapped. I couldn't hold it in any longer. Like I said, there's no justification; I should have gone to my confessor when I first realized my feelings and gotten a transfer, or at least gone on retreat or something. But please believe at least that our lovemaking was not premeditated at all."

She could believe that, but what difference did it make? It was what he'd done afterward that had done the most damage.

"Surely you can imagine how I felt after that. I was crushed, a lowly worm, I'd betrayed Rose and betrayed my vocation. I couldn't go on. At that point I did what I should have done sooner—I went on retreat, and ultimately asked to be released from my vows. I moved to the Midwest to make a new start."

You ran away. Like a great big coward. You ran away and left us—to them.

"It never occurred to me that Rose might have conceived from that one encounter. I swear to you, Kelly, I thought I was doing the best thing by Rose when I left. I figured she was young, she would get over me, she'd go on to have a happy life. When I heard she'd run away, I figured she'd run from me just as I'd run from her. I was so disgusted with myself, I never thought she might still love me, that I could leave the priesthood, marry her, and make her happy. I didn't think I deserved to *be* as happy as I could have been with her."

Kelly found her voice at last. "But then you went on to marry someone else. Kyle and Kiera's mother."

"Yes. But that was years later, after I knew Rose was dead. My mother told me that—she has second sight, you know. But even she didn't know about you. Only Esther knew, and she never told a soul." He shook his head. "To think that all those years we lived next to each other, each keeping our half of a secret, when if we'd ever put the two halves together—who knows, I might have been able to find you where she'd failed."

"But you didn't. You didn't find me until it was too late."

He looked up at her. "Kelly, I swear to you on my life, and I beg you to believe me—if I had known you existed, I would have moved heaven and earth to find you. Hell, too, for that matter. When I heard Rose was dead, I died myself—the old me died. If I'd known there was a part of her still living in the world, that I was responsible for, I never would have left you to be raised by—her murderer."

He dropped to his knees in front of her. "Kelly, if you'll let me, I'd like to be a father to you now. Not to interfere in your life and tell you what to do, but just to love you—to give you a family. Kyle and Kiera are thrilled to have you for a sister, and Mother will be too, in her own way. Can you forgive me? Will you be my daughter, in spirit as well as in blood?"

Kelly stared at the face before her, its lines etched more deeply than before, the dark eyes pleading. All her life she'd longed for someone who wanted to be a father to her.

But she'd longed for a mother, too, and that possibility had been taken from her forever.

She stood abruptly, forcing Aidan back on his heels. "Too little too late, Aidan. Way too late."

He drew himself up slowly and gazed at her with haunted,

glistening eyes, but she allowed no glimmer of relenting to show in her own. At last he turned and trudged out of the house.

When his footsteps had died away down the walk, she came to herself, looked at the book she still absently held in her hand, and knew attempting to read was useless. Her stomach revolted at the thought of food. The evening stretched out before her like a sentence to solitary confinement. Sleep was her only escape, but she knew it would elude her. She fed Ginger, took a sleeping pill, and went to bed.

CHAPTER 21

WHEN I ASKED Raphael for help, I didn't expect it to take the form of the first truly ferocious storm of the autumn. At eight o'clock, when Kelly went to bed, a light rain was drizzling through the still air, making a friendly kind of patter on the roof that helped to lull her to sleep, along with that pill she'd taken; but by midnight the wind was flinging torrents against the windowpanes. The trees in the yard swayed like drunken men, hurling their branches around as if trying to regain their balance. Kelly slept through it all, with Ginger curled protectively beside her.

After a couple of hours of this, I heard a loud crack from the dying oak next to the house—a long, slow, creaking noise that would shiver your bones like the sound of a hundred coffins opening. And then I saw it—that huge branch that hung right over the roof dragging away from the trunk. I threw myself toward it, though I knew I could do nothing, and cried out for Raphael.

Let it be, said his voice right beside me. *This is the Will. She will not be greatly harmed.*

So I watched, helpless, as that great bough pulled away from the tree and crashed right through the roof over Kelly's bedroom.

THE FIRST CRACK PENETRATED KELLY'S drugged unconsciousness only in the form of a firecracker going off in her dream. Not until the branch hit the roof did she begin to awaken, and even then her brain was too foggy to understand what was happening. But when the plaster cracked above her head, she collected herself enough to dive under the pillow as the bough crashed through the ceiling and came to rest across the foot of her bed. Ginger gave a tremendous yowl and ran out of the room.

She felt only terror as the rain of splintering wood and crumbling plaster fell around her. At last all sound subsided but the howl of the storm itself, and she ventured out from under her pillow. Miraculously, no heavy debris had fallen directly on her, but she felt an intolerable weight across her legs. There at the end of her bed was a minor forest where no forest should be.

She tried to pull her left leg free—a burgeoning pain in her right leg warned her off trying to move it—but it was wedged fast. She would have to call for help. She reached to the night table for her cell phone, but it wasn't there. Then she remembered leaving it on the dressing table, plugged into the charger. It might as well have been on the dark side of the moon.

"Ginger!" she called, and amazingly he put his head around the door and mewed. "Ginger, get the phone, there's a good boy." She pointed to the dressing table, then pantomimed talking on the phone. Ginger followed her motions with his eyes but did not move. Uncanny as he sometimes seemed, he was only a cat, after all.

She could scream for help, but who would hear her through this storm? Still, she had to try. She took in as deep a breath as she could and put all her force into one long cry. "HE-E-E-ELP!"

And to her astonished relief came an answering call. "Kelly? Hold on, I'm coming!"

223

It was Aidan's voice, and now she could hear him bounding up the stairs.

"Kelly?" He stood in the doorway, gasping for breath, shining a flashlight into the room. "I heard the branch fall and came as quick as I could. Are you all right?"

"I'm stuck. The tree's on my legs. Other than that, I think I'm okay."

He picked his way across the littered floor to the bedside, playing the flashlight's beam across the wreckage. "My God, you had a lucky escape. I should say miraculous. The main bough fell just clear of the bed—it's a smaller branch that's got you pinned. I'm going to try to shift it while you pull your legs clear. Ready?"

She nodded, setting her teeth. Aidan got down on one knee to get his shoulder under the branch. To move it he would have to rotate the full weight of the parent bough. He gave a mighty heave, and the pressure on her legs was lifted slightly. She wriggled her left leg free, but when she tried to pull her right, the only response was a sickening jolt of pain.

"I—I think my right leg might be broken. I can't move it."

"Try pulling your whole body back," Aidan grunted through his teeth. "Can't—hold this—much longer." The bough rose another fraction of an inch.

She sat up straight, put her hands behind her, and heaved her hips backward. As her right leg passed under the branch, her foot bent forward, sending a fresh wave of agony that nearly swamped her consciousness; but she was free.

Aidan dropped the branch with a thud and sat gasping for a moment. The rasp of his breath frightened her.

"We've got to get you out of here. More of the roof might come down any minute with all that water coming in." Only now did Kelly realize that the bedclothes were wet through, and the sound of falling rain was not all coming from outside.

"I'll have to carry you, but first we've got to do something about that leg." He sorted through the debris for a piece of lath, broke it to the length of her calf, then bound it to her leg with a pillowcase.

"Now put your arms around my neck." He slid one arm under her back and the other under her knees. "I'll try not to hurt you, but I can't guarantee it. Hang on tight, okay?"

He straightened slowly. With her head against his chest, she could feel his heart pounding wildly. There seemed to be something odd about its rhythm.

"I'm too heavy for you, Aidan. Put me down. I can walk—or hop, anyway, if I can just lean on you."

"Hop? down the stairs? No way. Don't worry about me, I'm not completely past it yet."

He settled her weight against him, sidled gingerly through the door, and set off down the stairs, holding her so that her feet cleared the banister. On the landing he leaned against the wall for a moment before finishing the descent.

At the third step from the bottom, he lurched and slid the rest of the way, losing his hold on her legs. The makeshift splint caught between the spindles of the banister as momentum dragged her hips downward. As a tidal wave of pain engulfed her, Kelly heard a siren coming up the driveway; then everything went black.

HOURS LATER, SHE CAME UP through a morphine-induced fog to consciousness. All around her were the sterile white walls and curtains of a hospital cubicle, and leaning over her was a face she had longed for even in her drugged sleep: Nathaniel.

"Nat," she said, essaying a smile.

He bent over and kissed her forehead. "I'm here."

"What happened?" All she could remember since leaving her house, beyond the excruciating pain of having her leg set before the morphine had taken hold, was an equally excruciating anxiety about Aidan. "Where's Aidan?"

"He's here in the hospital."

"I've got to see him." She pushed herself up on her elbows.

Nathaniel stopped her with a hand on her shoulder. "Sweetheart—he's not doing so well."

"What is it? What's happened?"

"He had a heart attack. The paramedics brought him around, but—well, the doctor doesn't seem too optimistic. He's in intensive care."

She sank back on the pillows, her eyes filling.

"Why did he do it?" she said. "It was too much for him. The paramedics were on their way—why didn't he wait for them?"

"It's a good thing for you he didn't wait. By the time they got up there, the roof had completely caved in. You would have been crushed." He took her hand in both his own. "Aidan did it because he loves you."

Her heart constricted with a pain even greater than that in her leg. If there was a God, surely he would not do this to her—take away her father when she had only just found him. "I have to see him, Nat. Now, while there's still time. I have to tell him."

He nodded, then rose and went to call a nurse. After many frowns and shakes of the head, the nurse relented and brought a wheelchair, and she and Nathaniel helped Kelly into it.

"I'll take it from here," he said, and with a skeptical frown the nurse stepped back.

He pushed the chair out of the room and down the hall to intensive care. Kyle and Kiera sat in the hallway outside Aidan's room, looking for once like twins by virtue of the dual anguish written plain on their transparent faces. To Kelly's astonishment, Jim was sitting next to Kiera. "I heard what happened and came to check on you," he said a bit sheepishly to Kelly. "But since you were well cared for . . ." He exchanged nods with Nathaniel.

"Father Herman's in there, hearing his confession and giving him Holy Communion," Kiera said brokenly. "But he's been asking for you."

Nathaniel wheeled Kelly close, and she reached out a hand to each twin. "I'm so sorry," she said. "I don't deserve that he should have sacrificed himself for me. I won't blame you if you never forgive me."

They took her hands, and Kiera stood to kiss Kelly's cheek. "Don't be ridiculous, it's not your fault the tree happened to fall on your bedroom. He would have done the same for either of us." She blew her nose loudly. "Anyway, his heart's been iffy for years. The doctor kept telling him to slow down, but he never would. It's not in him to spare himself when other people need him."

Kelly swallowed hard, then forced out the thought that tormented her. "Then you don't think . . . he did it just to prove to me . . . because I was so stubborn and hateful?"

Kiera and Kyle shook their heads briskly and spoke in unison. "Absolutely not. He did it because he loves you. Period."

Kelly buried her face in her hands. For the moment her anguish was too sharp to be shared.

She heard the door of Aidan's room open and raised her head. Framed in the doorway was a Kyle-sized figure robed in black, in the act of removing a gold-embroidered stole from around his bearded neck.

"Kelly, this is Father Herman," Nathaniel said. She was unsure of the etiquette for greeting a priest, but he put out his hand in the usual fashion, so she shook it.

"How is he?" she managed to croak.

"His body is weak, but his soul is at peace. Or will be as soon as he talks with you."

Father Herman stood aside, and Nathaniel wheeled Kelly into the doorway. A nurse, fussing with the instruments surrounding the bed, turned and frowned at them. "Are you family?"

"Yes." Kelly lifted her chin and her voice rang out strong. "I'm his daughter."

The nurse shouldered Nathaniel away from the wheelchair and with a jerk of her head sent him back to the hallway. She pushed Kelly up to the side of the bed and returned to her ministrations.

The figure under the blankets seemed to have shrunk since the night before. The face Aidan turned to her was grey and drawn, but when he saw her, his eyes kindled into life.

"Kelly," he said, so faintly she had to lean close to hear him. "Are you all right?"

"I'm fine, thanks to you. But they tell me you're not doing so well."

The corners of his mouth tried to lift. "I've had better days."

She took the still, cold white hand that lay outside the coverlet and stroked it. "Aidan—Dad—I'm so sorry I was rotten to you. I don't know what came over me. I should've been grateful to finally have a father after all these years. And now—can you ever forgive me?"

His eyes brimmed. "The question is . . . do you forgive me?"

"Oh, yes. Completely. Only don't leave me now. We need to have years and years together. We have to make up for lost time."

This time his attempt at a smile succeeded. "The years that the locust has eaten . . . I think we'll have to wait for heaven to get them back. I'm going to be with your mother now, sweetheart. You've got a good man in Nathaniel, and Kyle and Kiera will be your family. You'll all take care of each other . . . just fine."

She pressed her lips to his hand to hide her tears. The nurse gave a cluck of alarm and bustled out, to return moments later with a doctor. Then she wheeled Kelly unceremoniously out of the room.

CHAPTER 22

KELLY ATTENDED AIDAN'S funeral on crutches. The doctor recommended a wheelchair, but she didn't want to call attention to herself; this funeral wasn't about her. The crutches were bad enough.

But Kyle and Kiera insisted she sit with them in the chairs at the front of the church reserved for the family. Nathaniel sat next to her; he refused to leave her side, and no one questioned his right to be there. Eunice was wheeled up to the end of the row, looking so forlorn that Kelly felt it likely a second funeral would not be long in coming. She reminded herself that Eunice was her grandmother, too—in fact, the only older relative she had living now—and strove to be as solicitous for the old woman's comfort as she could be in her own crippled state.

When she had maneuvered her way to a seat, with another chair turned backward in front of her to prop up her throbbing leg, Kelly at last had attention to spare to take in her surroundings. She felt a stab of remorse that it had taken a funeral to get her here to St. Innocent Orthodox Church—to this place that was so important to everyone she loved.

The space was cavernous, tenebrous, dim, and cool, lit only

by pale, cloud-filtered autumn sunlight admitted through the slits of windows in the dome far above, and by oil lamps and candles that flickered along the walls, fitfully illuminating the ranks of frescoed saints that covered them. No pews interrupted the expanse of wooden floor; the half-open coffin held pride of place in the center aisle, with a few rows of folding chairs set up to each side. The chairs filled quickly, but people kept coming in, standing behind and around them until the nave was full. Aidan had been greatly loved.

Beneath the vivid scent of the flowers that topped and surrounded the coffin, Kelly discerned a fainter smell she could not identify, a smell that seemed as much a part of the building as the icon-covered wooden screen that sheltered the altar. Then the priest and deacon appeared from behind the screen, the deacon bearing a great gold censer on a long triple chain, and as he swung it over the coffin, that smell rose and swamped the scent of the flowers. The incense was sweet and yet pungent, joyful and sorrowful. The choir's chanting swelled to greet it, incarnating that joyful sorrow and calling all to a world in which death could be seen not as an end, but as a beginning.

Kelly neither knew nor cared how long it all went on; her grief, her sharp remorse, her bitterness, even her physical pain were subsumed in that otherworldly atmosphere, at once rarefied and thick with holiness. Incredibly, at this time when her earthly father had been snatched away from her, as it seemed, so pitilessly, she began to think it might be possible to believe in a heavenly Father whose every inscrutable act and thought was always and only Love.

At the end of the service, she took her place in the line of mourners who filed by the coffin to—in the words of the hymn that accompanied them—"give a last kiss to the dead." To Kelly's

231

amazement, most of them did exactly that, leaning over the coffin to kiss Aidan's forehead, or his hands and the icon held underneath them. When her turn came, she took a moment to gaze at Aidan's still, white face, from which all pain and suffering had been smoothed away; his lips even seemed to smile.

Setting her crutches aside, Kelly braced her hands against the side of the coffin and leaned over to brush her lips over the cold forehead. "Goodbye, Dad," she whispered. "I love you. Pray for me, if you can, from over there—and maybe I'll learn how to pray for you."

RAPHAEL GRANTED ME A VERY special boon—the right to be there with the angels who received Aidan's soul at the moment it left his body. I couldn't go on the whole journey with him, but I stayed until the funeral, while he was still clinging close to his old home. Just before they put his body in the ground, I watched his spirit go to each of his children in turn—Kelly first, then Kiera, then Kyle—and give them a bodiless kiss and a blessing. And I saw the peace and wonder that stole over their faces as he passed. He paused a moment to take a good long look at Jim Meriwether, then blessed him as well. Jim took hold of Kiera's hand and squeezed hard.

Then Aidan turned to me to ask my forgiveness for his sin with my daughter. I gave it to him, full and free. "I'm ready," he said to the angels. "It's time," they said, and his journey began. He'll be with June Rose before long.

My time isn't quite over yet, though. I still have to make it up with Kelly, and for that I have to wait until the house is repaired and she can come home.

SITTING BY THE WINDOW OF what had been Aidan's office, her casted leg propped on the daybed where she'd been sleeping for the last few weeks, Kelly looked up from her book and across the low hedge toward her own house. It was truly hers now; she'd called off the realtor as soon as she got back from the hospital.

When she first returned, the caved-in roof covered by a blue tarp had borne a sickening resemblance to an accident victim in a body bag. For the first few days, while the crew—of which Jim seemed to have assumed leadership, to Kyle's evident relief—was clearing the rubble, she could not bear to watch. But now the roof was restored to its proper profile, and they told her the interior repairs were well advanced. Her leg was almost healed as well. By the time her cast came off, the house would be ready for her return.

She'd thought at first it would be difficult to watch others doing work she could not take part in nor even supervise. In her old life, these weeks of enforced idleness would have been weeks of purgatory to her. But now she found herself curiously indifferent to the world that passed beyond her window. She watched the work next door as if it were a play, or perhaps a protracted episode of This Old House. She was quite content to sit for hours on end with Ginger—who had condescended to follow her here, to her amazement and joy—and to read the books Nathaniel brought her, to chat with him or Kiera and Jim when they joined her for meals, or with Father Herman when he dropped by.

Once she got past staring at his beard, so long and full that she half expected to discover a family of mice nesting there, Kelly found she quite liked the bearlike priest of St. Innocent Church. Though he shared her grief for Aidan, his natural jollity soon prevailed in their discussions, which ranged far beyond the narrow ground she had previously imagined religion would

233

cover. In the course of her life, she'd had brief exposure to various flavors of American Christianity, from the guilt-tripping severity of old-line Roman Catholics to the false backslapping cheeriness of TV evangelists; but never before had she encountered a faith that seemed to be grounded in joy and a loving acceptance of herself as a human being.

Once Kelly asked Father Herman why he spent so much time with her, as she was not a member of his flock.

"Well, it's partly selfish—I enjoy your company." His eyes twinkled as he stroked his beard. "But if I were to limit myself to ministering only to baptized Orthodox Christians, I wouldn't be much of a priest. The Church is not an elitist club for people who are already perfect; it's a hospital for those who need healing. And that includes just about all of us." His deep brown eyes grew serious, penetrating her soul as deeply as Nathaniel's grey eyes were prone to do. "You've seen a lot of healing already, I think. But you've still got some way to go. The Church can help you, if you'll let us."

Kelly swallowed, summoning her nerve for a plunge. Then Kiera spoke from the doorway. "I'll be happy to take you to church anytime, Kel, you know that."

But she wasn't ready to be that conspicuous yet. "When I get off these crutches, we'll see." *When I can sneak in the back without causing a stir,* she meant.

And Kiera had done so much for her already—giving her a temporary home, fixing her meals, helping her bathe and dress, driving her to doctor's appointments. Kelly had tried to feel guilty about it, but Kiera made that impossible. "Hey, what are sisters for? Think if we'd grown up together—you would've bullied me into doing a million things for you over the years. We're just making up for lost time."

Every morning, Kelly had to pinch herself to be sure she wasn't dreaming. She had a real family now—a sister, a grand-mother, a brother, a sister-in-law, a nephew. Mindy brought the baby over now and then; he'd recovered from his bronchitis with all the resiliency of youth. Kelly never tired of holding him, playing peek-a-boo with him, or lifting him so he could try the strength of his growing legs against her lap.

"You're a natural with him," Mindy said. "You should have one of your own." Kelly looked up from Mindy to Nathaniel, who had just come in. She felt her face go hot as his mouth spread into a broad smile.

Through all these weeks, the quiet contentment of her solitary hours kindled into joy in the evenings, when Nathaniel came to sit with her. Their talks ranged far, from the deeply personal to the universal, from their own past histories to religion and world events. His opinions did not always match hers but challenged them, offering a new perspective on questions she'd considered settled. He unfolded her like a rose, bringing the buried petals into fresh air and sunlight one by one. And he, though transparent, was deep as the sea; she dove and dove and could never get to the bottom of him.

Physically, he showed great restraint. He would sit next to her and hold her hand, and when he left for the night he would give her one chaste kiss on the lips. She sensed he was waiting for something, and knew it was right that he should; but she was impatient with her disability for this cause, if for no other.

Occasionally Jim would drop in during the evening as well, though he spent most of his time with Kiera. The first time he and Nathaniel were there together, Kelly was nearly mute with discomfiture. But the two men seemed at ease with each other. After half an hour or so, Nathaniel excused himself for a minute, and Kelly took the opportunity to say tentatively to Jim, "You seem to be getting along pretty well with—everyone."

Jim gave her a sardonic smile. "Yes, I'm finally moving on. That's what you mean, isn't it? I'm not jealous of Nathaniel, and I've found a woman I really like who might be able to love me back one day. Does that bother you?"

Kelly reddened. "Bother me? Why would it bother me? You seem happy—I want you to be happy. And Kiera seems happy too. It's just . . ." She couldn't possibly voice that "it."

He did it for her. "You wonder how I could get over you so fast."

She wanted to sink through the floor. "Well, yes, it does seem a little peculiar. I mean it would for anyone. Not because it's me." *Stop before both feet get stuck in your mouth, Kelly.*

He laughed. "Lighten up, Kel. I'm just giving you a hard time. The truth is, I'd come pretty close to getting over you those months we were apart. I realized we must not be right for each other, or the attraction would've been mutual. When I saw you again and you asked me down here, the old flame flared up for a day or two. But once I realized you were in love—and not with me—it died for good. And then when I saw Kiera—" He shrugged. "It was like something clicked into place."

"Yeah. I know what you mean. I had that same feeling with Nathaniel." She stared dreamily past him for a moment, then came back with a start. "I just wanted to be sure—for Kiera's sake—that you weren't, you know, taking her on the rebound. That you really care for her, for herself."

Jim sat forward, all mirth vanishing from his brown eyes. "I promise you I do, Kelly. You know yourself how much she deserves a man's whole heart, and she's got mine. One of these days I hope you and I will be related, and that will suit me fine."

She smiled broadly. "Me too." She said a silent, tentative prayer of gratitude that she could enter her new life without Jim's broken heart on her conscience.

That had been weeks ago. It would soon be forty days since the accident—forty days which, Father Herman informed her, happened to correspond with the period of Advent in the Orthodox Church. These same forty days were considered to be the time during which Aidan's soul, having left the body, would make its unimaginable journey with the angels to its permanent home. Coincidentally, forty days was also the time her doctor had prescribed for her to remain in a cast; but since the fortieth day would be Christmas, he had agreed to cut that time a couple of days short.

So today, at last, the cast was to come off, and she would rejoin the world of the living. She closed her book and looked around the small room that had been her home for this time out of time, that had at first been so full of Aidan but from which his scent was now beginning to fade. Her grief for him, which had begun so sharp and tinged with guilt, had been almost purged by the funeral, and the gentler sorrow that remained had been transformed over these weeks into a deep sense of his continuing presence with her. Almost as if she had grown up as his daughter, she could hear his voice in the back of her mind, advising and encouraging, lending a foundation and stability to what had been her rootless life.

Her gaze passed over his books, his icons and vigil candle, his computer and file cabinet, and came to rest on a framed photograph of herself and Aidan that stood on the desk. Kiera had snapped them unawares the day Kelly nailed her token post in the addition, in the brief moment when Aidan had put his arm around her shoulders. She'd been annoyed with Kiera at the time for catching her with her defenses down; but that photo was priceless to her now. Aidan's face, become so dear in its absence, smiled at her from the picture, seeming to give her his benediction: It was time to move on.

CHAPTER 23

IF THERE WERE such a thing as impatience on this side—if I still lived inside of time in a way that can make you impatient—these last weeks would have been awfully long. From Aidan's funeral until today, when Nathaniel's due to bring Kelly back home, I haven't been able to keep an eye on her; I've had to rely on Raphael's reports. And if you think it's frustrating trying to worm all the details you want out of a *man*—try getting them out of an angel! But at least I've known that she's forgiven Aidan, forgiven God, if you can put it like that, and accepted all the love that's offered her from Nathaniel and the McCarthys; and that gives me good hope she'll also be willing to forgive me.

The boys have done a fine job rebuilding the roof and Kelly's room. But it'll never be the same room, because all the furniture and decorations were destroyed, either by the cave-in itself or by the water that kept flooding in all that night long. But perhaps that's just as well. She'll have one room, anyway, where she'll have to start fresh and do it all to her own taste instead of taking my leavings. I hope eventually she'll make the whole house her own that way; that's the prerogative of a bride. And I feel quite sure she'll be a bride before too long. Maybe she'll even save that bedroom for a nursery.

NATHANIEL DROVE HER TO DR. Cuthbert's office and came with her into the treatment room, carrying a mysterious long, narrow package. After removing the cast, the doctor felt down the length of Kelly's calf, flexed her foot and knee, and pronounced her healed.

He handed her a standard-issue aluminum cane and said, "Now try walking." But before she could get down from the table, Nathaniel stepped forward and presented her with the package. She unwrapped it to find a cane he'd carved of Brazilian cherry. Its smooth round knob topped a shaft carved with an ornate "K" entwined in roses, the whole polished to a brilliant purple sheen.

"Oh, Nat, it's gorgeous!" She turned it over and over, absorbing every detail of the carving. "But when did you find time to do this? You've spent practically all your evenings with me."

He shrugged. "I don't need a lot of sleep."

She eased herself off the examining table and gingerly put a little weight on her newly naked right leg, the calf so thin and pasty white she hardly recognized it as her own. Leaning on the cane, she tried a few steps, then turned back to Nathaniel. "It's perfect." She kissed him, heedless of Dr. Cuthbert hovering red-faced in the background.

The doctor said, "No pain?"

"Not a bit. A little weak and shaky, but no pain."

"Right. Then you're good to go." He handed her a referral slip to physical therapy.

She set off down the hall, leaning on the cane with her

right hand and on Nathaniel's arm with her left. Independence tasted sweet after these long weeks, but one didn't want to carry it too far.

THEY STOPPED FOR DINNER, AND it was dark when they pulled onto Journey's End Road. Nathaniel slowed the truck so they could take in the Christmas displays in all the neighbors' yards. They came to Mrs. Perkins' yard last. She had apparently set out to out-decorate every house on the block and had done it as garishly as possible. Dazzling colored lights outlined every lineament of the house, fence, and sidewalk, while a corpulent, lewdly grinning Santa exhorted wild-eyed plastic reindeer to leap and cavort in frustrated immobility across one side of the lawn. On the other side, an animated chorus of snowmen with Elvis pompadours belted out "Jingle Bell Rock."

Kelly was still dazed by this display when the author of it appeared at her open front door, dressed in her usual prim style with the bewildering additions of a Santa hat and green, bell-tipped elf slippers. Mrs. Perkins waved with both hands for them to stop, disappeared into the house for a moment, then bustled out to the truck bearing a plate-sized bubble of green and red cellophane tied with a wide purple bow.

"Kelly, dear, I'm so glad I caught you," she said, panting. "I've been meaning to come over and tell you how sorry I was about your accident and your poor dear house, and of course, poor dear Aidan, but I've been so busy with my Christmas preparations I just haven't had a minute." She glanced toward her yard with modest pride. "Such a lot of work, and you know I'm not getting any younger, but I've been doing it for so long the neighbors all expect it, and I couldn't let you all down, now could I?"

She paused with a smile that clearly expected a compliment.

"It certainly is impressive," Kelly managed to say with a straight face.

"Well, I do like to make the season festive, you know. I feel it's our duty to brighten others' lives whenever we can, don't you? So as I said, I'm glad I caught you, because I wanted to give you some of my Christmas goodies. I make twelve different kinds of cookies and candy every Christmas and give some to all the neighbors. One has to do one's little bit, doesn't one?"

Kelly took the package and held it on her lap. "Thank you, Mrs. Perkins. That's extremely kind of you. And allow me to apologize for all the noise and mess you've had to put up with the last few weeks—I'm sure those roof repairs must have been much worse than the inside work we were doing before."

Mrs. Perkins waved an arthritic hand. "Tut, tut, that's nothing, my dear. Of course the house had to be repaired. That blue tarp was a terrible eyesore. You know I told Esther for years she ought to do something about that oak tree, but she was sentimental about it—I guess Victor had planted it when June Rose was born, and she couldn't bear to cut it down." Mrs. Perkins dabbed a tissue at her nose, and Kelly had the feeling a sniff had been narrowly averted.

Then Mrs. Perkins brightened. "But all's well that ends well, isn't it, and now it's Christmas and we can all be good neighbors together."

"Yes, indeed. Thank you again, Mrs. Perkins, and a very merry Christmas to you." Kelly felt a momentary qualm. "Do you have anyone to spend Christmas with?"

Mrs. Perkins fluttered her eyelids and dabbed again at her nose. "Oh, my, yes, don't you worry about me. My nephew and his family invite me every year. He has such dear children—three little boys, and all exactly like their father. I've knitted nice warm ski masks for all of them."

The reference to Mr. Perkins turned Kelly's stomach momentarily to stone, but the vision of three small copies of him bundled up in "nice warm ski masks" threatened to tip her over the edge into hilarity.

"I'm glad you have family to be with," she managed. "We must be going now. Thanks again, and Merry Christmas."

"Merry Christmas!" Mrs. Perkins called after them as they drove away.

AS THEY TURNED UP HER driveway, Kelly blew out a long breath that turned into a gasp of delight. Luminarias lined the drive and the path to the front porch; white twinkle lights rimmed the porch railing and the roof, while an enormous wreath of fresh evergreen studded with more twinkle lights graced the front door.

Nathaniel parked the truck and helped her out. She walked up the path, lost in wonder. Jim and Kiera stood on the porch, beaming.

"Beautiful! Did you two do all this?"

Kiera nodded. "And this is only the beginning. Come on inside."

The floor of the vestibule was spread with pine needles that gave off a delicious scent as their shoes crunched over them. Ginger, a big green bow complementing his orange fur, ran up and twined himself around Kelly's legs in greeting. Once past the inner door, Kelly felt she had entered a magazine spread. Fir garlands wound with burgundy ribbons twined round the banisters and draped the archways, between which a banner proclaimed, "Welcome Home, Kelly!" in gold letters two feet tall. Candles flickered warmly on every surface and in sconces on the walls. At the far end of the living room, a cheerful fire warmed the inglenook; before the front window glimmered a huge Douglas fir strung with twinkle lights and dotted with gold and burgundy balls. On the coffee table stood large bowls of cranberries and popcorn, along with a pincushion and a spool of thread.

"We thought you'd like to participate in the decorating, so we left the stringing for you," Kiera said. "But we'll help if you want."

Overcome, Kelly swayed toward Nathaniel, who caught her with a strong arm around her waist. "It's so beautiful," she said, her voice breaking. "It's so . . . I never had a Christmas like this. I never had a family like this. You guys are just . . . the best."

Kiera beamed, if possible even more brightly than before. "You two sit down. We'll get the cider—it should be hot by now." She pulled Jim by the sleeve after her.

Kelly sank onto the sofa beside Nathaniel and let her head fall to his shoulder. "If anyone had told me four months ago where my life would be now . . . It's incredible. I don't deserve all this."

He pulled her closer. "None of us ever deserves any of the good things in life. It's all grace."

She didn't answer. Her heart was too full.

After a minute, he said, "The tree's pretty, but it looks kind of impersonal now. It'll be better in a few years, when we've had time to collect some ornaments of our own."

"Mmm," she responded drowsily. Then his words registered in her sleepy brain. "Did you say 'we'?"

His eyebrows rose. "I guess I did. Freudian slip." He shifted to face her and took her hands in his. "I wasn't planning to say this quite so soon; I had an idea of saving it for Christmas Day. But I've blown my cover, so I might as well say it now." He grinned a little sheepishly, then grew serious again. "You know I love you. My life is yours, whether you accept it or not. But I hope you will accept it. I want you to be my wife, my soul's companion, the mother of my children if God sends them. Kelly, my darling, will you marry me?"

Kelly had thought her heart was full already, but now happiness came welling up inside her in a great wave and spilled in tears down her cheeks. "Yes," she said, and had just time to glimpse an answering joy in Nathaniel's eyes before he gathered her into a crushing embrace.

"I'm going to make you happier than you've ever imagined," he said exultantly into her ear.

"You already have, beloved." It was the first endearment she had used to him, and she savored its taste on her tongue. "You already have."

CHAPTER 24

THIS IS THE first moment since I passed on that I've longed for something I used to have on earth: I wanted a glass of champagne so I could toast Kelly and Nathaniel on their engagement. It would have been a little victory celebration for me, too, because I'm virtually certain now that my mission has been accomplished. I've been given permission to appear to Kelly tonight, and I think she'll be in a frame of mind to grant me whatever I ask.

Goodness, it's been a long road, and a winding one, and at times I thought we'd never see the end of it; but now we're here, I am a little sorry to have to leave. Not that I don't have all glory to look forward to for myself, but I'd like to hang around a little longer just to see Kelly married, and happy. But this is where I have to learn my last lesson in faith: I have to let go and let them work out their happiness for themselves, trusting God to keep them on the right path. One thing I can always do is pray for them, and know my prayers will be heard.

Now my moment has come. Lord, have mercy on me, a sinner. I'm getting visible.

WHEN JIM AND KIERA BROUGHT in the cider and saw their radiant faces, it was clear from the quirk at the corners of Kiera's mouth that she'd guessed what had transpired. She and Jim sipped at their mugs, then tactfully withdrew. "We'll make up the bed for you in Esther's room," Kiera said to Kelly. "Your stuff's there already." They slipped out of the house after that, leaving Kelly and Nathaniel to themselves.

They drank the cider, sampled Mrs. Perkins' surprisingly tasty goodies, strung the popcorn and cranberries and draped them on the tree. By that time Kelly had reached a drowsy state of swirling variegated hues of happiness.

Nathaniel helped her upstairs. She assured him she could manage her nighttime ritual, and they said a lingering goodbye, sweetened by the knowledge that reunion was only a few hours away.

The sound of his footsteps fell away down the stairs and through the hall. The front door closed, and Kelly was alone. But she knew that truly she would never be alone again.

She brushed her teeth, then went into the bedroom, dazed with exhaustion and joy. Just across the threshold she stopped dead. Kiera had left the bedside lamp on, and by its light Kelly saw the old rocking chair that stood facing the window. The chair was rocking, and the top of a head peeked over its high back.

"Kiera?" she faltered. But it couldn't be Kiera; the hair was white.

"Come over here, dear. I want to talk to you." The voice that issued from the chair was soft and warm, but with a resonance as if it were speaking in a cathedral.

Kelly felt she ought to be rooted to the spot with fear. But Ginger trotted placidly into the room and hopped up into the chair, purring loudly. Surely if Ginger had no fear, she need have none.

She limped slowly over to the bed and sat, then raised her eyes by degrees from the floor to the chair. In it sat a woman, familiar but unfamiliar, old and yet not old. Her skin had the translucency of age but the suppleness of youth, with a luminosity that belonged to neither. In Kelly's mind, all the photos she'd seen of Esther at different ages merged into one essential portrait and became the face that smiled at her from the chair.

"Esther?" she whispered, the hairs lifting on the back of her neck.

The woman nodded, stroking Ginger on her lap. "Yes, dear. I'm your grandmother. Don't be frightened. I've been here all along, you know—ever since you came to the house. Only you couldn't see me until now."

That was what had kept the fear at bay—she'd been living with this presence now for months, had come to regard it as an integral part of the house even as she labored to make the place her own. "Yes—I've felt you here."

"And I hope you know I'm only here to do you good." Esther smiled with a very earthly twinkle. "Esther the friendly ghost."

"Yes." Kelly took a deep, steadying breath. "I've felt that too."

"I've brought you here and have been allowed to stay with you for a purpose, dear. Two purposes. To make up to you for everything I deprived you of by chasing your mother away—and to ask your forgiveness." Esther leaned toward her. "Have I succeeded?"

Kelly searched her heart for the anger she'd felt against this woman when she first learned of Rose's fate, but found no trace of it. The fire of her ordeal had burned it out of her. And as to making up for what she'd lost— "I had nothing when I came here. Nothing that mattered. Now I have everything."

Esther's smile illumined her already bright countenance. "And do you forgive me?"

Kelly reached out toward her grandmother. "With all my heart."

Esther shrank back. "I'm so sorry, but you mustn't touch me, dear. It's against the rules. We don't have a lot of rules on this side, but that's one of them." She stood, and Ginger melted unconcernedly through her lap to rest on the chair. "I can bless you, though."

Kelly rose, and Esther moved her hand in front of her in the form of a cross. "I have one more thing to ask of you, dear."

"What is it? Anything—"

"It's very simple, but it will mean a lot to me. Will you go to church tomorrow night and light a candle for me?"

"Of course I will—but what—"

Esther raised her hand. "The candle will be a sign of your forgiveness. Its flame will reach all the way to heaven and open the door for me. I've been waiting in the Vestibule all this time, you see. But now it's time for me to move on inside."

Her gaze traveled around the room. "I won't be with you any-more, dear. But you don't need me now. Pretty soon you're going to fill this house with love, more than it's ever held before." She turned back to Kelly. "And when you have little ones to hold and tell stories to about the days gone by—save a kind word for me, won't you? And use that nice new kitchen of yours to bake them a Crustimony Proseedcake in my name."

"Yes. I will."

Esther took one last long look, then blessed her again. "Goodbye, dear." She turned and walked toward the door, but before she reached it, she was gone.

CHAPTER 25

KELLY SLEPT LATE the next morning, which was Christmas Eve. She awoke ravenous and thought nostalgically of the delicious and filling breakfasts Kiera had prepared daily while she was under her roof. Well, no time like the present to start learning to use that brand new state-of-the-art kitchen downstairs.

But as she left the shower, she caught muted sounds of sizzling and banging, along with the tantalizing odors of bacon and cinnamon rolls, wafting up the stairs. Her first mad thought was that Esther was cooking breakfast, but she dismissed that thought immediately. The cook was no doubt someone more substantial—Kiera, Nathaniel, or both.

She turned back into the bathroom and blew her hair dry, just in case. It curled on her shoulders now, which together with the radiance of her happiness lent a new softness to her face. She smiled shyly at her own reflection, then took her lovely cane and progressed slowly down the stairs.

She entered the kitchen as Nathaniel was setting the table in the breakfast nook for two. This was her first sight of the completed kitchen—the appliances had yet to be installed the night of the accident—and she caught her breath at the beauty of it:

the warm textures of wood, slate, and granite gleaming in the morning sun that streamed through the windows of the nook. And most beautiful of all was the man who bent over the table, setting out Esther's Fiestaware, surrounded by—

"Nat! You did it!" She limped as quickly as she could to the nook, and he stood aside, smiling, as she bent to examine the carved frieze that ran around the tops of the benches. Here were the grapes, the wheat, the chalice, and the loaf, just as in Nathaniel's own apartment.

"Merry Christmas," he said as she turned to him in rapture. "Don't think me presumptuous—but I knew this table was destined to be the site of many sacramental meals to come."

She let him know with a kiss that his presumption was forgiven. But the word *sacrament* reminded her of her promise of the night before.

"Nat, there's something I need to tell you."

"Can you tell me over breakfast? I don't want it to get cold."

She took a few bites to take the edge off her hunger, then told him about her conversation with Esther.

To her surprise, he registered no disbelief and little amazement at her tale.

"You act like dead people appear to their relatives every day," she said.

He shrugged. "Well, perhaps not every day, but I've certainly heard of it before. It isn't all that uncommon in Orthodox countries—people there are more receptive to the spiritual world. The fact is, love, the barrier between the living and everybody else—the dead, the angels, God Himself—isn't nearly as solid as it's made out to be. You'll understand that in time." He smiled, and Kelly shut her mouth and blinked. "So I take it you want to come to church with me tonight?"

251

"Is there a service?"

"Absolutely—the Christmas vigil. One of the most beautiful services of the year. Long, though—but you can sit down since you're still a gimp. I'm afraid I can't stay with you; I'll have to chant."

"You're a chanter?" Kelly wondered if she would ever cease to discover surprises in this man she loved so much but still knew so little.

"Yep. They let me off for Aidan's funeral, but I can't get out of it tonight. They need every voice they can get."

THE CHURCH WAS DIM AND cool, as Kelly remembered it from Aidan's funeral. But now it was festive with a towering gold-trimmed tree in the narthex, greenery draping the icons and chandelier, poinsettias grouped around the central icon stand and lining the foot of the altar screen. Kelly expected to do her candle-lighting inconspicuously at the end of the service, but Nathaniel led her straight to the candle box in the narthex. "The candles burn all through the service, and all those prayers are added to the particular petitions the candles are lit for," he explained, so Kelly took her two slender beeswax tapers and joined the queue for the candlestand in front of the icon of Christ.

"I don't know what to pray," she whispered to Nathaniel.

"Just 'Lord, have mercy on Esther and Aidan' is fine. He knows what that means far better than we do."

When her turn came, Kelly shifted her cane to her left hand and lit the first taper from the thick white candle in the middle of the stand, then shoved its other end down into the sand that filled the surrounding bed. She raised her eyes to the icon of Christ, and He looked down on her in compassion.

"I don't know what I'm doing here," she mouthed silently. "I have no right to be here or to ask anything of You, but I made a promise, and it seems to be important. So please, have mercy on Esther, my grandmother, and forgive her as I have forgiven her." She shook her head at the absurd presumption that statement implied, and lit her second candle. "And please have mercy on Aidan, my father. He paid his debt to me with his life."

She stood a moment to watch the flames of the two candles flicker and grow firm, then turned aside toward the seat Nathaniel indicated at the side of the church.

The service began, and soon the music that had so moved her at Aidan's funeral took hold of her again. She watched the flames of her candles glowing through the smoke of the incense, twining with the pale stream as it rose toward the dome, and Esther's words about prayers ascending suddenly seemed plausible, though still as inexplicable as ever.

At the end of the service, brief prayers were chanted for the forty-day memorial of Aidan's death—or as the prayers put it, his "falling asleep." Kelly watched the smoke swirling in the dome and imagined Aidan and Esther together, saying a final farewell to this world and moving on to whatever unimaginable eternity awaited them.

"Goodbye," she whispered to them. "Give my love to Mother."

She felt their answer like a warm breath on her cheek.

ACKNOWLEDGMENTS

THIS NOVEL WAS finished in 2009, my second novel to be completed. At the time, it found an agent but not a publisher, being too Orthodox for the evangelical market and too Christian for the secular market. I am deeply grateful to Ancient Faith Publishing for giving it a home at last.

I want to thank contractor and dear friend Mark Roberts of Felton, California, for his assistance with the technical aspects of house restoration (any mistakes are mine, not his). I also want to thank my dearest friend Molly King for her input as a person then undergoing the remodeling of her house (by Mark); my friends and co-strugglers of the Orthodox Writers' Week at the Beach for valuable insights along the way; my then critique partner, Charise Olson; and a number of other friends and family members who believed in this book from the beginning. This novel is dear to my heart after all these years, and I hope it will touch your heart as well.

ABOUT THE AUTHOR

KATHERINE BOLGER HYDE is the author of the Crime with the Classics traditional mystery series (Minotaur and Severn House, 2016–2024), the standalone domestic thriller *After He's Gone* (Severn House, 2023), and several children's books for Ancient Faith Publishing, most recently *Brave, Faithful, and True: Children of the Bible* (2023). She has been an editor with Ancient Faith and its predecessor, Conciliar Press, since 1993. Katherine lives in Vancouver, Washington, with her husband, John, and two only slightly mystical cats. She attends St. Nicholas Church (OCA) in Portland.

We hope you have enjoyed and benefited from this book. Your financial support makes it possible to continue our nonprofit ministry both in print and online. Because the proceeds from our book sales only partially cover the costs of operating **Ancient Faith Publishing** and **Ancient Faith Radio**, we greatly appreciate the generosity of our readers and listeners. Donations are tax deductible and can be made at **www.ancientfaith.com.**

To view our other publications,
please visit our website: **store.ancientfaith.com**

 ANCIENT FAITH RADIO

Bringing you Orthodox Christian music, readings, prayers, teaching, and podcasts 24 hours a day since 2004 at **www.ancientfaith.com**